ALWAYS HUNGRY

The cons had a saying about him inside. Chaingang had nothing but his hate, they said. In truth it was what nurtured and sustained him. He was motivated by it. He let himself open to the pain and fed off of it. He stored away fury. Make no mistake tonight, dear heart. Death waits. Behind you. In the shadows. . . .

PRAISE FOR REX MILLER'S
CHAINGANG

"Rex Miller's potential, there to be seen from the start by anyone who had the stomach for it, is fulfilled in chilling, chance-taking *Chaingang*. . . . Rex's characters *all* come to life on his pages—at least, for as long as it takes Bunkowski to annihilate them! . . . Miller's *Chaingang* knows everybody is complicated as hell—and in *this* world, the shadows are gigantic, and come out *after* you!"

—J. N. Williamson, author of *Monastery* and *Spree*

"*Chaingang* is outstanding! In the character of Chaingang Bunkowski, Miller has created a quintessential killer. Chaingang makes Hannibal Lecter look like Mr. Rogers."

—R. Patrick Gates, author of *Tunnelvision*

"*Chaingang* is a bullet of terror and suspense! Sleek, nasty, compelling prose. . . . A terrifying dark adventure story!"

—*Cemetery Dance Magazine*

PRAISE FOR REX MILLER'S
FIRST CHAINGANG NOVEL,
SLOB

Books by Rex Miller

Savant*
Chaingang*
Iceman
Stone Shadow
Slice
Profane Men
Frenzy
Slob

*Published by POCKET BOOKS

SAVANT

REX MILLER

POCKET BOOKS

New York   London   Toronto   Sydney   Tokyo   Singapore

This book is a work of fiction. Names, characters, places and incidents are products of the author's imagination or are used fictitiously. Any resemblance to actual events or locales or persons, living or dead, is entirely coincidental.

An *Original* Publication of POCKET BOOKS

POCKET BOOKS, a division of Simon & Schuster Inc.
1230 Avenue of the Americas, New York, NY 10020

ISBN: 0-671-74848-3

First Pocket Books printing July 1994

10 9 8 7 6 5 4 3 2 1

POCKET BOOKS and colophon are registered trademarks of Simon & Schuster Inc.

Cover art by Cathleen Thole

Printed in the U.S.A.

Special thanks to Doug Grad, and to Stan S. Lavsky, who urged his actors to "play well, or play badly, but play truly."

SAVANT

PROLOGUE

Merciful dog crap."

"You rang, your horse-ship?" The man at the desk next to Sonny Shoenburgen's aide asked.

"I'm supposed to reclassify about four hundred and seven fucking things in the Whirlwind. Like I have the time and all." The Whirlwind was a data warehouse for the combined—nudge, nudge, wink, wink—*intelligence* community. "Dead-and-buried *Sixties* shit."

"Phoenix?"

"SAUCOG," he said, giving it the onomatopoetic acronym by which the Special Advisory Unit was known around Langley, Fort Meade, Foggy Bottom, and assorted heirs and assigns.

"Downgrading or upgrading?"

"That's what's funny. I'm supposed to run down all this stuff on one of their assets, this fun guy who was a mass murderer they had doing wet work in Nam, Cambo, and Laos—now get this—I'm not supposed to NR the stuff. It all gets an 'Officially Deleted.' Is that brilliant?"

1

"That wouldn't red flag it much if somebody hit that a few times in a search. Jesus." They laughed.

"Do you wonder whose side they're fucking on sometimes? I mean really. What the hell are they thinking?" The other man held up his hands in the "I give up" position, shaking his head.

"Oh, yeah," the aide said, "Colonel Shoenburgen plays with some weird folks. This guy . . . I remember him from the newspapers. Remember 'Chaingang' Bunkowski?"

"Not so's you'd notice."

"He was one of the first ones they used in the program— whatdyacallit? The experimental thing trying to make assassins?"

"MK Ultra."

"That was the other one. I forget. Anyway, this guy was a Bundy—only he'd wasted like literally hundreds of people, so they said."

"Oh! Wait a second. This was the one that cut their hearts out and ate 'em—after he killed the people?"

"Right. The very same. We're talking major nuts. Total psycho killer. They got him off death row somewhere— Leavenworth or something. I dunno," the aide said. "They thought they had the perfect killing robot. So they set him down in these neat places like northern I Corps—with military cover, right?"

"Christ."

"He goes across the fence—okay? Long-range recon. He's like about seven feet tall and weighs a thousand pounds or something—just huge! *Stone* killer, okay? The idea being they'll turn him loose and let him waste gooks and do his own thing. The ultimate point man."

"Did it work?"

"I guess it must have," the aide said, looking at the printout. "DMZ. Quang Tri. Did a thing with SAUCOG in the Rung Sat. III Corps. He was all over the damn place. Problem is—he somehow got cut loose. Disappeared. Ends up back in the world and was greasing folks right and left.

"He's leaving his nice fat blood trails all over the Midwest all of a sudden. Mutilated corpses. The *hearts* were missing."

"Guess who."

"Yeah. Some detective finally got him. They found him in Chicago, down in a fucking sewer."

"So that's all ancient history. How come you gotta reclassify all the SAUCOG stuff? Nobody's ever gonna get that bilge downgraded. Not in this lifetime." The aide shrugged in response.

"Some cop poking around. Colonel says clean the fucker. It never existed." He fed a code through his desktop keyboard and accessed ultra–top secret storage.

"I just work here."

1
─────

Columbia, Missouri

The Show-Me Motor Lodge was a busy operation on the
outskirts of Columbia, a prosperous college town in the
American heartland. Conway Seymour out of Pine Bluff,
Arkansas—self-employed according to the register—spent
a couple of easy days there on R and R. All 469 pounds of
him kicked back on a Show-Me king-size Beautyrest, mother naked most of the time, his lips wrapped around a quart
of Wild Turkey when he wasn't eating.

The maid ignored the DO NOT DISTURB sign as was her
custom, and tried to open the door. The policy of the
Show-Me was make whatever noise was necessary to get the
guests on their feet again by eight A.M. or thereabouts,
so the staff could take care of business: cleaning, readying
the rooms, emptying out the disarrayed beds for the next lot
of paying customers. Hostelries, like restaurants, didn't care
for folks who dawdled. They took up space and they interfered with the flow of business.

To be sure, at six feet seven inches and the better part of a
quarter-ton, Mr. Conway Seymour took up space. But until

5

the maid tried to open Room 366 with her passkey he was just another sleeping bod to be evicted. The lock clicked open but she couldn't budge the door. Some wiseguy had jammed furniture up against the door or something. Well, she thought, I'll handle that.

"Anybody in there?" she screamed, in a voice that might have summoned a few errant hogs in its time, as she beat on the door with a businesslike fist. "Do you want your room cleaned?" That was always a good one. When they angrily complained she could say she was just checking. You don't want fresh linens and stuff—fine, she thought, sleep in your dirty bed and see if I care.

The idea was to roust the slumberers. The vacationers or conventioneers who'd had a few too many the night before. She'd teach them to shove a chair under her doorknob.

She waited for the door to open and some frazzled housewife or bleary-eyed Joe to growl "Didn't you see the sign on the door?" But there was no reply. She banged again. This time she heard a huge, deep basso profundo rumble out at her.

"GO AWAY."

"Yes, sir," she said, with mock politeness. "Do you want some fresh towels?" Drag it out and make sure he can't go back to sleep.

"GO AWAY." Something about the voice made her flesh crawl, and she was not easily frightened. The maid shrugged and rolled her cart down the sidewalk to Room 367, where she was able to admit herself and go about her business, the first order of which was to turn up the TV nice and loud.

But neither loud television sets nor screeching maids disturbed Mr. Seymour. When he sensed that she had removed herself from the door, his eyes blinked shut and he fell instantly into a deep, untroubled sleep. His flawless inner clock registered 0758 inside his subconscious, as it monitored his vital signs, and such externals as ambient temperature—whatever might constitute a possible threat to his welfare.

What would the maid's scream have sounded like had she been able to see the sleeping man, much less his dream, as he fantasized about a pleasureful kill? The massive hulk registered as Mr. Seymour, nude, an immense hairy mound of muscle covered in ugly truck tires of rubbery fat, obscene pink johnson stiffly erect as he remembered the last "live one" he'd consumed, slept without covers, comfortably cool in the frigid Show-Me Motor Lodge air conditioning. His fearsome mouth, the mouth of a human shark, gaped open in the blubbery rictus of a wet grin, and contorted his dimpled, baby face into a mask of hatred.

Every detail of the kill and the mutilation was replayed inside the depths of his dream. If only the maid could have seen what was inside the mind of the sleeping man in Room 366. Behind that door she so desperately wanted to enter, a bestial monster lay. The heart-eater slept now. And in his sleep he dove down into underwater Corpse City, breaststroking through the junkyard of glass-walled coffins.

The desk clerk and the manager would both recall Mr. Seymour, the "big heavyset gentleman" who'd been a guest for a couple of days. He had slept several hours past checkout the second day, finally pulling pants and shirt and shoes on, and driving to the nearest fast-food joint, a KFC, and immediately returning to the room where he devoured a twenty-one-piece bucket of chicken, three quarts of potato salad, and a six-pack of cold Cokes iced down in the motel bathroom sink. He killed the last of the Wild Turkey for dessert, and tidied up the room for the maid.

As a going-away present in memory of her special wake-up service, he took his giant fighting bowie knife and slit open the pillows, defecated in them, repacked the feathers and sealed them with duct tape before returning them to their pillowcases. He also slit the bottom of the mattress open and urinated in it, more out of principle than for effect, cleaning himself with the bottom of the drapes. He figured the room would start stinking real good in a few hours.

With that bizarre activity completed, he showered, shaved, dressed in his three-piece business suit and tie, and took his key to the front desk.

Mr. Conway Seymour of Pine Bluff paid and thanked the desk clerk, got back in his car, and drove to the self-service gas station across the highway from the Show-Me. There, he ceased to exist, and another "real big guy" materialized to pay for the gas with his credit card. The Visa/MasterCard Merchant Center recorded that the purchase was made by one Paul Grose of Little Rock, Arkansas.

The unusual aspect of this transaction was the date of the purchase.

According to authorities, cardholder Paul Grose, otherwise unconnected to the individual who had used his card, had been missing for over two weeks when the card was used. The scrawled signature on the receipt duplicate did not match that of the missing man.

When the driver of the vehicle pulled back out onto the highway, a Mr. Vernon Jones of Valdosta, Georgia was now behind the wheel. A huge, meaty hand flung the wallet of the missing Mr. Grose over the side of the first creek he crossed. The driver discarded I.D.s the way the average person throws away used facial tissues.

He drove four to six miles over the speed limit, picking up speed a bit as the evening darkened and the prevalence of truckers forced the stream of traffic to move a bit quicker. Booneville, where he'd spent some terrible time once— some twenty-five years ago—was far behind him, both literally and figuratively. He had made his way through Overton, Sweet Springs, Concordia, Odessa, and Grain Valley, as the night swallowed him.

It was dark by the time he reached the outskirts of Blue Springs, Missouri, where he topped off the tank out of habit, paid cash, urinated on the seat of the men's urinal and then across the sink, for no particular reason.

Daniel Edward Flowers Bunkowski, at age forty-one or forty-two, the records varied, had taken more human lives than any other person in modern history—some said he'd taken a life for every pound of his weight. As is often the case the myth did not match the horror of the reality. Personally, he'd quit keeping a tally in the mid-sixties, but he was certain the count was well over five hundred.

Daniel Bunkowski, a.k.a. "Chaingang," headhunter of mercenaries, executioner extraordinaire, butcher and heart-taker, was the worst serial killer of the twentieth century. In legal wheels and with his choice of disposable identities, he drove through the bright lights of downtown Kansas City, Missouri, crossed the river into Kansas City, Kansas, and turned down on a service road that accessed the river. He parked and got out of the car.

He knew this place. The hideous, violent history of his hellish childhood poured across his mindscreen. He stood, perfectly inert, an immense statue in the shadows of the river, soaking in the stinging memories.

The cons had a saying about him inside. Chaingang had nothing but his hate, they said, with the common wisdom of the joint. In truth, it was what nurtured and sustained him. He was motivated by it. He opened himself to the pain and fed off of it.

Overhead in the darkness, headlights of passing cars illuminated moments of moving time, as he saw it inside the strangeness of his mind. The traffic noise was a continuous humming sound and he willed it to feed him, as he stored away fury.

When he was ready, he returned to the vehicle, changed clothes, got back in the car, and resumed his journey back to the place of his birth.

Imagine that *his* headlights are those you see in your rearview mirror. Exercise the greatest care. Drive defensively and for God's sake don't slam on the brakes unexpectedly. In the vehicle behind you is a man-mountain of brutality; a gifted presentient with an I.Q. that warps every curve; a killer whose secret biochemistry deviates from every known pattern. A giant of destruction follows you, waiting for you to become vulnerable—to show him that you are a potential victim. Make no mistakes tonight, dear heart. Death waits. Behind you. In the shadows.

Kansas City, Missouri

One big man parked his wheels, but another got out and used the pay phone. It was yet a third who payed the week in advance at Mid-America Parking, a fourth who summoned the taxicab and rode to the Hyatt. Some might have found all this a trifle confusing, but juggling disposable personas wasn't even a flyspeck as far as challenging Daniel Bunkowski's mental abilities.

"Thank you, sir," the cabbie told him, pocketing a slightly excessive tip. The man who took his bags received a similar gratuity from the extremely large, but well-dressed Giles Cunningham, whose company, York Sprinklers, Inc., of York, Pennsylvania, had called ahead the day before.

The caller priced the clubrooms, but decided instead on a guest room accommodation for two evenings. The seasonal day rate at Kansas City, Missouri's Hyatt Regency was eighty dollars, which Mr. Cunningham felt was more than reasonable after enjoying their luxurious and remarkably comfortable accommodations.

"Hello." The gigantic figure in the three-piece suit beamed down at the woman behind the front desk. "My company has made a phone reservation in my name. Giles Cunningham? From York, Pennsylvania?"

"Yes, sir," she said after consulting the computer beside her. "We have you in one of our guest room accommodations, double-bed, single-person occupancy for tonight and Saturday night—is that correct?"

"That's it. I'll confirm checkout tomorrow, if that's okay."

"Fine. How did you wish to take care of this?" The young woman was quite professional and did not appear to be the least flustered by the sight of a human woolly mastodon towering above her. "Are we charging this to your credit card, Mr. Cunningham?"

"I'll just pay cash, if I may," he said expansively, pulling out a huge wad of what appeared to be hundred-dollar bills and dexterously peeling two crisp C-notes off the outside before returning it to his voluminous pocket.

She smiled professionally and began making change. He thought how easily he could reach over the counter, grab her by the hair, and crush her skull against the desk.

"Here you are, sir," she said, telling him his room number, in case he was too stupid to read it off the door opener. He thanked her and in no time was in an upwardly mobile elevator, looking down at the head of a bellhop some two feet shorter and three hundred pounds lighter. He imagined how pleasant it would be to twist the man's neck until it snapped, then shove the body up through the ceiling trapdoor.

"In town for the show?" the bellhop asked.

"Unn," Chaingang grunted in a tone that could have meant anything, yes, no, or fuck you.

"You brought that hot weather with you," the man said, smiling. He was the type who always joked in Chaingang's presence, made intensely uncomfortable by the awesome size of the man. Bunkowski stared down at him without a flicker of response.

The smaller man carried a heavy suitcase, a used knockoff of a Vuitton that had been purchased that morning in a pawnshop. The two-suiter was full of Goliath-size apparel just purchased at Mr. Hy's Big, Tall, and Stout Shop there in the Crown Plaza shopping complex. The sign read, MR. HY'S HAS SOMETHING OF EVERY SIZE! In truth, the shop had been able to fit Chaingang with shirts, slacks—to be hemmed to a basketball player's inseam length—socks, a tie, an *ascot* for God's sake—two sweaters and a blazer. They'd had to say no to the 15EEEEE footwear, so he would have to make do with his burnished oxfords and the combat boots which he routinely wore.

The moment he was alone in the room behind a closed door, he began peeling off his clothes until he was nude, and then surveyed the wreckage of his personal treasury. The center of the huge flash roll of hundreds that he carried was, of course, blank paper.

He'd spent the night in a fleabag motel over on the Kansas side, and bright and early had been up looking at the storefront and industrial rentals. A deposit had gone on a second-floor cubicle of office space recently vacated by a fly-by-night ad agency. A tattoo parlor had tried to make a go of it downstairs, but had gone in the toilet subsequent to the AIDS epidemic. It was a shade more than he wanted to spend but it was isolated and—as a plus—it had a small bathroom with a sink.

The Southwestern Bell folks would be getting a healthy deposit, too, since the "Norville Galleries," which would be occupying the office space, hadn't had previous phone service. A quickie printer was doing some signage and letterhead stuff, and within the next forty-eight hours or so the company would be open for business.

"What kind of business is this?" the landlord wanted to know, as he counted the money for the closet-size office on East Minnesota Avenue.

"I'm in the mail-order game," the big man informed him, giving him a moment of terrible anguish as he came down hard on the poor fellow's foot. "Oh, my Lord. I'm *sorry!*" He was most apologetic. He had kind of "lost his balance" and something like five hundred pounds of meat had come to rest on the landlord's bunions. The guy had wanted to ask about this mail-order business the new tenant was going to be doing, but by then all he wanted to do was put some distance between himself and the behemoth whose money he'd just accepted. The name of his reference had been one Giles Cunningham, of York Sprinklers, Inc. The landlord might or might not realize that he'd given the address of the Hyatt Regency Hotel.

Everything was going according to schedule, Chaingang thought, surveying his vast nakedness in the mirror. He cranked the air conditioning down another notch and picked up the telephone, summoning the front desk.

"Yes, this is Mr. Cunningham. I'm going to be getting a couple of telephone calls this evening—perhaps—and to-morrow, which will be for a business I own here in town called the Norville Galleries. If I should get any calls for the Norville Galleries, that's me." He made sure they noted his room number. "Kindly pass this along to the other opera-tors, would you? It's very important. I appreciate it. Thanks!" He waited a few minutes and called back and spelled *N-o-r-v-i-l-l-e* for the person on the switchboard, drumming the name into their head by repetition. When he went out later he would call for himself using another voice, and they'd ring an empty room.

He decided that the haircut was next. He put on a change of clothes and took the elevator back downstairs. The newspaper ad was set to hit in the next morning's *Kansas City Star* classifieds. One or two more details to attend to and the Norville Galleries would be well on its way. Another entrepreneurial success story: the American Mercantile Dream in full bloom.

2

Elaine Roach needed to find work in the worst way. But even as badly as she needed this job, and as intriguing as it sounded—when she'd responded to the Help Wanted classified ad in the *Saturday Star*—the idea of calling on a man in his *hotel* room was anathema to her. She was terribly nervous. While she was coming up in the elevator, her knees started knocking together and she became so suddenly chilled that she feared she'd get violently ill. She nearly punched the lobby button and rode back down, but having to face another Monday morning without employment was a fear as terrifying as this one. She screwed her courage and marched down the hallway, the scrap of paper with Mr. Norville's room number clutched in one of her gloved hands. Even her knock on the door was prim.

"It's open!" a voice screeched from inside. She saw an immense and flagrantly homosexual man seated on the bed speaking into a telephone. "Come in. Be seated," he snapped, the mouthpiece covered so the other party could not hear him, presumably, motioning her toward a chair with a limp-wristed gesture. "I'll be with you in a moment." He turned away and spoke into the phone.

"No—it's someone about the position. All right, I'll see you when I get to the Coast. Yes . . . Um-hmm . . . I don't have room for those in my warehouse locally. I'll let you know when we move to the new building. All right. See you in Los Angeles Tuesday evening. *Au revoir!*" He hung up dramatically. He knew approximately how long the desk clerk usually took to get to the phones at this time of the day. He'd mistimed it slightly, by chance, but his huge paw had covered the mouthpiece when he'd turned and blocked her vision.

"So sorry, my dear. I'm having a perfectly hectic day. My name is Tommy Norville," he announced and swished across the room to greet the woman, who stood up, no longer quite so nervous, but exceedingly puzzled. A 400-plus-pound simpering queen takes a bit of getting used to. They shook hands. He offered a massive hand as if it had no bones in it, and when the woman took it she felt as if she'd grabbed a fat ten-pound perch as he gave her his best impression of a dead-fish handshake.

As usual, he'd sized her up instantly and she was perfect. Utter perfection. The woman was wearing a hat such as nobody had worn in twenty years and white gloves!

"I'm Elaine Roach," she said. "I phoned you about the position in the antique gallery," she told him unnecessarily. An unattractive woman, made more so by a severe hair style—prematurely ugly hair—she was a spinster in her early fifties who could easily pass for Social Security age, due to both her appearance and deportment.

"Yes, Miss Roach, I think your qualifications may do." He turned in a dainty pirouette like an elephant in a tutu, and swished back across the room, bidding her to sit with a limp paw that gestured as if it held a fairy wand. One fear—her greatest, in fact—that of being raped, was no longer relevant.

Norville was dressed flamboyantly, in what she thought of as "sissy businessman" clothing, his hair cut very short on the top and streaked, the twenty-dollar drugstore bifocals down on his nose. They were the kind with the cord attached, and they gave his dimpled face a sort of benevolent and oddly feminine look. He wore a silk shirt, a turtleneck sweater under it that accented his hugely fat double chin, with a loud pocket silk flowing from the pocket of his blazer.

"I haven't worked since I lived in Portland," she said in a quiet voice, her eyes downcast. She was used to being turned down.

"Excellent," he simpered. "Your head won't be filled with wrong work concepts." He was a master at camouflaged doublespeak. After a few minutes in his presence one almost began to make sense out of his utterances, so seemingly connected were the cleverly pseudologic patterns. "Do you have family here?" he asked pleasantly, crossing his legs and almost suffocating as he did so.

"No. Not anymore. Everyone's passed away. My brother and his wife and their two children are all I have, and that's who I was working for when I lived in Portland. If I may ask, what exactly would this position with your antique gallery entail?" She was seated so primly it was all he could do not to walk over and touch her, just to see how high she would jump. Her legs were squeezed so tightly together it was absurd. She held a huge purse in front of her private parts, clasped in a death grip by those hands encased in the stupid white gloves. He couldn't have selected someone more ideal. Chaingang thought he might be in love!

"Of course. Primarily you'd be responsible for keeping our financial records, which are simple in the extreme. You'd open our small amount of business mail that comes in from the periodical auction, cash the checks and so on, and answer the phone. It would not be a demanding job for more than a few days each month—the sort of business when things are hectic for a couple of days and then you just sit around idle until the next auction comes up." Consciously, he was forcing his word patterns to match hers. The question that began "what exactly would this position with your antique gallery entail?" was echoed, for instance, in the phrase "the sort of business when things are hectic." He had matched the rise and fall of her speech cadences precisely.

He was also matching his voice and its rhythms to the effeminate clothes, the sissified speech affectations, and the woman's obvious expectations, based on her call—and now on her body language—but he was quite careful not to lay it on too thickly. All he wanted was enough to counterbalance her natural fears, offset his massive size a bit, and give her something to remember him by. He was more animated than usual, and he never allowed his rubbery face to sink into the look it normally wore when in repose.

"There is one other thing I wonder about—and it's something I would pay extra for, in fact considerably extra. A telephone. You know, I was going to break my long-standing rule and install a phone in the gallery itself, but I detest doing that. They're so intrusive! And—no more than we'd use it, I wonder . . . would you consider renting me the use of your phone for one day each month? Say for an additional two hundred a month?"

"Oh, certainly. I have a private line at my apartment, and you could use it one day a month. Would the calls be local?"

"Um. I wouldn't be using it to call out. We'd be receiving calls on it. I could run the number as our auction line."

"Of course. That would be fine." She shook her head. "I wouldn't charge that much, though. Not just for you using it one day a month."

"I appreciate that, Miss Roach. However I would like to pay it for this reason. Occasionally—I mean, perhaps two or three times a month—I might get a customer inquiring about an item listed in the mail auction. And if you didn't mind, here's what I'd like you to do: You answer the telephone in your normal way, and if they ask if this is the Norville Gallery you tell them yes, but that the director is out, and that I will return their call. Each evening I would give you a call and you'd pass those numbers along to me. You'd seldom get such inquiries, so it wouldn't become a bother. But if you'd be willing to allow the use of your phone in that manner I'd make your salary fourteen hundred a month instead of twelve hundred a month."

"Certainly," she said quickly, mentally counting the financial windfall. They spoke some more about the gallery and what the auctions were like. He'd chosen his person well. Elaine Roach was rather at ease now, evidently pleased by the nature of the work and the pay scale.

"It's done then." He stood up heavily and she got to her feet. "I'll start you on salary instantly, and I'll call you in the morning with your first day's duties." He saw something in her face, sensitive to sea changes as ever. "Monday, rather. I forgot what day it was." He said this in a hushed, prim voice, and she nodded her understanding. She had nothing against a homosexual employer. Perhaps she would find this a pleasant association after all. She mentally made a note to remember to use the word "gay" instead of homosexual.

"So, Mr. Norville, I'll be working out of my apartment essentially, and not at the gallery?"

"Yes. Pretty much so, essentially. You'll make a trip to the bank and post office now and again, but for the most part you'll just stay all nice and cozy, in your apartment." She brightened as he fed her lines back to her. Clearly she was someone who didn't relish being back out in the work force.

The job sounded wonderfully ideal to Elaine Roach, who had not been treated kindly by her fifty-four years on the planet. It was almost too good to be true. She also thought she sensed Mr. Norville's genuine pleasure with her qualifications and it was reassuring that at last she had met someone whose needs she in some way filled.

They said their goodbyes, and he came back inside the hotel room. If she learned at some point that Giles Cunningham was the name on the register as occupant of the room in which she'd met Tommy Norville, it could be explained away in the most understandable terms. Giles and Tommy were roommates. He would wait awhile and Tommy

Norville would now cease to be, for a bit, except in print and over the phones.

For the moment, the image that stared back at Tommy Norville in the Hyatt Regency's mirror was one that bore surprisingly little resemblance—size aside—from that of the man who had not long ago occupied Cell 10 in the Violent Unit of D-Seg at Marion Federal Penitentiary. Clothes did indeed make the man. The bleached, newly shorn hair, and such touches as the "seamstress" bifocals, made a remarkable change. But it was his movements, in character, that added texture to the Norville persona.

Chaingang had observed an actor on a television talk show proclaiming what a terrific training ground the daytime soaps were for thespians. He'd watched a few minutes of these programs and found their broadly played, scenery-chewing histrionics laughably inept. Along with his many unique gifts, Bunkowski had the natural skills of a consummate actor: keen powers of observation and mimicry, a predisposition for thorough preparation, the ability to instantly summon up stored emotion, and the feel for a character's center. The acting and reacting he'd seen on the daytime dramas had been ludicrously unconvincing.

He intuitively knew that he'd hammed up the Norville character. If he played him again—and he would—the next time he'd not draw on such a broad stereotype. He filed away a quick critique of his kinesiology and a mental list of suggestions for how he might better locate Tommy's center, when next he came to life.

With that done he shed the character as much as possible. A cap would cover the hair when Giles Cunningham checked out, and he would forget to drop his door opener at the desk. The bellhop who took his bag to a waiting cab would find himself the beneficiary of another oversize tip, with a request to return the key card with thanks. The bill had been prepaid with checkout in mind. The fewer persons who saw Mr. Cunningham prior to his becoming nonexistent, the colder a trail he'd leave behind.

As always, his computer sorted options and retraced movements, calculating the time it would take the authorities to follow his paper trail along the interstate highway. He felt fairly confident that he'd lost his trackers, but for once Bunkowski couldn't have been more wrong.

Blue Springs, Missouri

In the parking lot of a shopping mall down the highway from Blue Springs Antiques Barn, the gigantic killer pulled out photocopies of ads, familiarizing himself with his merchandise, both real and imagined, seeing where the holes were in his presentations.

The first auction would be Wednesday night at six P.M., closing at midnight, Central Daylight Savings Time. By then the results of the first series of letters would have arrived and the collectors wishing to respond could reach Elaine Roach by telephone.

These were memorabilia collectors of one kind or another whose ads Tommy Norville had seen in various publications. It didn't matter what you were looking for, so long as it was shippable, the Norville Galleries probably had it: militaria, clocks, china, cut glass, French cameo, antique firearms, Indian Americana. Name a category and he stocked it in depth. Your top want, in each instance, was the item that caught his expert eye. You were prepared to pay the maximum for X item and he had X item in his next auction—what a coincidence! You could phone your bid in Wednesday night. In some cases, he even sent a Polaroid of the item in stock.

The ideal merch was something for which ten different collectors across the country lusted. By some coincidence again—on those particular items—there would be ten winners! He looked at the ads and computed the logistics of the come-on. First there would be a week while the invoices were mailed out to the winners. Allow another ten days for all those "winning" bidders to respond with their remittances, and he estimated a three- to three-and-a-half-week window between that moment and the time the money was in his pocket.

He was already sending in the ads for the direct priced-sale offering of collectible weaponry that would run more or less simultaneously. Tommy Norville had learned all these fields in the same way he'd learned everything else of a survival nature, and he knew everything from toxicology to locksmithing; he'd force-fed it to his brain.

For the past week, he'd been all over the Kansas City area, driving as far as fifty miles out to visit promising shops and galleries, photographing rare merchandise. Especially weapons. He'd even taken a few illicit shots in museums. The dealer's shops were much more lenient about permitting a would-be customer to "keep a visual record" of such-and-such for his files. He'd learned there were dealers called "runners" who used such a technique, finding scarce items, running to find a buyer, then running back to buy the item only if they had a money-in-hand sale.

He read ".69-caliber flintlocks. Beautifully dec. 18th century. Gold-washed barrels and mounts." The rare pair of cased weapons represented an expenditure of $6.50 in gasoline, Polaroid film, and a flashbulb.

"Unique .55-caliber flintlock has solid ivory stock with silver and gilt inlays, enamel niello work and gorgeous cloisonné. Clean, superb, no cracks. Ivory ramrod is original. Fourteen-inch barrel octagonal at the breech. Lockplate has no bridle on frizzen. Ivory stock/carved dragon's head butt makes this a museum-quality flintlock." A gun collector's wet dream. Indeed, it was museum quality, all right. The nearby Patee Museum is where he'd obtained the photo.

The next half dozen with pictures were firearms that could actually be purchased from dealers within ten to fifty miles: an unusual wheellock from around 1600; a Japanese match-lock long rifle from the same time period, dripping in ornate brasswork; a little sterling sash pistol; a sheathed hunting sword dated 1550. Pieces Tommy Norville could actually buy and sell. Weapons with checkable histories to lend credibility to his scam.

The remainder of the auction was composed of fantasies, pure artifacts of the imagination, and scarce goodies with pictures and/or descriptions cribbed from other collectibles auctions.

".58-cal. cased set of flintlock duellers by Wogdon. Extraordinary presentation set marked 'to the inestimable Conan Doyle *from his admirer.' Signed* Wogdon. *Museum qu. pair of cased duellers. Pristine mint, lavish gilt and sterling inlays on long, slim barrels. Gold-lined b. vents. Set, complete with documentation from the author's estate, accompanied by engraved, gold powder flask, rod, and inlaid bullet mold. Rare wood presentation case with brass corners, carved* Sherlock Holmes *image on lid of case, marked inside,* Wogdon, London."*

A more experienced weapons buff would have realized that Wogdon was not making cased dueling pistols when the creator of Holmes and Watson was alive, but nobody's perfect.

Fantasy listings would be certain to elicit a few outstanding bids, and they would gain attention for the priced-sale items to be offered at the same time.

When the first week to ten days' worth of remittances from the auction and the sale ads had been banked by the trustworthy Miss Roach, Tommy Norville would have her make a withdrawal. Shortly thereafter, the up and coming antique weapons dealer who ran the auction galleries would cease to exist.

A dissimilar-appearing but equally large man had once hired a nice lady to aid him in much the same type of enterprise, working from a nearby post-office drawer she had rented, and utilizing a bank account and telephone in her name. He'd netted over eleven thousand dollars profit from two sales of "rare regulator and advertising clocks."

When a chief postal inspector and local authorities finally got around to following this paper trail, they'd end up with a perplexed Elaine Roach, whose sissified Tommy Norville description would be somewhat at odds with the tenant of the upstairs office on East Minnesota Avenue, should they even track him to that particular lair. It was all most confusing. Daniel Edward Flowers Bunkowski was rebuilding his war treasury.

3

The next few days found Daniel Bunkowski busy with the details of his mail-order scam, and searching for a likely rental location for his safe house. Because the East Minnesota Avenue office had running water and toilet facilities, he could make do with a sleeping bag on the floor for a couple of weeks. Sometime in the next three weeks, however, he needed to find a suitable place where he could hunker down when he "ran his traps," courtesy of Elaine Roach, and pulled the lion's share of money out of his auction remittances. At that point he needed to vanish.

An extremely large but well-spoken gentleman with a full beard, who did something academic and terribly vague for a living, put a deposit on a small rental property in Overland Park. Two months in advance, as agreed, with the first month's rent effective in thirty days. It was adequate for his needs of the moment, and the terms fit his window of logistics. If he had to bail out in three weeks rather than four he could always extemporize for a few days. He was the very definition of "field expedient."

With safe house rented, office and temporary dwelling paid for, ads in the mail, Elaine Roach with her nominal make-work, letters of auction solicitation out, Bunkowski had time. Time to kill, that is.

For the first time since they'd freed him from Max Security in Marion, Illinois, once again blessed with an official sanction to go out there and take lives, he'd analyzed his choice of an escape route. As always, he made such decisions instinctively, but with the constant spoonfed data from his mental computer, acting in sync with whatever presentient vibes were brought forth.

It had been the most natural thing to decide on a northerly course as an exfiltration route from Southeast Missouri. When the Waterton spree reached a climax he'd prepared a suitable identity, legal wheels, and without much analysis headed for Kansas City. Now, with a bit of time on his hands, he could ponder the why of it. He'd been heading for Kansas City, perhaps, because it was home, as much as the beast could be said to have a home.

He had time now to reflect on his early life, something he seldom cared to do. It had been a horror-filled hell of torment: at the hands of a perverted "stepfather" of sorts, a cruel foster mother, and the older boys who turned his early reform-school years into a nightmare without end.

As a little boy he had been kept virtually the slave of cruelly twisted desires, made to feel that he was less than an animal. He was watered and fed from the dog's dishes, kept in stifling closets, tethered to the family bed, and sometimes chained inside a suffocatingly hot "punishment box."

As the child was pushed over the edge, used, abused, tortured to the edge of insanity and beyond, he adapted. Mutated. Survived by escaping into a secret world of the mind.

There, inside a room that most would describe as imagination, there was an inner room, and his insanity or fear had unlocked this place. There—inside a room most of us will never see—many paranormal things become possible. The mastery of one's life support system, the controlling of the vital signs, mind over matter, eidetic recall—many things denied the ordinary human being.

Inside this secret place, he'd taken the first steps toward mastery of the will—steps that would lead a nine-year-old victim to the darkened basement of a third-floor walk-up where a bottle of hydrochloric acid waited. Small fingers had reached the bottle, held it carefully as the bruised, battered little boy made his way back up to the third floor, and down the filthy hallway to the rooms where the drunken man lay in a collapsed stupor.

The man, nude, his blue tattoos of frightening serpents and fearsome objects covering an expanse of leathery skin, sprawled across the bed on his back. The child was rock steady as he removed the stopper, and with fingers wrapped in rags pulled back eyelids and poured. He could no longer hear the screams of the one he called "the Snake Man." Too many years, and hundreds of other screams, had dimmed the brightness of those delightful sounds.

When Dr. Norman had found him, languishing on death row as only Chaingang could languish, he'd known the huge killer was more than merely abnormal. He suspected that Daniel was one of the rare human specimens known as physical precognates. From that moment on, there'd been a bonding process between the doctor and his—for want of a better word—subject. And there'd been questions, hundreds of them, many of which had gone unanswered: What about Chaingang's siblings? Were they alive or dead? Had Daniel ever attempted to seek out his biological mother? Was he furious that she'd abandoned him at birth, forcing him into the horrible childhood he'd had? Had he ever thought of tracking her down? Had he wanted to look up the vicious foster mother who'd allowed these horrors to be perpetrated? Was she alive? What about the man he'd blinded? Did he lust for the Snake Man's heart?

Under drugs and hypnosis, over dozens of interviews, debriefings, interrogations, Q and A of every type, and what could be termed "therapy," Norman learned a few things. The records were long gone as to the identity and whereabouts of the biological mother who had abandoned him at birth. Similarly, if the data had ever been known, there were no records identifying a biological father.

The Snake Man was believed to be deceased. The records showed that he had ended up a pitiful wino, a blind beggar who existed from one jug of cheap muscatel to the next. It was of no consequence—Daniel said. But the doctor never fully believed him.

Chaingang either had no siblings or had no interest in finding them. At one time, he would have loved to find his real mother and go "rip her womb out," but too many years had gone by. The truth is, inside, Daniel had never really lusted for revenge on these old figures from his past. He had so much intense hatred for *everyone* that years of mayhem had acted as a kind of diffusive influence, spreading his rage out. He wanted vengeance against mankind, not just some old lady in Kansas City.

On the other hand, it was always somewhere down in the dark recesses of his nasty brain fissures, the simmering hatred he felt for his "foster mother"—what a joke—and the nameless, faceless "others" he could no longer hope to identify, much less track. As long as he was here, and had a few days to *kill,* why not do so?

That night he found his foster mother. She hadn't aged a day—inside his mind—not until he first laid eyes on her. The sight of her brought back all the memories in a furious flood of remembering: the urine stench of the closet where she liked to keep her big bad boy, the rough pinching hands and the cigar-smoke breath of the Snake Man, and the way she'd laugh when the man used him, the look of the dog's food-and-water dishes and the taste of the dog food, the sunlight through the grimy window that beckoned to him when he was chained to the bed, the look of the peeling wallpaper and the feel of the sharp springs beneath the bed.

He could see it all at the first moment he saw her face. The cracks in the linoleum beneath the old oilcloth-covered table. The black of the filthy sink where the porcelain was long gone. The smells in the darkness: feces, smoke, whiskey. The cardboard box beside the bed where the bad things were. How he hated to see the Snake Man reach into that box for things he'd used to hurt the little boy; things to whip, stick, burn. The Snake Man loved inflicting pain.

Little Daniel could see the rust on the hinges of the metal punishment box, the air holes where he pressed his little nose and mouth, the feel of the suffocating heat, the memories of the little dog and his other pets—the silverfish and cockroaches and bedbugs and rats that were so much a routine part of his young life . . . all of these things poured over his mind.

"Call me Mrs. Garbella," she had told the child when they first met, smiling with mock sweetness. Later, when he'd mispronounced her name, she'd slapped him, hard, nearly knocking him unconscious.

The face is one he would have remembered anywhere. He'd forgotten just how ugly the old bitch was. She'd been no prize in her thirties, but now—in her late sixties she was a certifiable hag.

"Whatya want?" she snarled at him through the cracked door held closed by a flimsy piece of chain which he could have bitten his way through.

"Don't you remember me?" he asked in his most dangerous rumbling bass. She glared out at him a moment too long and he smacked the door with the flat of his right hand, a hand the size and density of a twenty-two-pound shotput, and the cheap chain arrangement popped loose from the wood as the door smashed in at her.

He was in. Slammed the door shut. Started to demand that she get on her feet, but even at her advanced age she was still mean enough she wanted to fight, and she managed to struggle upright again and charged into him snaggletooth-and-nails, clawing and biting this monster of an adversary.

She *scared* him. Later, he attributed it to the element of surprise, but really the little boy hiding inside him somewhere was momentarily frightened by her unexpected retaliation and he reacted too swiftly, the huge fighting bowie knife—a razor-sharp blade that could cut two inches of loosely swinging hemp—slashing into her with all the force of a quarter-ton death machine.

Compute the foot-pounds of pressure times the kinetic energy, multiply by the stink of the closet where she kept him, squared by the sum of the hours he'd spent inside the box under the bed, and you can begin to understand the ferocity with which he swung that mighty blade. The single slice decapitated the old woman, and her head hit the floor like a big ugly ball before the body could topple. Chaingang's right hand and arm were painted with her blood, which was spurting from her neck with every beat of the woman's dying heart.

Headless, she was even uglier than in life. He wanted to pick the head up by the hair and sit it in the toilet, as a last gesture of his disdain, but he couldn't overcome his revulsion enough to touch her again.

He kicked the severed head of Nadine Garbella into the closet and slammed the door on it, washed the blood off in the sink, and exited the scene of the accident, careful not to step in the widening pool of dark steamy blood.

An accident had happened, all right. She'd died without knowing who he was. He woke up on top of a sweat-drenched sleeping bag in a darkened office on East Minnesota Avenue, shaking with rage, still inside a monster's North Kansas City nightmare.

4
___

Washington, District of Columbia

The man who'd carved the conglom known worldwide as
EMARCY TRANSCO from ore-rich North American gold-
fields, M. R. Sieh, had sired one son. His namesake had
come out squalling and fighting, tough as his daddy and ten
times as smart, and when the old man passed on, "Junior"
was running the show from a seven-thousand-dollar contour
recliner.

The mercantile exchange challenged him, but not so
much as government service did. He was drawn by the
power magnet and from his first contact, a European
ambassadorship that he'd purchased—unapologetically—
with EMARCY TRANSCO funds, he'd been hooked.

Now, at sixty-eight, he was among the three most powerful men in American government, yet his name remained
largely unknown to the general public. Long ago he'd
discovered that the real power brokers were without a
profile. The names you knew—one or two rich oddballs
excepted—were those of figureheads. Serious men understood the need for anonymity and total discretion.

M. R. Sieh, Jr., adviser to five presidents, secret manipulator and possessor of phenomenal wealth, had a mind that had not been dimmed by time. As a matter of routine he continued to write the odd, unexpected memo to various senior traders in which they'd be asked to "rethink" their short position on zero-coupon treasuries, Japanese puts, or whatever the latest fiduciary fad entailed.

His obsession had been the gathering of intelligence. That obsession had led to the formation, in the years prior to the Vietnam War, of America's most secret intelligence agency; the forerunner of what became SAUCOG.

Reluctantly, Sieh had reached an uncomfortable conclusion: that there was in fact a need, arguably, for sensitive covert missions that utilized assassination as a final solution. However Hitlerian that sounded, however misanthropic it would appear on paper, the realities were that governments—like society itself—sometimes felt obliged to kill.

When the act was performed on a large scale, it was given other names, such as "war." When the killing was done as punishment, it was called "execution." But men often found reasons for legally if not morally breaking the commandment "Thou shalt not kill." The words, that is to say the euphemisms, used to describe the act in covert intelligence operational jargon varied with the fashion of the times, and the bureaucratic level of the language. "Wet work" was now passé. "Termination with extreme prejudice" had seen a moment of currency. "Sanctions" and "executive action" had each been in vogue for a time. Briefly, the language had taken a hard right turn in the late Eighties, and there'd been a passing flirtation with mobspeak, in which such transitive verbs as "drop," "plant," and "clip" found their way to D.C., Langley, and environs. But these were fads of the moment.

The style of the Nineties was sign language. The spoken word was out, and while one still spoke of contracts the meaning had changed. One was now a contract player. Agencies or special units no longer "held paper" on a certain party. Degrees of prejudice were expressed with hand signals. The extended first finger and cocked thumb to the head, universal cliché for handgun, was today's *"adios"* sign. Tomorrow, it would be something else. The "cutthroat" finger-slash, perhaps.

M. R. Sieh, Jr., was far removed from such crude activities. Had he been approached by the misguided souls who had seriously embarked on a venture to establish a school for government assassins, he'd have simply quashed it. But the thing had somehow taken root in a few like minds within the SAUCOG hierarchy, and incredible things were permitted to happen.

A mass murderer, a psychotic killer of monstrous notoriety, had been freed from prison, given weapons, and encouraged to kill more or less at random! Sieh had forced himself not to demand every head involved in the lunacy, which, of course, had ended in a bloody debacle, and one—on top of that—in which the killer had supposedly escaped! The reverberations had finally reached him, it had become such a monumental fiasco.

"You're telling me that the thing was *not* a disaster, Dr. Norman?" Sieh spoke softly into a scrambled telephone.

"That's correct, sir. The entire mission was conducted with total security so far as the real point of the exercise, or the true degree of surveillance the subject was under."

"I must say," Sieh enunciated carefully, "I have a certain admiration for a person who can remain so detached that he can refer to the random execution of dozens of innocent individuals as an 'exercise.'"

"I know how cold that sounds," Norman said with equal care; he did not know the identity of the man on the phone, only his level, and the doctor would do nothing to further jeopardize his precious program. "I assure you if I had the luxury to be appalled by slaughter I would be. Let me remind you of my original mandate: to create an experienced cadre who might one day perform sensitive government work involving *human extermination*. The concept was to film, tape, and otherwise chronicle the activities and special techniques of the most adept assassin known, to do

32

so in a relatively isolated area within the best security fence we could erect, one that would still let the subject act and react under field conditions."

"Again, Dr. Norman, I repeat my question—how was this not an unmitigated disaster? The subject penetrated the fence."

"No, sir. Not in the least." Norman's notes were in front of him. This was the easy part. "When the idea for the program—to study the subject—was first initiated, it was many years ago. It was a matter of waiting for the technology to catch up with the plan. Over time we were able to develop an experimental drug that proved to be sufficiently effective that the subject could be manipulated to a degree. We had the various surveillance, monitoring, and weapons systems necessary. Eventually, a laser implant was perfected and we had our technology.

"Only one other man besides myself and the director of Clandestine Services was allowed to know the true control mechanisms, or the real operational scope involved. Remember, sir, we are talking about a subject who has killed hundreds of persons—over five hundred at least—and who has many unique skills. Subject has a genius-level intellect. His I.Q. goes right off the graphs. He is, in my considered opinion, *presentient.* If you hope to hoodwink subject with some run-of-the-mill confidence game, you will lose. Therefore a great deal of thought, preparation, and—yes—cold-blooded calculation went into the execution of this operation.

"Please remember that we were planning to let a killer loose and—forgive my bluntness—allow him, encourage him to destroy human beings. The plan was not without precedent, by the way. Both the MK Ultra and Star Racer programs were antecedents. But neither was so—to use your word—cold."

"Mmm." The man on the other end of the line made a soft monosyllabic grunt that he was still listening.

"We tried to choose an area with an extraordinarily high incidence of animal abuse. Incidentally, the child-abuse

33

numbers were abnormally high there as well. Waterton, Missouri was the target community the computers found for us. The profile was right both for initial manipulation of subject, who we felt would first target the animal abusers, and as an isolated agricultural community with a low population density. We could encircle a twenty-five-mile radius, which subject understood to be his comfort zone—or kill zone—and maintain full-time surveillance with two hundred operatives."

"But you had an implant performed, sent the subject in—drugged—to an area where he was supposedly turned loose, you had him electronically monitored, two hundred armed men and women encircling him and even with all that he escaped."

"No, sir. That's the point. He was permitted to appear to escape. The entire purpose of the . . . operation was to see how he would escape. This was the field exercise. To observe him under those conditions and see how his superior cunning and intellect would deal with the problem. He dealt with it quite well, as you know, and appeared to manage a neat escape and evasion. With a bit of help from us. That was the tricky part."

"Are you saying that you helped orchestrate his escape?"

"We indeed helped him appear to escape, not the same thing at all. He's been under constant surveillance ever since he left. I'm looking at him at the moment—as we speak." Dr. Norman allowed a tiny coloring of satisfaction in his tone. "He could be extinguished at a single command from me."

"But for God's sake, man, why haven't you given the command?"

"The plan is not to destroy subject, sir. The plan is to observe him. It was never just to observe him killing our preselected targets and targets of opportunity. We want to see how he thinks, schemes, plans, how and why he chooses the targets he does, how he improvises in the field, how he—"

"But why wasn't anyone else within the directorship of SAUCOG or Clandestine Services told about what was involved here so that it could be—properly contained?" For once Sieh was at a loss for words.

"I can only say that we—the director and myself, as head of the program—decided that the need to know did not exist. Not in this special case. It was my feeling, and I continue to believe, that the fewer who knew of the real plan the greater the chance for its success. The more one understands our subject and his capabilities the more one would concur as to the need for total security, even within the unit."

"What did you mean—you were looking at him at the moment?"

"I'm surveilling him electronically, just as other—um—assets are. On the OMEGASTAR system. The movement detection monitor. His implant mechanism makes it impossible for him to conceal his location. We've been with him every step of the way."

"I'm familiar with your mobile tracker unit, but didn't that malfunction? I was told that's how he got loose."

"The fabled 'bobble in the power' I believe it was called? Hmm. No. I'm afraid we engineered that, as well."

"Umm." The line was quiet for a second. "And you can have this subject disposed of when the program's goal has been achieved—you're certain of that?"

"He's in one of our asset's crosshairs every second of the day and night." The doctor had begun to improvise. But he had work to do. He couldn't sit and chat on the phone all day long.

"Where is the subject now?" Sieh asked. There was a brief pause while Norman prepared his dissembling response, but it was enough time for Sieh to understand that he'd asked a question whose answer he had no need to know. "Yes—all right," he said softly, as if Dr. Norman had responded. "It sounds like you've been on top of this all along."

There were a few more assurances on Norman's part, and

without further amenities the call ended. The doctor returned the telephone to its locked cupboard, and resumed working on his paper, the title of which was "Demystifying the Physical Precognate," which he would one day publish as part of his *Man and Mythology* series. He wrote a sentence and read it back:

"The Easy-Option/Quick-Fix Generation is a world choking on the quicksand of its own stupidity and arrogance." The telephone call had irritated him. He crossed the sentence out and began anew.

Far from Marion, Illinois, M. R. Sieh, Jr., had turned to a report from one of his EMARCY TRANSCO troubleshooters. He read a sentence that began *"American Barrick, Chelsea Metals, Echo Bay, Homestake Mining, Newmont Gold, Pegasus, Placer Dome—"* He caught himself reading the same names over and over, not really seeing the sentence. He had found the call both terribly upsetting and, in another way, at least partially reassuring. Overall, it was a troubling and horrifying business, and one that he was certain was doomed to failure, yet he felt powerless to act on his hunch, and he was a man who found the feeling of powerlessness to be an alien one.

He tried making notes for his memo. He wrote: *"Short pos. in subordinated bank debentures, LDC paper. Long pos. in cyclicals."* He capped his pen. He felt old and suddenly very tired. Perhaps he'd take an early nap today and put all this nasty business out of his mind. He stared out at the beautiful view of countless cherry blossoms in bloom.

The call had upset Dr. Norman equally. He looked over at the large green screen. There was a tiny, white, glowing blip dead center. He watched Daniel, whom he knew was in Kansas City, through the miracle of the OMEGASTAR, the *O*mni DF *MEGA*plex *S*ecure *T*ransceiver *A*uto-Lock Locator *R*elay unit and movement detection monitor.

Daniel Edward Flowers Bunkowski was alive and well. In the nation's capital, M. R. Sieh, Jr., wondered what sort of a world it was in which scientists held human life in such cheap regard, and then he realized that science hadn't changed all that much.

In Marion Federal Penitentiary over in Maximum Security, Dr. Norman was capping his own pen.

Neither man was trivial enough to consider that the word "capping" was a euphemism for pulling a trigger.

5

_____

Fort Worth, Texas

To the little boy who peers down into the heart of the immense cathedral, it is as if he views a sea. A sea of humanity. Into this sea it has begun to rain rich, full, vibrating organ notes, notes that fall slanting through the stained-glass sunlight that pierces the body of crucified Christ, washing over the sea with throbbing music, drenching it in a flood of spine-tingling sounds. "Know the _fear_ of God!" the voice intones.

Seven lamp stands, he sees. One like a son of man, clothed in a long robe and with a golden girdle around his breast. "His feet were like burnished bronze, refined as in a furnace, and his voice was like the sound of many waters; in his right hand he held seven stars, from his mouth issued a sharp two-edged sword, and his face was like the sun shining in full strength."

The apparition of the Deity speaks. "Behold I am alive for evermore, and I have the keys of Death and Hades." The child trembles with dread. A pervasive sense of fear shakes his body as he is pulled to his feet and propelled forward, down through the vibrating sea of faces.

"Bobby Price." The man speaks to him from the pulpit in a voice of concentrated thunder. "Bobby."

Pressure on his arm. His hand caught in a hard clenched fist that pulls him along, drags him down the center aisle toward the mouth of the river of sound. He has never known such terror.

"Bobby!" he says again. Motes of dust sparkle like dying stars in the angled rays, wheels of blinding color lance his eyes from dying Christ imprisoned in stained panels high above. *"Do you renounce Satan?"*

The Price mansion reeked of old money, serious money, which in the Metroplex generally meant cattle or oil. The Price fortune had been built on black gold: petrodollars, and lots of them. Two petroleum tycoons' heirs merged, via marriage, into one—the Tinnon/Price consortium.

John R. Price and the illustrious Olivia Tinnon of Dallas, Curaçao, and Barbados, leveraged their way into one another's lives. It was a loveless marriage from the beginning, a union that pregnant Olivia described to a sister on her wedding day as being "just like the oil bidness. John is light, sweet, crude and dirty."

Bobby Price seldom saw his preposterously rich jet-set petroheir-and-heiress parents. Pampered and spoiled by nannies, given everything, he was simply one of those sick aberrations for which there appears to be no scientific explanation.

But the little child would long remember standing naked on the front-hall stairs, where two women teased him, promising him he would never be a complete man. He would often recall the bitterness of his tears as he stood beneath the dark oil portraits of stern ancestors, listening to the taunts of the maid and the nanny who had found him nude on the stairway.

Later, he would also fix on the moment when the nanny had caught him trying to peer up her skirt, and had opened large, fleshy legs to reveal the frightening black cavern hidden in her bush, telling the boy he'd fall in that hole and nobody would ever find him.

Funny how little it sometimes takes to change a child into what will someday become a twisted sociopathic menace.

Women speak of their biological clock. Bobby Price had one, too. On the surface he seemed to be a perfectly normal child, but if you placed your head to his heart and listened carefully, you could hear the little boy ticking.

From the first time he took one of his father's hunting rifles into his small hands, it was love at first sight. Where children from more prosaic backgrounds grew up with Red Ryder BB carbines, Bobby was given an expensive "varmint" toy, one that fired the genuine article—.22-caliber long rifle ammo.

Bobby took to the weapon like a duck takes to the wet stuff, and—unsupervised and indulged—he began to kill. "Shitbirds," he called them. Within a few weeks the "shitbird" population in the Price section of suburban Fort Worth had dwindled alarmingly.

Bobby Price had found his calling. He loved to kill. *Loved* . . . to kill. It became his philosophy, his raison d'être, his religion. His obsession with weapons had begun in earnest.

When Bobby was fourteen he had grown bored with slaying birds and animals. Already the veteran of two wild-boar hunts and innumerable big-game hunting excursions, Bobby became fascinated with the prospect of taking down some two-footed trophies. He started scoping traffic and snap-shooting an empty Weatherby-Magnum at the passing cars.

One day it was just too much for him. A farmer came chugging along in an old beat-up pickup truck, and he could no more have stopped himself than the man in the moon. He snapped a .357 round into the empty chamber, snicked that oiled bolt into lock 'n' load, and squeezed one off. That time he ended up in an asylum. Daddy saw to that. Daddy and Daddy's legal talent.

When he came back out—still in "deep therapy," of course, he went to work for some people there in Texas, who thought "Shooter" Price was just what the doctor ordered.

Not long after that he was arrested as a prime suspect in a mob-style execution, and again Daddy's lawyers went to work. It was a bit tougher this time. Bobby was seventeen. A lot of people thought Bobby should get the electric chair. But then a lot of people suddenly came into a whole bunch of money, and changed their minds.

The deal was this: Bobby could walk, but only on one condition. The kid had to join the U.S. Army. There was a nasty little war going on in Vietnam. One outfit in particular liked the cut of Shooter Price's jib. They all agreed—this li'l ol' boy from Texas was nothin' but a flat-out born killer.

Quang Tri Province, Republic of Vietnam

The Sixties found Bobby Price in I Corps Tactical Zone, killing for peace. Diem and Kennedy were but two of the better-known casualties of that time. SAUCOG, a mysterious and clandestine intelligence group, in league with the Clandestine Services unit of a monolithic "fact-gathering" agency, had found several mutant personalities, some of whom had been institutionalized at the time.

A plan had been devised for inserting "killer robots," as one unfortunate memorandum phrase had described the action personnel, into situations involving highly sensitive operations: assassinations, over-the-fence jobs, torture and terrorism; no act was to be beyond the purview of this special unit. In a war where our allies were often our enemies, a sanitized hit squad was worth its weight in gold.

The mandate appeared to be presidential, and the combined forces unit had drawn on both military and civilian resources. It was a mixed bag of horror stories.

In a secure Quonset hootch within the perimeter of the spook complex near the Quang Tri airstrip, admittance to which required special clearance, an old man and the kid—known to his colleagues as Shooter Price—talked about a unique weapon system. The old man did most of the talking.

"The .50-caliber sniper weapon is nothing new. As you know there have been isolated kills made with the so-called Ma Deuce—the M-2—and the Hotchkiss .50 is performing admirably as you can attest." He turned and removed what appeared to be a large map cover. Bobby Price saw a cutaway schematic of a firing device.

"Ray guns—electrical guns more properly—fall into three groups: rail, coil, and polarizer. That's a rail. Those are capacitor banks." He pointed. "You understand what a capacitor is?" Shooter nodded, but the old man ignored him. "Umm. No matter. You couldn't move this, much less carry it. You need conducting rails for the projectile to ride, and this is where you shoot your current, which creates a magnetic field. It travels along here, and *BANG!* Fires your weapon. Not practical. Too big. Wears out quickly." The old man turned to another cutaway in color.

"In a conventional firing device you need three things to operate: a furnace, a projectile, and a pipe. You burn something or create heat, expanding gases blow your projectile out your pipe. *BANG!* How fast the projectile comes out—that's your bullet velocity.

"The coil is good, see, because it isn't limited by the same laws that govern velocities in conventional furnaces. We go now from one mile a second to two miles, three, maybe *four* miles a second! We call that hypervelocity.

"Energy waves travel through here." He pointed to the drawing of the coil gun. "And the force of the magnetic field propels the projectile at hypervelocities of such speeds you can penetrate anything.

"You ever heard how a hurricane drives pieces of straw through boards?"

"Yes, sir." Price hadn't but he wanted to show he was paying attention.

"Same deal." The man shook his head and long gray hairs misbehaved. "Hypervelocity. It makes the projectile penetrate the target according to a different set of physical laws.

"In theory, if your bullet was dense enough, you could put

a coil gun on a satellite, send it in orbit around the earth, and you could fire a projectile that would penetrate the globe and come out the other side of the planet! In theory, that is. If it didn't burn up on the way—and so on . . ." The old man trailed off, mesmerized by his own ideas.

"This is the polarizer. Magnetic field. Super velocity. More durable than a rail gun. Smaller than a coil gun. Only problem is the energy eats the bullet. It gets the furnace so hot—so to speak—that when it pushes the projectile out the pipe the projectile itself disintegrates because the air becomes the target." He'd completely lost Shooter.

"So here was where a light bulb lit over my head. Look at the *projectile* the light bulb said to me, not the delivery method. Put something that makes its own little furnace out there on the tip of the bullet, see? When the hyperspeeds heat up the projectile, *BANG!*—the combustible material fires! Now you got your furnace here, and here—burning up the air on the way to the target. *Excelsior!"* The old man gestured wildly in the air, looking like a mad scientist in a comic book.

"SHARP-HEX! Stands for *S*uper-*H*ardened *AR*mor-penetrating *P*rojectile—*H*igh *EX*plosive. Tungsten-carbide kinetic energy penetrator with an incendiary detonator on the tip." He showed a large-scale cutaway of two cartridges. "APEX! *A*nti-*P*ersonnel Projectile. *EX*tended Range. This one'll go through anything. This one not only explodes what it strikes, it destroys itself in the process. Amazing projectiles," he said with undisguised pride.

"Only problem is in the delivery system." He turned to his final schematic. "It's like the old story about the electric car. They cost a cent and a half per ten thousand miles. The only trouble is the extension cord costs fifty thousand dollars. Same deal. The furnace and the pipe cost the U.S. government a quarter of a million dollars. Only one field model has been produced. Nothing else like it exists anywhere on earth. The U.S. M-3000 .50-caliber single-shot, hypervelocity, extended-range, flashless, *S*ilent *A*nti-

*V*ehicle/*AN*ti-*T*errorist Weapon System. SAVANT for short. The death ray!"

At a location known officially as Fire Support Base King, a sprawling hilltop jump-off point just south of "the Zone," SAUCOG's sniper, Bobby Price, was given his first secret mission in which the SAVANT weapon system would be utilized.

A spike team of mercenaries and other headhunters drawn from the Combined Forces Special Unit, both civilian and military personnel, was to be aborted. Post-Diem liaisons had caused both the team's operations and its goals to be a political liability.

The world supply of ammunition, four hundred rounds of SHARP-HEX and APEX cartridges, was now in the care of the sniper. He had run only eleven practice rounds through the weapon before he reached a feeling of confidence that the mission could be easily accomplished.

Bobby Price and SAVANT waited in a forward gun pit, not far from the landing zone where the team's two choppers would be arriving. Behind him a squad of snake eaters and two tank crews sighted their weapons from a protective treeline.

But not all of the members of the spike team were aboard the unmarked skinships. One man was missing.

In deep sleep, the missing man had envisioned the stalk of a wounded enemy. The hunt took him down into the core of a dark fragment of a time when he'd tracked one of the little people, following a blood trail that led to a clearing where the blood drops suddenly stopped. Where had the wounded man gone? In his dream, a thought occurred. What if one took a bottle of blood and made a trail, smallest drops last, coming out from an ambush site, a man backtracking in his own footprints leaving a trail of sprinkled blood drops?

As the thought crossed his mindscreen, the man jerked awake from the folds of his imagining, a sniper's sights lingering on the back of his head.

The thing that had saved him before saved him now,

nudging him awake in the darkness of a spike-team hootch. It prickled his skin as he waited, vexing him, prodding him to his huge bare feet. It would protect him from his own side.

Silently, like a great fat cat, he began to ease his way out into the night, loaded with duffel, weapon, 15EEEEE boots, surprisingly graceful and sure-footed, a dangerous dancing bear. Outside he froze. Waited. Listened.

The thing that warned him on a level he could never totally identify pushed him in the direction of the perimeter. It would not be as tricky to get out as it would be to get in, but damned near. He knew where the mines and traps were, where the guard posts were, the location of the listening post out beyond the edge of the distant trees, but it would require all his skills to make it out through the tanglefoot, concertina, razor wire, and assorted protective fencing, out beyond the danger of "friendly fire."

The immense human-shaped mass tiptoed through the tulips, glided, slid, crawled, rolled, picked his way through the wire, moving as if directed by an inner gyro, his mental compass taking him deeper into the shadow of Firebase King's perimeter.

Trees. Foliage dripping from recent downpours. He moved through the treeline, away from Firebase King and the fate that his presentience foretold, stopping again at the far side of the woods to watch and listen to the sounds of the night around him, slowing his vital signs, forcing himself into a state of bioelectrical calm, patient as the most efficient animal predator, tuned to the darkness that surrounded him.

From the edge of the trees, he saw a patch of open paddy that he would have to cross, an extremely perilous place, but beyond that there was a wash of sand, then a steep slope covered in tall sawgrass. The slope led to the river, swollen with monsoon-season rains, a brown swift-moving snake that could take him out of harm's path.

They hoped to kill him. To kill all of them. He let a bit of his rage creep back, inflaming his calm, giving him an edge of anger. When his killer instinct was all the way up again he let the shadows swallow him up, and he willed himself across the paddy, willing himself into a state not unlike invisibility, a feral, invulnerable, massive component of the Asian night.

Within minutes he was gone. A quarter ton of killer had disappeared. Vanished from sight. All that remained was a whisper in the sawgrass.

It was a hell of a place for tanks, the tank commander thought, standing in the hatch of "Tracks from Hell," perched on the treeline's edge. Pogues back at Battalion Headquarters were fucking terrain morons, and he'd said it a hundred times to anyone who'd listen. He watched the grunts settle in with guns up. The tanks were security for the squad, and for the sniper down in the gun pit.

The radio crackled before he heard the skinships. With these people—the outfit he worked for—you didn't ask too many questions. They said two unmarked Hueys were gonna get lit up, you lit 'em up. Arty from FSB King, tanks, and a couple of fire teams? Shit. Those old boys were history.

"In position," he said, keying a handset.

"Hellstorm, we copy." An anonymous voice crackled in his ear. He signaled, and inside the steel monster beneath him compensating idler wheels whirred, final drive sprockets revolved, gloved hands on steering control assemblies touched transmission and throttle, and the powerful turbine moved "Tracks from Hell" forward, past the edge of the treeline.

The youngster at the gunner's station watched the primary sight. Computer-operated laser rangefinders and thermal imaging systems locked on to their targets.

The tank commander, his thumbs caressing the butterfly triggers of his M-2, patted the big .50, and climbed back down out of the turret, pulling the hatch shut. Inside the monster it stunk of mo-gas farts, hot oil, and heavy-duty payback.

The two targets hovered expectantly in the hidden sights of several tons of friendly fire.

It was a hell of a place for tanks, that was all he could think of.

Down in the gun pit, Shooter Price, a pair of North Sonic IIs keeping only a part of the machine noise out of his ears, laid the crosshairs of a Laco 40X sniperscope on the lead bird and his trigger finger exerted three and a quarter pounds of pressure. SAVANT spat death.

A covert op had become a herd of rogue elephants—a liability. . . . Now it was terminated.

But not quite.

6

Fort Worth, Texas

Nanny is behind the wheel. She will not ride in the chauffeur-driven limo, not to a place of worship. It is not seemly. She would be embarrassed if her girlfriends would see her and the little boy get out of the rich folk's ostentatious car. And she loathes the filthy-minded chauffeur as well.

Her voice is loud in his ear as she sings the doxology in the pew at church.

"Praise God from whom all blessings flow . . ." The words, without true meaning, run together inside his head.

They drive past Sunday lawns manicured by workers of dark skin pigmentation and she turns the radio sermon on. A preacher from some distant station in West Texas is pleading for money. Bobby gazes out the window at the lush streets lined with weeping willows, magnolias, frangipania, bougainvillea, yuccas, and their more exotic cousins. The yards are landscaped here and lawn jockeys still wait at curbside. The homes have names. Entrance archways proclaim this is Fandangle and Fandango, Twin Forks and Twin Pines, Cedars and Big Oak, Rocking R and X-IT, San

Sebastian and San Ciello, Chisholm and Lazy L. The men are named Clint, Bubba, Billy Bob Ray, and Billy Ray Bob.

The neighbors here may be faceless strangers who own an immense Arabian horse stud ranch.

Dappled sunlight filters down through three-hundred-year-old oak, and mighty Dutch elms that arbor the clean streets as they wait to die of Dutch elm disease, and catches in the turrets of the catty-cornered mansions.

"Hal-lay-lool-ya!" Nanny says to the radio, enthusiastically, startling the boy.

The men are real men here, and they swill down the Pearl and the Lone Star to chase their Dick'l 'n' branch wattah. There are no beauty salons in evidence. These rich suburbs are unsullied by either mine, mill, factory, plant, or other industrial blight. This is serious old-time money.

Bobby Price has his childhood memories. He was almost seventeen when he and his father's lawyers decided he'd best opt for military service.

He remembered Beaumont, the Panhandle, Big Bush, Baghdad on the Bayou, Waco, San Antone (where you could still shoot a black panther with it declawed in the cage, and call it sport), Lubbock, the Cowboys, White Rock Lake, South Oak Cliff, TCU, SMU, the Metroplex, River Crest Country Club, where a girl once reached up the leg of his swimming trunks to see what was "hidin' in that ol' hair." She had told him something he would file away forever:

"Lord, Bobby, they ain't but two things he didn't give you and both of 'em was a dick."

He recalled the doctor who had written ". . . *it will not be possible for him to achieve penetration.*" He would prove that good medical man wrong a hundred times. He would do some damned flat hog wild penetrating before he was done. (In 1966 he was driving a blood-red 'Vette with dual glass packs—as phallic a ride as there was back then—the sort of kid who'd never be street legal, and he was afraid of nothing.)

"Olivia," he called his mother. She was distant and beautifully cool, and the wrinkles had fallen from her face and neck to gather on hands encrusted with platinum and rocks from Harry Winston and Van Cleef and Tiff's. "Ma'am" was the intimate form of address permitted her only child.

The dining room was a long expanse of table with the tallest throne chairs at either end. Heavy, carved, ecumenical TexMex and El Grecoesque murals, tapestries, and ancestral oils mixed among the open beams, adobe moderne, and the showpiece wall of leaded glass. Here, in these rich Texas suburbs, the "cathedral" ceiling started.

In the dining room, Bobby Price sat in solitary silence, hypnotized by the images in the colored glass, hearing the man ask him the question from the pulpit again and again:

"Bobby . . . have you renounced Satan?"

Kansas City

Bobby Price, a.k.a. "Shooter," woke up, as he sometimes did, instantly and fully awake. The first thing he did was eyeball DeMon, the detection monitor, which confirmed for him visually that all was well. Big Petey was status quo.

The beeper and the sensor alarm would have had him on his feet had it been otherwise, but he liked the reassuring visual confirmation. He wore his monitor the way some folks wear their wedding bands—everywhere.

His beeper lay alongside his pocket change on the motel dresser: a few coins, a pen and notepad, a wristwatch that cost more than a poor man's annual income, a pair of North Sonic plugs—the tools of his trade.

He hit the cold floor and did twenty slow push-ups. Then five the hard way, one handed, his weight balanced on the fingertips of his right hand. It killed him to do those and he let himself drop to the filthy carpet for a moment, remaining in a prone nose dive for as long as he could stand it, letting the foul odor of the carpet cleaner, room deodorizer, booze spills, and the residue from a carload of tobacco ashes force him to recoil away from the floor.

Bobby was on his feet, breathing deeply. He went over and hit his weights, doing a few slow, *s-l-o-w* serious reps with the special fifty-eight-pound job. Arm curls that made those powerful bikes and trikes pump. As always he tried to do one with the left arm and couldn't get the chrome off the floor. He breathed some more, did a few squats, then went into the doorway of the bathroom for isos.

Bobby put everything he had into the isometrics, breaking a sweat as he pushed against the immovable forces, doing the iso groups the same way he did everything else, with total dedication and concentration.

He finished. Showered quickly, warm water then ice cold, surveying the clean, lean, mean Shooter Price in the door mirror. He didn't like himself nude, so he toweled off, pulling on a pair of royal blue briefs that hid the useless appendage that had controlled so much of his life.

In the mirror, he examined himself again. The reflection was that of a trim, muscular, extremely good-looking man in his mid-thirties, which wasn't bad for forty-one. Well-developed upper torso, arms, and legs. A self-confident face that could be described as "handsome," and few would challenge the adjective. Five feet six inches. Well, he would be, as soon as he dressed. He wore shoes with high Cuban heels. Short? Okay. But perfectly shaped. The 159 pounds distributed properly over his frame. And with the briefs on, he couldn't see the tiny sleeping bird that mocked him from its hairy nest, the superfluous and recalcitrant hunk of meat that was a source of great puzzlement to all.

Chisel-featured, flaxen-haired, brilliant, fastidiously well-groomed, he was and always had been tremendously attractive to women. And like so many persons who appear to have been wound too tightly, his energy force gave off a strong animal magnetism. So both his physical appearance and the coiled-spring ambience of Bobby's inner conflicts produced the expected dynamics. A long succession of beautiful and sexy women had been left unfulfilled and puzzled by the inexplicable impotence of Shooter Price.

Completing his morning ritual, he dressed in elegant

Neimann's doeskin slacks, a sandy tan cashmere sweater, and four-hundred-dollar handmade Italian loafers, then filled his pockets and stepped out into the sunlight, pulling the motel door closed and locking it.

He unlocked the gleaming bone-colored M-30 and slid into the cold seat, kicking on the engine. He touched a button watching the windows disappear, as power augers released the top. It was too humid, he decided, and he raised the top back up, pulling out of the motel parking lot, the three-liter V-6 growling out into the stream of late-morning traffic.

Big Petey was a dead white blip on the OMNI, which was on Locator/Focus-lock, Automatic, and Monitor B. The OMNI paged his beeper if Big Petey, his private name for P.T.—primary target—went into motion beyond a proscribed radius of his current location.

Bobby Price flipped open his gold-trimmed alligator-hide notebook to the last entry: P.T. had been out of action since 0140. He clicked his slim gold pen and jotted down the time.

Big Petey, Shooter Price's special assignment, was none other than Daniel Edward Flowers Bunkowski.

For three days Petey hadn't moved and Price was getting antsy. "Get a life," he told himself, staring into the face of the OMEGASTAR. Inside his head, he had this big boy down pat and cold. One of his tricks to keep fresh and sharp over long, boring plants, which was the jargon for what the TV shows and films call "stakeouts," was to continually recite the tech manuals, running the nomenclature and specs through his mind like worry beads; his private sniper's litany:

"OMEGASTAR *provides the* SAVANT *operator with a complete menu of sensors and monitors, tactical communications linkages, auto-paging, and EW Countermeasures, all housed within a single device to assure successful tracking and targeting.*" It stared back at him: its two bright eyes as much living optics to Price as a person's; the blue DeMon and green LocLok eyes—meters—around the nose of the Mobile Tracker Paging Unit. Freq dial. Power indicator, a complex bank of tuners. All the colored lights of the intrusion detectors, channel lights, and heat detectors glowed orange, yellow, and red like the string of lights on a Christmas tree.

"User/Operator-friendly, the complete four-in-one console, housed in transit case with all fitted accessories, weighs less than twenty-five pounds. The Auto-Lock locator for the movement detector, when synced to the portable pager and sensing units, eliminates the need for hands-on operation of the tracker, as well as the need for "around-the-clock" eyeball surveillance presence." Bet your sweet taters it did.

The master on/off switches were shielded in individual hazard covers, red rubberized hoods that protected each toggle from being thrown accidentally. The mouth of the tracker system's face was a perpetually open *O* of glowing green, a white blip visible in the center of the OMNI's bull's-eye. There were jacks for the various commo-links that could act as message channels to the Newton Secure Sig-System, and a scrambled landline plugged into the tracker's ear.

"OMEGASTAR Mobile Tracker is manufactured by Signatech Electronics, Inc., of Davenport, Iowa, and is available in Sea Blue, Sandstone, or cream finish. Unit accessories include Mini-pager, Beeper, Light shields, Mesh net, Ghillie cover, and Cammo-fittings in Snow White, Sand, Woodland Green, Light Brown, O.D., Black, and other optional combinations, as well as the Executive Attaché Transit Case into which the entire unit is housed."

Bobby Price was Dr. Norman's ace in the hole. Bobby and SAVANT, the silent and astonishingly deadly .50 sniper weapon, with the tracker continually monitoring Daniel Bunkowski's implant signal, made it possible to let Chaingang roam and kill.

It mattered little to Price that he was an instrumental part of what was—arguably—one of the most malevolent programs ever initiated by the military or intelligence community in the name of science and/or national security. What mattered was the work. To Shooter the work was everything.

The decades since Vietnam had been long, boring ones for him. There had been moments of excitement—yes—with long, slow dry spells in between.

He'd remained with the parent company for the whole time, taking contracts during the Seventies and Eighties, but basically just sitting on his butt most of the time. He had filled his life with expensive toys, cars, babes, hobbies, books, theater, films—and travel.

He'd lived on Ibetha before the hustlers moved in; St. Tropez before the tourists came; Barbados before the rowdies found it; Puerto Vallarta before the hippies arrived; Cancun before it became a spring-break shithole.

To many persons, Bobby Price's life would seem idyllic. But without work—*the* work—he was a lifeless shell inside. The operational challenge of the stalk infused him with energy and purpose. He would have paid *them,* truth be known, to retain his position as SAUCOG's senior sniper.

The weapon system had been his baby for a quarter of a century, and in all that time the R and D guys had been unable to come up with anything that could touch it. She was still the queen of long-range killers, and would probably reign so as long as she remained operative. A second model had been contemplated, but prices had gone through the ceiling. To build her a twin for the Persian Gulf War, for example, would have cost five million dollars. She was a unique piece.

Would SAVANT ever rust or break or fall apart with age? No. Not with Price's tender, loving care and normal maintenance. She was made to function for many more years. What of the remaining hundred-and-some special rounds? Would the old ammunition begin to malfunction with time? Nobody knew for sure, and the inventor of the system itself was long dead.

In the Eighties, the company had ordered a small run of SHARP-HEX and APEX ammo manufactured—just in case. And Shooter's stash had been upgraded with two cases of new Red Rock Match Grade (Silent/Extended Range) .50 sniper rounds, hand-delivered by the arsenal's courier. But

Shooter, a professional worrier, never fully trusted the new stuff and continued to use the old rounds without incident. So far there hadn't been a cough in the carload.

It had been interesting to watch Chaingang in action during the first phase of this operation, which had taken place in a small Missouri farm town. Price had been kept busy, driving the country blacktops and gravel roads parallel to the primary target's movements, as he wound along his river routes or made his way across farmland. Petey had been a busy boy.

It was funny about the relationship between a sniper and his target. When you were hunting it was one thing, you took the target down at the first opportunity of a sure shot. When you conducted surveillance, it was a test of one's professionalism. You watched the same P.T. through that Laco 40X, or across the open blade sight, over and over, and pretty soon your trigger finger got very itchy.

That's why Shooter never watched Petey too long through the weapon. He'd follow him on the tracker, stay close enough to take a shot should the order ever be issued, and be pleased to "blow him up real good," but until that time he was a big, fat golden goose. Also there was a bonding, albeit one-way, that had gone on over the years. In an odd, ironic way it was almost as if Shooter viewed Chaingang as an old pal.

Sure, he thought, examining his reflection in the mirror, Bunkowski was a repulsive slob of a psychopathic killer but . . . since when was killing a crime? He broke himself up, laughing inside his mind, locking the door and slamming it behind him. He was heading for the rare bookshop, doing what he always did when he was bored—looking for ways to spend money.

"Hi." The girl seated behind the bookstore counter smiled up at the face of the handsome guy who'd just walked in. What a hunk, she thought, suddenly feeling very hot. She'd been reading a romance and it was as if the guy in the book had come to life, blowing in off the scorching streets,

55

ready to sweep her off her feet—the only difference being that the one in the novel had dark hair. She immediately scoped in on his ring fingers, and brightened at the absence of jewelry. "Anything special?"

"Just looking," he said. "I have lots of interests."

"Make yourself at home." I'll bet you do, she thought. "Feel free to browse." She put a little laugh into her voice.

"Thanks." He moved past her. Athletic-looking guy, maybe thirty-four, thirty-five. Unmarried. Probably not gay but you couldn't always tell. Really cute. She stood up and checked her image in the mirror, busying herself with a stack of books behind the counter. Touched her hair and adjusted the blouse she was wearing, a scoop-necked, off-the-shoulder peasant blouse which she wore demurely.

He zeroed in on familiar titles. Common stuff like *Sniping on the Rhine* and *A Marksman's War Diaries*. Immediately, he found a title he'd been looking for: *Sniper's Journal: Bound Volumes XI–XIX*. He'd heard of these but had never seen them. They were published by a small-press zine that had reproduced sections of lost material. He opened the leather-bound collection of magazines and thumbed through it. Most of it was stuff he'd seen or owned in the original, but he saw an article entitled "An Authentic Account of Sharpshooting in Mexico." Damn!

"How much is this one?" he asked the brunette girl with the nice chest.

She quoted him a price that he thought was way out of line and he let it show in his eyes.

"Wow!" he said, keeping his tone friendly. "That's pretty high—I'll have to think on that one."

"Sure," she said. He went back to the bookshelf he'd been examining, and she watched him carefully put the volume back where he'd found it. "I'm sorry about that. I don't own the shop or I'd make you a better price."

"Oh? This isn't your place then?" he asked conversationally.

"No. I manage it for the owner."

"I was in here once before—I don't think I saw you. I

would have remembered," he ad-libbed. "What's your name?" He didn't care but he could never stop himself. He could smell it on them when they wanted him and it was always worth trying again.

"Melissa."

"That's a nice name."

"Thanks."

"Mine's Bobby."

"Hi, Bobby," she said, thinking how inane she must be sounding. "I don't remember seeing *you* in here before either."

He had tuned out on her. In between McBride's *A Rifleman Went to War* (1935) and McMullen's *W.W.I Sniper* (1918) was a book he never expected to see.

McLeod, W. D. Edward, *Queen's Log.* Jesus! Every collector wanted this one. *Queen's Log: A Personal Narrative of Marksmanship Under Siege by the Zulu Nation,* the full title. Five hand-drawn, tipped-in maps of the Roarke's Drift battlefield. His skin felt ice cold in the summer air conditioning.

"How much for this one?" he asked her.

"Um. That's uh—" She double-checked her typed inventory list to be sure. "Twelve-fifty." He didn't react, so to make certain he understood she said in a soft voice, "One thousand, two hundred and fifty dollars." Only the two of them were in the shop. She was sure he'd be irritated or amazed, but he nodded instead.

"Okay. I'll take this. I'll probably be getting some other books so—is it all right if I leave this here for the time being?" He had placed the book toward the back of the long counter.

"Sure. That's fine."

"That's one I've been hunting," the good-looking guy said, heading back toward the books. Obviously, he was a real collector. She wondered if he'd try to write a check and how she'd handle it when she had to tell him no.

He went back to the stacks with his heart beating. What a find. Twelve-fifty was way, way low. He was so pumped up he bought a dupe of Idriess's *Sniping: With an Episode from the Author's Experiences During the War of 1914–18*, a common little publication, because it was in perfect condition in the dust jacket. He was stoked.

"This is a great store. And I love the name of the place: Dog Soldiers!" He laughed and the girl made an appreciative chuckle.

"Thanks." She felt tongue-tied. One of the sides of her blouse was riding a bit low on the shoulder. She didn't care.

He looked for another ten minutes and came back to the counter with an autographed first edition of Daoust's *Cent-Vingt Jours de Service Actif: Récit Historique Très Complet de la Campagne du 65 Eme au Nord-Ouest* (1886), *Shooting to Survive: Indian-Fighting at Adobe Walls and Buffalo Wallow*, an original *FMFMI—3B* manual, *Memoirs of a Marksman at Peachtree Creek*, and an ultrarare edition of *Tagebuch: Eines Ordonnanzoffiziers Von 1812–1813* that made Bobby's ticker start thumping hard again when he saw the hand-drawn map in color! He loved this store and everybody in it.

"You must be a real collector," she said, not keeping the awe out of her voice. He had peeled off twenty-seven pictures of the late, great Benjamin Franklin, then went back and got the bound book of *Sniper's Journal* magazines, which brought his purchase to nearly three thousand dollars. Hardly the biggest sale she'd rung up but Bobby Beautiful paid for these as if he were buying an armful of paperbacks at B. Dalton or Waldenbooks, instead of plunking down three grand for a few books and booklets. He was gorgeous, single, and rich. She wasn't going to let him out of the store alive.

"Didn't you see anything else that you liked?" she asked him boldly, the heat evident in her voice. Not caring about what a bimbo she might appear, or how far the blouse was slipping down as she leaned forward on the counter.

"I saw a lot that I liked." He had ferocious eyes, and he ate her up with his gaze—just the way the man in the romance novel had devoured the heroine. "I didn't think I could afford it. It looked too special," he said. She thought she was going to have a heart attack.

"You're never going to know unless you ask." She colored at her own chutzpah. She boxed the books very carefully.

"I need somebody who really knows these things to act as a guide. You know what I mean? Like—well, you know this stuff. I wonder if I could get you to help me? Say, later, when you get off work? Would you have time to advise me in these collecting matters?" Why did he go through this over and over? He knew it wouldn't amount to anything but he insisted on putting himself through it. Maybe he'd get one who'd do what he wanted without having to pay for it.

"But we hardly know one another," she said, coquettishly, telling him yes in every other way but words.

"Sure we do. I'm Bobby. You're Melissa. What more do we need to know?"

"Are you married—for one thing."

"Uh-uh." What an airhead. He was already regretting it, but the blouse and bra had fallen away from her breasts and he couldn't help but notice a distinct nip in the air. "Are you?"

"Free. White. Twenty-one. Female."

"What time do you get off . . . work?"

"Four-thirty. I live down the street."

"Hey—that's great. Would you mind if I drop by? Take you out for *dinnah?*" he asked. She thought his accent was cute.

"That'd be nice."

"Seven?"

"Sure." She was used to eating at five, but for him she'd eat at midnight. "Sounds great."

"Okay, Melissa. Sounds real good. Where do you live?"

"Oh, yeah!" She snapped out of it and wrote her address and phone number down, then her name, in big, circular, loopy script, and dotting the *i* of Melissa with a small heart. "See you tonight, Bobby." She started to ask him his last name and decided she didn't care. Bobby Beautiful was his name.

She smiled and he blew her a kiss goodbye. She watched him through the front window, grateful the boss hadn't been here to overhear her coming on to a customer. He drove a sharp convertible—it figured he'd have great wheels—she wasn't sure what kind.

Why did he go through the motions? he asked himself again. He wasn't stupid—why do it? They wanted the same thing. He couldn't give it to them. They never liked what he liked. Why didn't he pay for it? Because it wasn't any fun to pay for it. One of these days he'd find a girl, just like the girl that . . . he whistled the last five syllables to himself. Loading the books in the trunk, packing them in a cammo-cover and wedging the box in with SAVANT and the tracker, the items nearly filling the small trunk of the car.

Fuck her, he thought, as he drove off. Knowing that he couldn't. His mind now on the rare books.

Bobby woke up in one of those terrible fuzzies between sleep and the fully awake stage, head pounding softly with the dull precursor to what could be the front edge of a bad dream, but he forced the thoughts through, replaying a totally real experience from his groggy memory banks.

As he pushed himself up from the carpeting he took stock of his surroundings. Melissa's place. The bedroom white with a surfeit of wicker and bric-a-brac. He got back on his bare feet and went in and urinated, splashing into the center of the bowl, flushing, running water. Melissa said something from the next room, a sleep-muffled comment, which he ignored.

Their coupling had started out as it often did, with an exchange of tender kisses and endearments, the romantic prelude to lovemaking heating up into a wild mating game. Four days of this.

She was dressed in a flimsy camisole top, spike heels, and nothing else. He loved the way the sharp heels felt against his legs and feet. He was ready to be punished.

"Stand up," he said to her, warming inside.

"Huh?" She didn't understand. What was wrong?

"Stand up in the bed. Come on."

"Right now?" She couldn't figure him out. Bobby was so weird.

"Yeah." His voice sounded hoarse. "Come on." She stood up on the bed as he directed.

"I'm going to punch holes in the bed with these heels."

"Turn around. Let me see you. Yeah. Turn—like that."

"You like me like this?"

"Put your foot here." He offered his testicles to her.

"Do *which?*"

"Yeah. Put your spike heel right on me there."

"I might hurt you, Bobby."

"That's okay—come on. You won't hurt me."

She tried to comply, gingerly placing her shoe in contact with his genitals. "Put your weight on it." She did and he moaned.

She thought she might have hurt him and she dropped down on her knees in the bed.

"Please, honey—let's just make love, okay?" She tried to kiss him and he pushed her roughly away.

"Make me call you Mistress Melissa and squeeze my balls real hard."

"No," she whined. "I don't want to do that. Please? Just hold me."

He held her, but he had grown very cold. She tried kissing him again, then she lowered her face over him, letting her hair sweep along his flat stomach and thighs. It was a trick of hers, and it had enflamed other men. But when she tried to take Bobby in her mouth he merely rolled over away from her. He had lost all interest.

In the bathroom mirror, Bobby Price's reflection was pale, but his face felt suffused with something akin to anger—a combination of embarrassed guilt and rage. He wanted to strike out.

Four times they'd been together and he'd get her so hot she thought she'd go up in flames—then he wouldn't do anything. She'd never been with anybody like Bobby. She knew that she had a body that turned guys on. But he never got—excited. He was so small. She wondered how big it was when it was erect. She'd been with another guy who had a small one when it was soft but it was plenty big when he got a hard-on. He was so uptight. She had to make this new man in her life respond. Maybe if he could relax . . .

"Bobby?"

"Huh?" He came out of the bathroom with his clothes back on.

"Don't go, honey," she said. "Let's have some wine."

"Um." He grunted, wishing he had an excuse to hit the bitch. She returned with a tray. Two wine goblets and a little plate of snacks. Cheese and crackers and stuff. "Sit on the bed there. No. I'll sit and you be the priestess." She had no idea what he was saying. He took one of the wine goblets and sat on her bed. "Now . . . you put a cracker in my mouth." For some reason he started rubbing himself, trying to get turned on.

"Huh?"

"Feed me a fucking cracker. Stand in front of me and act like you're feeding me a cracker." He was a puzzle to her, but she stood in her little see-through camisole and the spike heels and started to comply, holding a cracker in front of his mouth as if he were a parrot or something. A cockatoo.

"Corpus Domini nostri Jesu Christi custodiat animam tuaam in vitam aeternam," he intoned. She recoiled in shock.

"Don't!" she said. "That's blasphemy."

He'd had enough of her ass. Price stood up and, for no real reason, tossed the wine into her face.

"You dirty—" Wine dripped from Melissa, her camisole, staining bedclothes and white wicker. She came at him, a tough girl and a strong fighter, and he took a couple of punches before he had a chance to clobber her a good one with that weight-lifter's power arm. She went down in a wine-stained heap on the bedroom floor and he turned and walked out, forgetting her the second the door closed.

He unlocked the car, plopped into the seat, keyed the

ignition, and then the engine roared to life as he sped away from the apartment house.

He drove north in silent rage and self-pity, finally getting his shit together when a familiar street sign nudged him. He realized he was on busy Linwood Boulevard, and he drove a few blocks and turned. Bobby knew what he was going to do before he did it, and when he saw the field in back of the gas station he turned, taking a service road until he'd reached just the right isolated spot.

He parked on the shoulder and opened the trunk and got the big case out, carefully stepping over a barbed-wire fence after he'd snagged his shirt on the top strand in the darkness. With a small penlight he worked his way to a position where he could look back down the hill on a side road. There was a brightly lit tavern and another business of some kind next to it, and a few cars in the gravel lot. He opened the case.

"The U.S. M-3000 .50 SHERFSAVANT Weapon System, is referred to by the abbreviated acronym SAVANT. It is a unique sniper rifle with a maximum effective range of nearly two miles, well over three thousand meters. With Laco 40X sniperscope it weighs 29.5 pounds. The rifle is equipped with a fiberglass transit case with fitted sponge rubber compartment liners. The cased weapon system weighs approximately thirty-one pounds." Bobby said his rosary as he assembled the piece by touch.

"Classification and type: silent, extended range, covert. Operation: bolt-action. Caliber: .50. Capacity: single-shot. Length: 48 inches. Barrel length: 27 inches. Scope and Optics: Laco 40X, Lenses are Magni-coat. Reticle: mil dot duplex. Silencer and Flash Suppressor: Ultronics. Eye relief: 3.5 inches. Lands and Grooves: 9. Twist: right hand, 1 turn in 9 inches. Trigger pull: 3.25 pounds. Magnification: 40 power. Ammunition: Red Rock Match Grade (Silent S-type). Main elevation: Ballistic comeups built in. Elevation, fine-tune: adjustable. Windage: adjustable. Muzzle Vel: hypervelocity. Manufacturer: USARCO Mfg. Division of Quad Cities Tool

and Die, Rock Island, Illinois." "Tool and Die." He liked that. He always enjoyed saying that to people who asked him what line he was in. "Tool and die," he'd tell them, meaning it.

The stock and shoulder rest had been custom-molded to fit his face and body, and the finger indentations and palm moldings on the grips in back of the trigger housing and forward of the action had been cast from his hands. Sighting the piece in darkness was as simple as pulling on a pair of comfortable old leather gloves. She fit him perfectly. But the stock hurt him a little when he put his face down close to his main squeeze, and he whispered to her, "Not you, baby. Melissa hurt your daddy." He fondled her knurled bolt, snicked it, and a big, hard sniper round filled her oily mouth.

"Anti-Personnel APEX(X) rounds consist of a full steel-jacketed shell containing propellant, *A*nti-*P*ersonnel *EX*ploding projectile (*ex*tended range), high explosive, and detonator." He looked down through the calm green of her and clearly saw a man step out of the tavern and into the parking lot. There was no one else in sight. *"When a round is fired and the bullet strikes the target a detonator causes the high explosive charge to explode the fragmentation material. This material consists of soft, scored* penetrators *that fragment like miniature bomb shrapnel, and which are designed to tumble at hypervelocities, mushrooming and disintegrating at the point of impact. This round is particularly effective against human beings and other soft targets."*

"Corpus Domini nostri—" Bobby Price whispered to the soft target below as he applied the requisite three and a quarter pounds of pressure to his favorite squeeze.

7

Victor Trask was feeling semi-shitty. He'd woken up with a terrible, pounding hangover and since he didn't drink that was not a propitious beginning to the day. Neither did it auger well that he cut himself while trying to shave his face, the right side of which was pockmarked with old acne scars. He knew that others, women particularly, found his face appealing—women used words like "character" and "interesting-looking" when describing him—but he thought he was ugly as sin, with a face like the landscape of the moon. Actually he wasn't half bad-looking. His features were sufficiently chiseled and decently proportioned to give him a craggy profile, and he'd been blessed with a tight cap of hair that never seemed to be in need of a comb. Trask, true to his inner character, tended to see only the worst. He saw the salt and pepper in his prematurely graying hair, the residual complexion of a zit-ridden childhood, and a bulbous "clown nose." Pulling clothes on he briefly examined himself in the door mirror and saw a thirty-six-year-old guy with a body the color of a dead bluegill. Make that carp. He had to get out in the sun one of these days.

He hated the sun. It was so . . . sunny. He was a night guy

and had nocturnal inner rhythms. It was three in the afternoon, which was like seven A.M. to him, and he had a half an hour of Kansas City traffic to negotiate before he was safely ensconced in the KCM building. The kids were out, which probably meant the traffic would be even worse, if that was possible. He put three Tylenols in his mouth and drank a swallow of tepid water from the tap. Breakfast. He wanted coffee but he would be half an hour late as it was.

He'd been a news announcer and writer for Z-60 for two years—his tenth and eleventh year in the business—when Chase Kincaid, KCM's program director, and also national P.D. of the Karrash chain, had brought him in to work for a guy who was then managing editor of their Kansas City news department. He did three on-air casts a night, good bucks, and no hassles. It had been like the early days at WNEW in New York, where a buddy of his had done the nine-to-midnight radio news. Three casts a night, and you split, the guy told him. "I work fifteen minutes every three hours, sleep all day, and at nine I go down to the Village and hunt for virgins." He was kidding but once it had been almost that big a skate.

D. Andrew Karrash had been a wrestling promoter, of all things, and had made his fortune back in the early days of television. He'd retained the rights to the early grudge matches between the vintage mat stars and the "freak shows" like tag teams and battles royal. When MacLendon and Turner and other broadcast pioneers such as Storz were experimenting with formats in the early days of all-news radio and TV, Karrash was recycling his old Gorgeous George kinescopes to "U"s, independent UHF channels, and other small and medium market properties who were seeing numbers in trash sports.

Karrash's chain ended up with three major market stations, of which KCM was the flagship. When Andy Karrash became ill and retired, less than a year after Trask moved to nighttime news at KCM, there'd been a tremendous shake-up. First, KCM had gone all-talk, under the national ownership of Rogers Communications, a New York–based publishing house expanding into broadcasting. The absentee owners had so far kept Chase Kincaid as local program director, but nearly everything else had changed.

A big-time TV and radio anchor had been imported to helm the news department, and Trask's easygoing boss had been axed. The new managing editor, Adam David, from Pittsburgh, was a top-notch air talent and writer/producer, but about as laid-back as sulfuric acid. To say that Adam David took himself, and the news, seriously, was like saying that "the universe is rather a large place."

All-talk could be a mind-bending concept. At KCM, it was an often uneasy melding of entertainment and hard news, and the two sides of the coin were not necessarily comfortable bedfellows. Louie "Captain Kidd" Kidder, a venerable Midwestern radio and television old-timer, had been brought in to set the tone of the station. In a market that ranged from "more music/oldies" to hard rockin' country formats to zany morning men, Louie Kidder's homespun, gentle wit and thoughtful insights were a welcome breath of radio air. From nine A.M. to three P.M., KCM's airwaves were filled with a basic news and "human interest" mix, some of which involved feeds and special packages such as business and financial/investment news, sports, weather, and various remotes. At three the talk turned to telephone call-ins. The three-to-six and six-to-nine shifts were helmed by men and women who were adept at eliciting the greatest amount of heat, if not light, from the topical subjects of the moment. The midnight phone show starred popular Kim Streeter, who was thought to have one of the three or four sexiest voices of any woman on major market radio. She sounded like the most beautiful, sweetest angel who ever drew a breath. In fact, Kim Streeter was beautiful in the face, and had an angelic personality to go with it, but she outweighed Vic Trask by ten or twenty pounds. This eclectic hodgepodge appeared to be working, if the ratings and word-of-mouth were barometers. Into this stew was stirred the legendary Sean Flynn and company.

Flynn had once been a king of talk, working almost as

much as Larry King, with a profile the equal of King's or Tom Snyder's, having made his bones in the competitive Chicago market. Rogers Communications had brought him in from a night gig in some southern armpit of a market, and told him—in effect—do or die. It was his last shot to regain his crown and he came at it with a vengeance; a bright guy who'd fallen down the well of alcohol abuse, he hit the air boldly, with such a cutting-edge intelligence and sense of awareness that he made the nine-to-midnight gig his own overnight. The numbers were astonishing. He nailed the position with his first killer sweep book, a ratings response that two competitive stations sued over, forcing the survey companies to recount. The second count was even higher for Flynn. The guy *owned* Kansas City at night!

Within twenty-four hours of the announcement of the resurveyed numbers, Sean Flynn, forty-four-year-old has-been alky, and two Jewish attorneys from Krelberg, Boda, and Kamen—whom Flynn referred to over and over as Nafka, Kafka, and Putz—with a set of contractual demands unprecedented in the mid-echelon annals of KC broadcasting: *astronomical* money; a stepladder clause linked to the ratings books; grandfathering out the exhaust pipe; a pay-to-play page that made the guys from Rogers wince every time they thought about it, and demands for a producer-writer staff, for God's sake, began a three-day haggling session that ended up with Sean Flynn owning the store.

Flynn took Trask off the air and gave him a title—senior researcher—and they hired a producer from Memphis, a bird by the name of Babaloo Metzger, who had a rep for big numbers and a tough-as-nails shop, and Metzger brought in his own researcher from the Tennessee station, a woman named Barb Rose. Bookings were to be handled by Kincaid, various newsroom personnel, and Flynn had his own private secretary/receptionist/booker/handler/woman-of-the-night named Jerri Laymon. Sean Flynn's "America Tonight" became Sean Flynn's "Inside America," with important guests, open phones, in-depth interviews, and preproduced pieces, and the ratings went all the way through the roof.

It was quite odd—all of it. Victor Trask, headache forgotten, zooming around the tailgaters in the direction of downtown Kansas City, had the odd sensation of being fairly successful in a job he didn't totally understand. Beginning his thirteenth year in a business that made him, at thirty-six, wonder what he wanted to do for a living "when he grew up." And for all that, it was rather satisfying. He genuinely thought "Inside America" was entertaining radio, and this was at least as much fun—if harder work— than the news gig. The job also paid more, you could come in late, or leave early, if you didn't do it too often, and there was no heavy lifting.

He tuned the band of the radio, flipping across the polluted Missouri air:

"Love thirty and the match. We'll be going to Lion, France, on Monday to bring you—" Trask twisted, with a grimace, reminding himself to tell the news reader he'd mispronounced a word.

". . . all you talk about is fish and seafood . . ."

". . . on Power ninety-nine! No showers showing within twenty miles of Kansas City and . . ."

". . . Royals lead. It's two and oh!"

". . . Sweet Home Ala-bah-ma! . . ."

". . . I-70 just three miles past the Truman Sports Complex. Come on down and check out this selection. You won't—" He clicked back to FM and got some easy guitar he couldn't identify and filed it all away.

Victor Trask was an observer. He noticed things. He would have made an okay cop or a P.I., he thought. Maybe the investigative reporting part of this research gig was what held such appeal for him. He liked the hunt. The dig. Yet, in personal relationships, he hadn't shown any of the same dedication, or tenacity, or grit. He'd in fact screwed away a perfectly good marriage—boring and dead-end but perfectly good—because it seemed as if he could never get into his home life the way he could his work. He was a workaholic, he supposed. Not for the money. That was obvious enough. He liked to keep his mind occupied.

Now his wife was a memory that would have faded completely but for odd moments when a desire to see or talk to his daughter brought the exes into brief contact again. Neither of them could believe they'd ever been married and had lived together for six years, a couple of lifetimes ago.

He finally made it downtown in one piece and went through the usual ritual of the parking garage. Lower-level employees (and you couldn't get much lower than Trask: a few news readers, apprentice engineers, various and sundry copywriters, purchasing assistants, receptionists and typists, and a couple of security guys shared the lowest plateau) could not park in the postage-stamp rectangles reserved for KCM's "key" employees. These were the executives; anyone with *chief, manager,* or *director* in their title; the station controller; Mr. Kidder; Mr. Flynn; the VIP rectangle; and of course the account execs. Even the engineers had two spaces! When contract renewal time came around, if he had the clout and the numbers were still up, he was determined to somehow lobby for a parking space. It would be the equivalent of a raise both in money and prestige, but to Trask the awarding of a space epitomized the tacit acknowledgment of worth. Not to mention the implication of a degree of assured tenure.

Trask came into the station through the big, showy front doors, a massive pair of bronze slabs in "lightning-bolt deco," waved to the guy at the security desk, and walked across the long foyer to the elevator. All you saw here were giant plants and the ultramodern artwork and sculpture that dominated the length of KCM's entranceway. From the front doors only the unobtrusive security post, the front desk—always staffed by a bevy of lovely youngsters who came and went with the tide—and the plush seating arrangements in the first-floor lobby waiting area were visible. If one made it past the guard and front desk and turned left, the richly appointed VIP waiting area beckoned. Beyond that was a door that led to the sales area: the sales manager's offices off to the right, the sales receptionist and account executives' offices to the left. Coming back toward the front of the building one would pass sales lounge and bathroom, the big sales conference room, and what they called no-man's-land. Here, at the front of the building, but inaccessible from the front doors or foyer, was the general manager's huge sanctuary, and sandwiched between various utility and storage rooms was the room that housed the internal closed-circuit internal security monitors, and, some said, the audio equipment. It was generally thought that every word spoken in the building was recorded, and— presumably—monitored.

Inside that room abutting on the visible security desk in the foyer, was an invisible room of which Bill Higgins, head of KCM security, was lord high chamberlain. "Inspector Higgins of the Yard," as they called him outside the station, was a pleasant-looking balding man with a mustache, to whom no one but the G.M. and—rumor had it—Rogers Communications, conversed. While it was necessary to have security because of the controversial nature of some of the programming, the way it was handled added to the feeling of paranoia that helped to keep KCM's employees on their toes.

Trask had his I.D. on his shirt, but neither the front-desk guard nor the receptionist needed to see it. Both of them knew his face as he knew theirs. His ride in the elevator was a solo one, so his first words inside the station were spoken on the second floor when he got out and smiled at the beautiful girl at the desk. "Good morning."

"Good afternoon, Vic." She smiled, and he winked at her. All men winked at her—it was a law. Her name was Monica Bonebreak but they called her Monica Heartbreak, a former Miss Congeniality in the Miss Missouri contest, and if she was a loser, thank the Lord that Vic had never met the winner. He always had to fight to get his breath back as he walked past her.

The "program floor" receptionist sat with her back to a

long glass wall that ran the length of the building. Behind the glass, one saw Adam David, if he was at his desk, flanked by all the news editors and news readers/reporters, the wire service room, and the editing facilities. All of this was backed with a display of electronic gear, world maps, and a long bank of clocks that gave the time in Tokyo, London, Paris, Moscow, and so on. Everyone who worked at KCM was *very* ashamed of the clocks, but so far they had been a legacy that Rogers Communications insisted was "part of the KCM-age." If it wasn't broke, don't fix it, so the hokey Dave Garroway—era clocks stayed.

Free-form seating and more silver and bronze sculptures flanked the artwork at the receptionist's desk. Glass walls were at either end of the long entrance area, and a visitor could see Production Studio C to the right, the back of which contained an impressive library, and the announcer/engineer area, and to the left were the double-paned hallways that separated Broadcast Studio A and Master Control from the civilians.

Out front, it was all spacious and artsy-fartsy, but Trask no longer worked out here. He walked around the lounges and stopped at Production where he saw a news reader working at the mike. He cracked the door to Engineering.

"Is he doing anything I can't interrupt?"

"Naw," the engineer grunted.

"Thanks," Trask said. He went in to where the man was getting ready to record. "Hi."

"Hello."

"'Scuse me. Hope I'm not screwing you up?"

"Uh-uh. Watcha need? I'll be done in five minutes."

"No. I don't need in. I was listening on the way in. It's *Lee*-ohn. The city in France?"

"Huh?"

"You pronounced it like *lion* in a zoo—it's *Lee*-ohn." He gave the word its French pronunciation, the second syllable nasal and thrown away.

"Yeah, so?" The guy shrugged and opened his eyes wider, obviously pissed off.

"Hey—not meant as a put-down. I just thought you'd want to know." He turned to leave, feeling like an idiot.

"Do you say 'he drives a Le Sabre'?"

"Yeah." Trask smiled.

"Why don't you say he drives a *Luh-sob-ruh?* That's the way it's pronounced in French."

"Yeah, but—"

"Do you say *Pah-rrryeeee?*" He exaggerated the French pronunciation. "Nobody would know what the hell you were saying. Are we in France? Nooo. We're in fucking *A-mare-ee-kuh*. Okay? That's why we don't use French on the fucking airsville." The man smiled but clearly he was torqued off.

"I gotcha." Trask wanted to say "Yes, but," and explain the logic, but he knew what this guy was like. His name was Michael Melody—his real name—and he was an asshole. "I didn't think. Stupid!" He hit his head with the flat of his hand.

"You got a Band-Aid hanging from your face," the news reader told him as he eased out the door, "by the way."

"Thanks," he said, noticing his goofy reflection and peeling the small strip off and wadding it up in his fingers. He was glad that when he'd smacked his head in that gesture he hadn't given himself a headache again.

Jesus.

Trask walked down the hall past Production Studio B and Engineering, the Talent Lounge where the lesser air people hung out or had small cubicles, past Kidder's and Flynn's suites, and into the guts of "Inside America." Three offices, of which the largest was the producer's, were located across from the Programming Department's bathroom. Visitors to the P.D.'s office, the controller, bookkeeping people, copy chief and copywriter, purchasing assistant, and news readers all shared this one bathroom. The door was directly across from Trask's office. He was wedged in between the "Jew and Jewess," as Sean Flynn called them. (Flynn called the triumvirate "two Jews and a snooze.") Babaloo Metzger, whom he didn't trust, and Barb Rose, née Barbra Rozitsky,

73

his sworn enemy, were on either side of him, and all day long people went to the crapper across from his office.

He had one hour before the production meeting. They were set for tonight and tomorrow night. They need a guest, a topic, a theme. Flynn was antsy.

He looked at his bulletin board, skimmed through his files, eyeballed notes. Somewhere, there was a clipping in this stack of garbage—yes! There! The words "Black Dahlia" leaped out at him. A highly publicized 1947 murder case. He had a slant. He'd interviewed a guy with LAPD Homicide and had some notes which he began to shape for the production meeting. A team of volunteers had been called to the sight of this ancient torture/mutilation/slaying, because a woman had said she had memories of her father "killing women." They were going to dig. They didn't find anything. But Trask thought he could get some good stuff out of the person with whom the woman's therapy sessions had been conducted.

Four P.M.: Metzger knocked at his door, rubbing the indentations made by his glasses.

"Let's go."

"Okay." Trask got up and gathered his notes. They waited for Barb Rose to join them. She was an attractive, dark-haired woman with good features, a wide mouth, and carefully coiffed hair. She could have been any age from twenty to forty—one of those faces. She dressed upscale, and the largest pair of earrings Trask had ever seen on a white woman dangled from her ears.

"Hi," she said to both men. "You look like you cut yourself."

"Uh-huh," Trask said.

"Umm." Her tone said it all. Too bad it wasn't lower and more severe. Why did they compete so fiercely? "Had any coffee yet?"

"No. Been too busy." God! He wondered if she was actually going to be nice and get him a cup of coffee.

"You look like you need a cup," she said, ever the comic.

They made their way into the Programming Conference Room, a somber place about the size of a railroad car, with a dozen or so chairs scattered around two scarred wooden tables placed end to end. Downstairs, the Sales Conference Room looked like the meeting space of a major bank. Upstairs, the conference room resembled the kind of place the border police bring people suspected of drug smuggling.

The three of them took seats as far apart from each other as possible, and waited for Flynn. He soon came, accompanied by the Mystery Tramp, which is what they called Jerri Laymon, who brought his coffee and various papers. She was a sultry, mysterious woman who was quite pretty but who wore dark glasses most of the time, and at night. Everybody thought Sean Flynn was putting the pork to her. Trask and Flynn thought Babaloo was porking Barb Rose. Nobody thought Trask was doing much of anything, except maybe with himself.

Flynn, handsome, gray and silver-headed, with a dark black mustache, his silk tie askew, read quietly, then—not looking up—said, "Who's got something for the hole?"

"I do," Barb Rose said, and everybody looked at her. "Remember the so-called Black Dahlia murder?"

For ten minutes Barb Rose did a presentation based on Trask's notes. There was no way she could have come up with all the material independently, since some of the stuff had been gleaned from a phoner Trask did with the West Coast homicide dick. She had to have had a bug in his office or a tap on his phone. Or somebody else did and she had access to the tape.

"I don't think it's strong enough, even with the tie-in to the local case and the therapist. I do like the therapist interview, and that's strong material on the business about regressing a patient. Let's go at it from a 'Scam or Science' angle, you know?" Flynn pitched his voice down a register. "Psychiatry and hypnosis, how much of it is real, how much is pure hogwash? Something along those lines. Get that old

Bridey Murphy thing and get me the background on how it was brought forth, later proven a hoax and so on." He looked at Trask, who was itching to say something.

"What? You got something?" Sean Flynn asked.

"Yeah. What you just heard." He slid all his notes across the table and glanced at Barb Rose, whose face was a mask. She had a pair, he'd give her that.

"Nu?" Flynn glanced at a couple of the pages.

"So doesn't this strike you as a tad odd? We've got the identical shit?"

"Okay," Flynn said with a smile. "So?"

Trask just stared at him and shrugged.

"What's wrong?" Barb asked innocently. "Did he come up with similar stuff?"

"Yeah," Flynn said. "Coincidences happen. What can I say. Let's get on with it. Here's the way I think the show should come together: first, you guys get me somebody who . . ." Victor Trask tuned halfway out as the meeting continued and Flynn put the "Discoveries Made in Therapy" program together.

They eventually went back to their cubicles and Trask made a cursory search of his phone and office. Nothing looked out of place, but how would he know if he saw something? He gathered up a briefcase full of papers and looked at his watch: six-fifteen P.M. Buzz, his old engineer buddy, was still working dayparts last he'd heard. He'd check at the "Zoo" first.

Trask left the KCM building and found a pay phone. It was still bright daylight at six-twenty. He dropped money, dialed, and after a half-dozen rings, a young girlish voice answered.

"Z-60."

"Hi. Is Buzz Reid working, do you know?"

"Is who working?"

"Buzz Reid? Engineering?"

"Um. One moment please." The line went dead. He waited. It was hot and smelly in the alcove where he was calling. There were two coin phones side by side, with a small divider for privacy between them. Old tobacco smoke and God-knows-what-all made him wrinkle his nose. There were no directories, which had gone the way of phone booths years ago. Vandalism had seen to their demise. Most of the public phones near KCM were card-type or third-party-billing-number-type. Again, coin ops had been phased out because of vandals. He flipped his pen out and scrawled the word *vandalism* on a pad. This was the kind of stuff he fed off of. He might be able to get a show out of that one thought. Now he'd start a file on the topic and see just where it led him. He was writing *locked churches* when a voice said hello.

"Buzz?"

"Yo."

"Vic."

"Hey, man. What's up?"

"Not too much. I wondered if I could buy you a cold one when you get off? Talk about a couple things."

"I can't do it tonight. I got a game."

"When?"

"I'm going to be leaving in about . . . fifteen or twenty minutes, matter of fact."

"Would you have time to grab a cup cross the street? Five minutes or whatever? It's kind of important."

"Yeah, if you wanna come on by right now. I could give you ten minutes or something. Say—meet me at Sammy's in five minutes?"

"I'll be there. Thanks." Trask hung up, started to walk, and changed his mind. Went around the corner and saw a couple of taxis in front of a nearby hotel, got in the first one and had them take him the eight blocks to the greasy spoon across from the radio station. He got there before Buzz Reid did. He had his coffee in front of him when the engineer walked in.

"Hey, stranger," Reid said, settling down beside him in time to have a cup of coffee set in front of him. "Thanks."

"I appreciate it," Trask said. "I know you're runnin' but I wanted to shoot the shit a minute."

"No problem." Buzz was notorious in Kansas City radio. He was forever trying to get guys to screw his wife, a plain woman in her thirties, who, Trask recalled, had long red hair and an Olive Oyl shape. Reid and his wife were "into swinging," so he claimed. Trask had always managed to slip out of such invitations. It was all but impossible to fire an engineer, but his sexual "misconduct" had somehow gotten him terminated from KCM, in spite of a ferocious shop steward and an unforgiving union, back in the days before they'd worked together at the Zoo. He *hated* KCM, and had a great deal of expertise in what Trask thought of as "bugging."

"You remember how you always used to say they taped the phone calls and stuff at KCM?" he whispered to the small, thin man at the counter beside him.

"Um."

"Is that something you knew for a fact or were you saying what you thought they were doing?"

"Fact. They tape everything. Not just the phones."

"How did you know? Mind if I ask—confidentially?"

"I heard the fuckin' tapes is how. Jimmy Olfanski who used to be the chief at KCM showed me all that shit downstairs. I heard private conversations made in the sales manager's office, in the fuckin' control room. Et cetera, et cetera."

"Downstairs."

"In the manager's office it used to be. Now it's all in the security room down there next to the supplies 'n' shit. Everybody knows about it. They been doin' that shit for years."

"And they play all that back and listen to it? Everybody's conversations? Why?"

"Who the fuck knows, man. They like to keep an upper hand. You know how management is, pops. Always fuckin' with everybody's head. They sit down there and watch the tapes, I guess, and make random checks and that. Old Inspector Higgins his bad self. I guess that's what he does all day. Sits there watching the tapes and jerkin' his wire."

"Watching—you mean they got videotapes?"

"You see the cameras, man. What did you think?"

"I knew they could see, but I never imagined they would be taping with video. What the hell's the point of it all? What do they expect to see or hear?"

"Hey. Go figure. I suppose . . . employee theft or some shit. I really don't know. I know I could sabotage the shit out of their security systems and they'd never fuckin' know what hit them."

"Yeah? How would you do that?" Trask asked.

"I know some shit about that place, man." Buzz Reid leaned close and whispered conspiratorially, "I know how to get into Security . . ." Trask just looked at him. ". . . from above, baby."

"How?"

"Engineering."

"Yeah?"

"You know where the equipment room is across from those offices like Copy and Purchasing?" Trask nodded. "In the early days that's where the other stairwell was. You could drop a ladder down through the back of the equipment closets and climb right down to the ceiling of the security room, pull the partitions out—" Reid proceeded to detail a break-in somewhere between Topkapi and the Brink's job.

"Judas! I wouldn't have the *cojones* for that, brother."

"Well, anyway—it could be done easily. Tear all that Big Brother bullshit up, man."

"Is there a way to stop that sort of surveillance? You know—make it so they can't hear what you're saying over the phone or in a private conversation in an office?"

"Sure. In theory, they got every kind of bug jammer you can want—stop any sort of pickup from phone taps to reflection bugs. Cost you a few hundred bucks to get a real good one, but they're available."

"Um."

"I got to get my ass in gear, man. Anything else?" Reid took a last sip of coffee.

"No. But I may call for more advice."

"Anytime. Whyn't you come out to the house sometime? Party with us."

"Might just do that one of these days. Hey, Buzz, I really do appreciate your time. I'll holler at you again, maybe."

"Sure thing. Good to see you." Reid got up and waved a salute.

"Same here."

Trask took a mouthful of cool coffee and held it for a few seconds, not wanting to swallow.

8

Back at KCM that evening he found a "progress memorandum," as Flynn liked to call them, from The Man himself, telling Trask—in effect—you're letting down, looking for excuses; get your shit together. Not in so many words, but that was the sum of the long memo. He'd have been willing to bet good money that Barb Rose hadn't been sent one. He knew Flynn always checked with Metzger when he was sending memos or whatever, so this was probably a joint venture. He could recall phrases Babaloo had used in various shitty conversations they'd had: "open up the topics" and "start looking for larger themes" were two that echoed.

Specifics? Make-work. Time-consuming legman/leg woman stuff that he found interfered with the more serious business of digging. Stuff Barb should be doing, he felt. And then there was a page on what Flynn called "Factlets," the little stuff that he would use to weave into the nightly commentary that made people think he was a genius. In the middle of a discussion of The Impatient American, and how we wanted instant rewards and instant gratification, Flynn told a shrink guest, "Did you know, on average, we spend three years of our life waiting for traffic lights?" The shrink laughed, called him on it, and he produced the clinical verification off the "top of his head." Trask's work. You couldn't give him too many Factlets, he had a consuming obsession for the damned things, and they were a pain in the butt to find. Once one had exhausted the obvious printed/ recorded sources they were hard-won nuggets.

The memo was the perfect ending to a really semi-shit day that had become the genuine article. He went home in a blue funk, his head full of microphone paranoia and Factlet phobia.

He had cleaned all the loose notes out of his office. Anything that he might use toward creating a great theme. It boiled down to a stack of newspaper and magazine clippings, book reviews, and cryptic annotations that referred to sound bites on scraps of half-inch home VHS tape that he'd collected over the past year or so.

The next project he'd build at home. If he used the telephone he'd dial from card-op public phones and use his credit card or bill the calls to the station line. He'd dedicate himself to coming up with something that would pull his rear end out of the flames. He wanted to save his job—at least until he figured out what he wanted to do for a living.

Understandably, the first theme was Big Brother. Surveillance. He seriously toyed with the idea of paying Buzz or some unsavory character to climb down the "Engineering ladder" to the internal security vault and get proof of the station's spying on its employees. Wasn't there a Missouri statute against "entrapment" or something? He could check all that out. Build a case. A brief against KCM! File it on the air over "Inside America," and—when it got humongous numbers and regional press—it might be enough that they wouldn't have him killed. What the hell was he thinking? His big theme was to indict the people who employ him? That made zero sense. But still—he'd let it simmer.

He began taping streamers of news clippings around the apartment in categories: *Mistrials and Plea Bargaining— the Courts in Trouble, Child Abuse, Pornography, Censorship, Adolescence in the American Value System.* It was a personal favorite, but he wondered how it would play in the Kansas/Missouri radio ether: the concept that we'd rather squander millions on parades celebrating a tiny war that had no complete resolution, pretending it was the heroic victory of all time, when Vietnam vets had only begun to be honored, than feed the poor. . . . He junked that one immediately—too much realism! Pretty soon he'd covered all the walls and was starting a series of file folders with the offshoot topics that ranged from Abortion to Zoning.

So many of these big topics had been done and done and redone and done to death. Could he really stand one more show about the pornography shops, television, the NEA, movie ratings—all of that? Borrrrring. He went around the room pulling down the environmental stuff, the porno stuff, and pretty soon the walls were visible again.

This wasn't the way to go about it. He'd start with categories and get precise definitions, then open them up. He looked at a stack of notes and the one on top read Vandalism. He pulled down a dictionary and turned to the *V*s: Vulgarity, Volumetric analysis, Vitriol, Violins, Violence . . . He stopped his thumbing backward through the dog-eared book and read:

> "**Violence:** *N* (1.) Physical force exerted to abuse or injure. (2.) Instance of a physically forceful treatment or action. (3.) Effecting injury by physical force, brute strength, brutality, physical assault. (4.) Unwarranted or unjust use of physical force or savagery. (5.) Furious, turbulent, or physically violent act of destruction or fierceness."

He read on through the synonyms and variety of meanings: "Excessiveness, rage, brutality, assault, vehemence, fury, destructiveness, force, rampage, savagery, frenzy, fervor, attack, severity, onslaught, turbulence, bedlam—" There was a word or definition explaining violence for nearly every clipping he had! Bloodbath, mad passion, craziness, deadly force, rebellion, street gangs, child abuse, spousal abuse, animal abuse, rape, hysteria, bestiality, explosions, desecrations—it was all here under this one mad umbrella. *Violence.* Even vandalism!

Certainly, there were topics that didn't fit, but even those that fell immediately outside this category pointed him toward specific future show subjects: "Waste and Corruption," "The Japanization of America," and others instantly gave him slants he'd not looked at before. He'd tapped into the talk-show gold vein.

Violence was the broad background theme for thirty shows—at least. Trask had a month of material he would do in advance, and blow the minds of Flynn, Metzger, and everybody at the station. He would ask for a parking space in the lot, and—in lieu of a raise—Barb Rose's head on a silver platter. No, too violent. He'd ask for a pay-to-play contract clause but settle for the parking space.

Suddenly every story in his stack in front of him, from "Mistrial in Rape Case" to "Infant's Body Believed Placed in Trash by Parents," all went back up on his apartment wall. Subdivided into appropriate categories—a few of which were arguable—it appeared at first glance that Trask had the makings for nearly six weeks of fascinating late-night shows—all on the same universally encompassing theme.

The day that started semi-shitty for the senior researcher at KCM Radio had ended solid gold.

The next day Trask called in sick and stayed in his apartment "on aspirin and vitamin C, to shake this cold" that was coming on. The fact is he probably didn't have much more than that, in the form of a glass of orange juice, and four cups of coffee which he took time out to fix from a jar of instant, as he worked on his files, from before sunrise to one o'clock the following morning.

When he finally stopped to take a deep breath and examine the results of his work, he wanted to call Sean Flynn, who'd probably just be returning to the studio from his nightly post-show donut and coffee, to tell him to "clear the decks for the next two sweep periods!" He was bursting to tell somebody about what he'd stumbled across, but he knew it would be professional suicide to do so. Metzger and his pal Ms. Rose would get cut in on it and he'd be left right where he was.

What he did instead was set his alarm for eight A.M., and he went into the bedroom and crashed for a deep seven-hour sleep. He was up the next morning and writing, still rubbing sleep from his eyes, stoked as he hadn't been since his early years in the business. Victor Trask had come alive!

The focus began with an international overview of violence, cribbed mostly from TV news and talk shows, and an interesting study he'd wangled from the local sheriff's Homicide unit.

From there, it focused on Kansas City, and the statistics on property crimes of burglary, larceny, auto theft, arson, robberies, assaults on persons, rape cases, attempted murders, homicides, and suicides. His source on this was an FBI press kit, and the K.C. cops were using it to help bolster a political fight to stem budget cuts.

Violent crime was up over ten percent overall, with murder having jumped nearly fifteen percent in the past year. In a period of twelve months, Kansas City, a town of—according to a recent census—slightly less than 450,000 citizens, had recorded nearly sixty thousand violent crimes. That was just within the city limits. The K.C. metro area, a vast sprawl of densely populated suburbs, wasn't included in the survey. The city alone showed that approximately one out of every seven persons had recently committed or would commit a violent crime. And those were just the crimes reported. Rapes and assaults went notoriously unreported. Violence—it appeared—was genuinely epidemic in proportions.

What Trask's discovery had been, however, was not in the sheer numbers, but in the nature of the crimes. His file headed Violent Deaths was the key to the "exposé" aspect of this series of interlinked shows he was outlining. It would be what other media would tag as the core of the programs which would deal with escalating violence in America. If his conjecture could be proved it would bring both Sean Flynn's program, and by projection *himself,* to the attention of the entire country. Trask saw something nobody else had seen, or so he believed. He saw a single thread of motive weaving through some of the most violent murders.

How was it possible he'd found something the Kansas City cops had missed? This was nothing to rush to the station with. It was the chance of a lifetime, the "beat" of a career, and came with its own built-in public forum. All he needed was time to put his case together.

First things first: If Rose had an ear on his phone or in his office, he could have it uncovered, but if she did—and he knew that she did—it had to be with Metzger's tacit approval. If the producer was as close to the woman as it appeared, Trask would accomplish little by exposing her spying and thievery. Perhaps Metzger hadn't encouraged it, or even known about it, but he would probably protect her. She was a tough cookie. Like so many in broadcasting, she had limited talent but a terrible driving ambition. She probably saw the bug or wiretap business as industrial intelligence—just good business one-upmanship. There was also the possibility that Babaloo and Barb were a secret coalition, and the plan was to undermine Trask for whatever reason. It really didn't matter. What he had to do was now create a false agenda, which they would then find.

By memoranda and scraps of notes, by phone calls made out of his office at KCM, by a select batch of tapes left on his desk, he would create this fictitious slate of projects to be discovered and—for all he knew—purloined.

The odd thing was that when he'd got a slant on the violence theme, so many hitherto boring subjects began to fall into logical order. Slant was everything. When he saw how these other topics could be interwoven he seemed to get new perspectives on a wealth of tried-and-true topics from *organ donors* to *organic farming.* They all fell into place for him. It was tough to find shows he didn't want to research, all of a sudden. These new slants brought a hot light to these well-trod issues, making them interesting and provocative again. A topic as yawn-inducing as *tabloid news* had now become *name fixations.* He could imagine a clinically analyzed piece on our penchant for celebrity trivia that worked on a different level than the superficial one. We loved to hear, see both film and video, and read gossip about the Donald or the Kennedy family. But the why of it was linked to root causes more substantial than what might first appear to be the case: he could see ways this report might be part of an overall look at the human condition that would be tremendously thoughtful and thought-provoking—if not meaningfully revealing. Everything always came back around to the same basics such as sex, politics, and religious beliefs or personal philosophies—or the lack thereof—but it was the way in which those basics were probed that could make a talk show thrilling or lackluster. Trask knew that he'd touched a rich nerve near the pulse of mankind's existence, and he had that same scent in his nose that archaeologists must get on a hot dig. He smelled secrets and buried treasure.

9

The telephone in Elaine Roach's apartment had the bell position muted to its lowest point, but still she jumped when it rang.

"Hello," she said.

"Miss Roach, this is Tommy Norville."

"Oh, yes, sir!" Her voice brightened. One of the boss's infrequent phone calls.

"Well, how did the first auction night go?" he asked, with just a hint of sibilant simper and pseudo-world-weary petulance in his voice.

"Very well. Sir—I'm glad you called and I certainly hope you won't be angry with me but I—uh—had to take the phone off the hook at two-thirty A.M. I just couldn't stay awake any longer. I hope it's all right?" He could hear the nervousness and fear in her scratchy voice.

"Of course, it's all right. You mean you were still getting calls as late as that?"

"Oh, yes, sir. I think they must have tried to phone me all night, for when I put the phone back on this morning at seven-thirty, it rang instantly. A man in California said he'd been dialing and getting a busy signal all night long."

"Hmm. Amazing!" he said through fat pursed lips.

"Of course, I didn't tell any of the ones who phoned this morning that I took the telephone off the hook last night."

"Well," the effeminate-sounding man told her, "you certainly didn't get much sleep." He wanted to ask about the auction response but he decided he'd go gently. "Perhaps tonight you could retire earlier, Miss Roach. And then, of course, you'll have a couple of weeks to recuperate before the next round of telephone calls."

"Yes, sir. Oh, by the way, you might want to know that we had many calls on one of the items, Mr. Norville. Number forty-one? The cased dueling pistols that belonged to Sir Arthur Conan Doyle?"

"Oh?" He kept the interest out of his tone. "Did they fetch a decent price?"

"Oh, yes, sir! The highest bid was from a man in New York who bid $24,500 for them."

"Pardon?" He had to make a noise that sounded like a loud cough, and he covered up the mouthpiece of the phone while he laughed. He loved making fools of the monkey people.

"A man in New York bid twenty-four thousand five hundred for them. And we had about two dozen bids on that item. Next to number forty-one item number three was the most popular, it appears—" Then she began to give him an accounting of the telephone auction. He let her ramble on for a while.

"That sounds excellent, Miss Roach. And you emphasized we would need cashier's checks or money orders, did you not?"

"Yes, sir. And I told them we had to be in receipt of payment within ten days as per the stipulation in our printed terms. Everyone said they would comply. Several persons wanted to know when their items would be sent out, and I reminded them that you will notify all winners within one week, and that it will take about two weeks to process the winning remittances, so with packing time one could safely say approximately six weeks from the time their remittance is sent." She was maddeningly pedantic and precise in spelling out everything she'd enunciated or done in the last twenty-four hours, but that was exactly what he'd wanted. Nothing would reassure a mail-order customer more than a nice, long phone conversation with somebody as obviously straight as Elaine Roach.

He realized that it was doubtful anyone would be writing him a certified check for $24,500, not for a sight-unseen item from an auction with whom they'd had no prior business, but if her figures were any indication, he knew that his war treasury would soon be healthy again.

Daniel Bunkowski had no interest in profit for money's sake, but he had a need for operational funds, and the response to his first mail-order auction had been satisfactory. As soon as he'd notified all the winning bidders of their good fortune, he'd be ready to resume the so-far-fruitless search for his foster mother of years past, Mrs. Nadine Garbella, for whom payback was long overdue.

Kansas City, Kansas, 1958

Little Danny Boy waits, hurting, fearful, trembling from the anticipation of what terror awaits him as much as from the cold. He huddles in the closet with Gem, the little dog who is his only companion. The closet is cold, pitch black, foul with the stench of urine. This is where the Snake Man often makes him stay. He and the dog huddle together for warmth and companionship. His small, plump fingers curl in the mongrel's matted hair and he strokes the dog gently, whispering to it reassuringly with his mind.

The most recent welts have begun to scab up now, and he hopes he will not be whipped. Pain is only part of it, he realizes in some undeveloped pocket of his mind. There is the sense of dread that chills him. It is easily as difficult to bear as the physical abuse and pain, although his child's thoughts do not consciously make such distinctions.

For a time he called it the Dog Boy, but once the Snake Man called *him* that, and now he calls it Jim, which—later

—he will misspell. Typical of his strange mental capacity, he will retain the spelling of a word—the one that means "precious stone or jewel." Because the two words sound much the same to his ears, he spells the proper noun *G-E-M*. Later he will learn that the word means "something that is prized for its great beauty." It will be an appropriate name for this dog, which he regards as a beautiful animal. He prizes it above all else, this young child who doesn't know an antonym from a homonym, his gem of a dog, and now he hears the threatening voice of the hated Snake Man and he and the pup both tremble at the sound.

To whom will he appeal? He has pleaded with Mrs. Garbella a thousand times and her answer is to give him more of the same, or—if she is too tired to lash out at him—laughter, which can sting almost as much as a switch, when it is the court of final resort. He and Gem will appeal to a higher authority, to the place inside his head where the others live. To the place where he and the dog can escape.

Marion, Illinois—30 years later

Some believed he was retarded. Some said he was a genius. They said he had a raw intellect that zigged off of every chart, zagged off every graph. He was said to possess a mind that was incredibly keen and a sociopathic brutality. They called him the Beast.

Dr. Norman headed the R and D team that found him, and hid him in a special kind of housing. A place from where it was believed, prayed, he could not escape.

Norman had first learned about the Snake Man, and the tortures Daniel had suffered in the loving care of his foster mother, during one of their initial hypnosis sessions in which he'd employed the experimental drug known as Alpha Group II.

The software containing that memorable interview resided in a secret place, inside a smudged, worn Manila envelope marked *Bunkowski,* and what appeared to be a man's name, *Max D. Segmarion*. A closer inspection revealed that the label read *Max/D Seg/Marion*. Shorthand for "Maximum Security, Disciplinary Segregation, Marion Federal Penitentiary"—the most dreaded, hardcore solitary "hole" in the prison system. A violent unit designed for the only man ever given a level-7 danger rating: Chaingang Bunkowski.

The cassette in the old envelope was a working copy, a second-generation dupe of a master which resided with the other treasured matrices in a vault. It was on this interview tape that he'd speculated that he might have taken down one "monkey man" for every evil pound of blubber and muscle on his then 420-some-pound carcass.

The heavy hitters who were on the subscription-distribution list for this bizarre information, planners in the clandestine intelligence think tanks, came to an immediate consensus: He was running a gigantic shuck on his case handler.

Only Dr. Norman there in the Marion "shop" believed. He felt the power of Chaingang's aura in the same way that a woman feels a man's vibes and attunes to it, calling it love. In a sense, he loved Daniel, whom he felt was the oddest of deviates—a *physical precognate*. A genius who could physically foretell peril to himself. Norman was certain that his strange and mysterious early warning system was what had allowed him to murder so wantonly for extended periods, in spite of law enforcement's concerted efforts to stop him.

Now Daniel Bunkowski, a mountain of fat, hard muscle, and kill lust, sat moldering away inside the Max, while Dr. Norman's colleagues tried to decide if he was for real, and Dr. Norman worked on a plan to watch him in the field.

The first time Norman managed to break through, his "proofing session" as he'd later call it, was Alpha Group II Interview #8, in which for all to hear he captured the true essence of the beastly killer on tape.

"Daniel?"

The doctor's voice. No response . . . the tape reels revolve but there is only the light machine hiss of the playback.

"Daniel, can you hear me?"

"Rrra." The lion coughs on tape.

"Daniel, it's your friend, Dr. Norman." Norman knew this tape from memory—it had played inside his head many times. "You know you can trust me." There is the sound of breathing. Deep, relaxed breaths of the drugged, hypnotized mass murderer. "Daniel? Can you hear me?"

"Mm."

"Daniel, do you feel good? Are you relaxed?"

"Mm. Feel good."

"Daniel . . . Dr. Norman would never hurt you the way that your foster mother and her friends hurt you when you were little." He could recall the way the beast clenched his hand into a huge, hard fist and how he was so thankful for the chains and straps that restrained him. "Those bad people hurt you. The Snake Man. He *did* things. Awful things to you, Daniel, and you had to punish him for it. Remember?"

"Mm."

"You learned many lessons when he hurt you, Daniel. Lessons about survival. How to remain still. You learned how to control yourself inside, didn't you?" No response. "You could lower your— Daniel, you learned to regulate your heartbeat and . . . breathing rate, didn't you?"

There was a loud and frightening noise as if an engine had started or the lanyard on a chainsaw had been pulled. But it was a human bark. Daniel's laugh chilled anyone who heard it.

"I agree." The doctor laughed gently. "Your friend Dr. Norman agrees that it is very funny, Daniel. I am pleased you were able to construct these defenses against the bad people. Remember how you told me about you and your little dog? How you'd stand in the closet hiding from the Snake Man?"

"Mm."

"You learned to get revenge, didn't you, Daniel?"

"Yes." Very clear, the deep basso profundo like a steel column in the listener's ear. "I poured acid into his eyes and listened to his deathscreams." Deathscreams? But the Snake Man was blinded, not killed.

The noise again. The coughing bark of the lion's laughter.

"You know all about acid, don't you, Daniel?"

"Yes."

"Chemistry, math, the general sciences, engineering, physics, biology, biochemistry, you know many things. I am proud of you, Daniel," he said on the tape, meaning it. "Your new friend Dr. Norman is quite proud of Daniel. How did you acquire so much knowledge? Do you read a lot?" No response. "You don't tell just anyone about how smart you are, do you, Daniel?"

"No."

"It is our secret, Daniel. I know you camouflage your intelligence but you know many things, don't you, Daniel?"

"Yes."

"Tell Dr. Norman, your friend. Tell me your secrets, Daniel. What do you know?"

"Many things."

"*What* things?"

"Chemistry, math, the general sciences, engineering, physics, biology, biochemistry, I know many things." Daniel played with him. Repeating his words back to him. Teasing him. Buttfucking the doctor in the brain. Showing him his eidetic recall.

"I love it when you share your intelligence with me, Daniel. Your friend Dr. Norman loves to see how smart his friend Daniel is. You have a wonderful brain. Dr. Norman is proud of you."

"Chemistry, math, the general sciences, engineering, physics, biology, biochemistry, Safar, Rabi I, Rabi II, Jumada I, Jumada II, Rajab, Sha'ban, Ramadan, Shawwal, Dhu'l-Qa'dah, Dhu'l-Hija . . ."

"That's right, Daniel. You have a wonderful brain."

"Cold chisel, blacksmith's chisel, bricklayer's chisel, box chisel, floor chisel, beveled firmer chisel, socket paring chisel."

"Tell your friend, Daniel, how you predict—uh—tell Dr.

Norman how you know when something is going to happen?
Can you tell me that?" No response.

"Daniel?"

"Mm."

"Tell me."

"Nnn."

"Tell Dr. Norman more of the things you know." No
response. "Please tell your friend Dr. Norman about how
you learned to punish the Snake Man?"

"Yes."

"You know many things, don't you, Daniel?" He thought
he'd lost him.

"Many things, Dr. Norman, such as but not limited to the
following: paramagnetic resonance and the spectra of
diatomics, the role of the mystagogue in televangelistic
fund-raising, procambium, protophloem, and cellular phe-
nomena, theoretical fluid mechanics, noncyclical phylogeny
and cenogenesis in numerical humankind, orthogonal poly-
nomials, classic profiles of psychologically externalized
business failures, elliptical intuits and precognitives, fric-
tion, viscosity and hysteresis, application of quantitative
prediction to the 'Rossler Effect' in found objects, funda-
mentals of resupination cosmology, employment of
steerable null processing group equipment, statistical mechanics in orbital angular momentum theory, field expedient timers utilizing piezobuzzer voltage pulses, analysis of
EMP frequency radiation, quotient grouping in vector
algebra, countermeasures to defeat clue sprays and detection powders, half-rhombic directional theorems, DNA
intermediaries from the cosmic ocean, hypno-inducing
properties of crystalline hydrates, behavioristic variationals
in catabolism."

The sound of a deep breath sucked down into huge lungs.
"Identification of human and animal spoor." This would be
the first of many such interview sessions in which Daniel
would open up a random corner of his dark mind for Dr.
Norman. "Inconstants in motor vehicle identification and
postal indicia as boundary-value problems, utilization of

passive infrared external sensors as detonation devices, contemporary uses of figs, pomegranates, poplars, oaks, cypress, ashes, and other organic materials in blood rites, offal, tripe, ascarids and other lumbricoids as bait, chemistry, math, the general sciences . . ." Chaingang Bunkowski's gospel.

Three decades later, Daniel continues to play his own tape inside his mind, just as Dr. Norman was sure he would: he hears the "deathscreams" of his torturer each time he kills and it is the very heart of pleasure. Remembered pleasure. Imagined pleasure. Yet something is missing. Perhaps it is payback.

Compute the hatred he feels for his foster "mother" and the crimes she committed and allowed to be perpetrated against him by this formula: Apply the rules of kinesics and physics to the laws of mass and motion, multiply by the origin and intensity of rapid movement, governed by the rules of impetus and inertia, and add the sum of vengeance squared. Take this to the cube root of fear. Divide by madness. Add bloodlust. Compute the hypergolic synergy as you would for the explosion of typical rocket fuel.

That is how much hate boils inside Daniel Edward Flowers Bunkowski, and that is how many pieces of flesh he will tear from Mrs. Garbella before he allows her to die.

10

An enormous man named Mr. Bentley, driving legal wheels, headed west on 670 across the stretch of oily water that separates Kansas from Missouri. His I.D. would convince the casual inspector that Mr. Bentley was a prosperous insurance man from St. Louis, dressed for fishing.

He crossed the river in a stream of traffic and turned right looking for Mrs. Garbella. She'd moved around a bit, understandably, over the years. The street signs indicated that he was at the corner of Fourteenth and Bunker. Bunker was a name out of his horror-filled past, and just the word sent a jolt of rage through him.

Say the word and most have some association: Hitler's Bunker, Archie Bunker, but to him it is a synonym for hell. Bunker—even now it can reach whatever vestiges of the little boy that still reside deep inside his massive hulk. The name is a fanged, slithery thing that crawls out of the past, snaking through his memory banks. Terror Avenue.

In his fishing clothes, Mr. Bentley parks, locks the vehicle. A decrepit river-front building, once a cheap hotel, now a sub-poverty-level rooming house. Each time Mrs. Garbella moved she dropped another notch down the scale. This is the bottom of the poverty chain.

He wears a voluminous jacket, too much clothing for the sizzling temperature, but he appears impervious to such mundane externals as heat, and the huge, canvas-reinforced pockets of the jacket bulge with weighty goodies. Many pounds ascend rickety stairs to the second floor. *2C.*

A shotput of a fist the size of a small ham threatens to take the peeling door off its rusting hinges. Slow movement inside. The occupant takes her time getting there. He realizes she must be nearly seventy. Late sixties, perhaps. The door cracks open and old eyes peer through from the darkened interior.

"Eh?" the crone cackles from the safety of a chained door, much the same as in his dream about her.

"Hello. Remember me?" he asks in a rumbling, deceptively soft voice. "From many years ago?" He pushes his way in.

"Please—please don't hurt me. I don't have any money. You've taken everything. Please go away." The old woman begins crying.

It is not Nadine Garbella. He is so disappointed. And now here is some old crone blubbering, and he'll probably have to take care of her—seeing as how he's thrust his way into her life.

"I'm not going to hurt you," he says gently. "I thought Mrs. Garbella lived here. Where is Mrs. Garbella?" The tears flow and she crumples into a chair.

"Stop crying, please. I must find Mrs. Garbella." The woman seems to be having a full-fledged nervous breakdown. "Stop it." He gives her a light shake, but a light shake from him is equivalent to a roller-coaster plunge and she momentarily stops but begins gasping for air. "Let me get you a glass of water. This is all a mistake." He searches for a glass in the tiny apartment. He must interrogate this old witch before he can put her out of her misery.

"Please—" She tries to beg him, her sobbing getting worse.

"Listen. Listen to me!"

She gasps like a fish on land.

"Here. Drink." He gives her a filthy cup of tap water and she tries to peck at it like some ancient bird, but immediately resumes soft, monotonous sobbing. Somewhere outside he can hear the intermittent pop of firecrackers in the July streets.

"How long have you lived here?"

"About a year," she says, managing to show coherency for the first time, between gasped sobs.

"Where is Mrs. Nadine Garbella?" Sobbing. "Do you know?" The old woman shakes her head. "What is your name?"

"Ethel Davis," she says and another big flow of tears begins.

"Why do you keep crying? I promise you won't be hurt. Listen, it is important I find Mrs. Garbella, the previous tenant. Where did she move to? Who would know?" Tears.

"Who do you rent this from? Who's the landlord?"

"The boys let me live here."

"What boys?"

"The ones with the bicycles. They're bad boys."

"Did you ever see Mrs. Garbella?" She looks like she's about to die on her own. A few more minutes of this and nature will take its course, he thinks.

"They killed my little cat. My poor little cat!" This starts her off again. He stands there, a monumental mountain of patience, biding his time.

"Who killed your cat?"

"The boys."

He gentles her down, the way one would gentle a wild animal. Reassuring her that everything will be all right. He learned that this pathetic old crone moved into what had become, essentially, an empty, condemned building. But the building had occupants. A biker gang was evidently using it for a combination crack house and torture chamber.

When the "boys," as she called them, weren't otherwise gainfully busy, they liked to take neighborhood pets and play with them. Play, he gathered, involved throwing dogs and cats from the roof. They had extracted some pitiful sum of money from old Ethel for her lodging, and when the well ran dry they decided to take a measure of revenge on her. She had one possession, a cat. They told her they taught it to fly, and laid what was left of it on her doorstep as a parting gift.

She had thought they were back for another round of fun when Mr. Bentley forced his way into her sad life.

"Are the boys up there now?" he asked.

"Yeah." She nodded, still trying to stem the tears.

"Here—for your door." He peeled some small bills off his roll. "Get another cat," he told her, turning and leaving. She watched this huge apparition's back fill the doorway, waiting a long time and not touching the money that had fallen to the floor.

To understand the why of it—why Chaingang let the old woman live, why he gave her money for the broken door, why he didn't shake the bag of wrinkled skin until the secret of Nadine Garbella's whereabouts fell from her, why he did what he now did—took a degree of understanding not even Dr. Norman could claim.

Only the beast himself knew why he was motivated to kill. There are obvious possibilities: it had been a long, dry spell without killing, and he'd been in close proximity to the monkeys, the hated ones, for periods of forced interfacing. He was tired of taking monkey shit in any form. He was tired of sleeping on the floor of an office overlooking East Minnesota Avenue. He had been screwed with and manipulated once again by The Man. He was crazy as steel cheese—that was part of it.

Sure, as a boy his only companion had been a mongrel pup, and there was the thing the shrinks call transference, and the thing that made him believe animals were better than humans, and the fact that no animals had ever done to him what people had done. But that didn't begin to cover his true feelings.

Chaingang roared his parody of laughter when he saw the

bulls gore the onlookers in Pamplona on TV. He wanted to take the ears from every matador, and every other spic piece of shit in those arenas, blow all those chili-sucking grease-ball beaners to a place beyond Latin hell, and it was not a figure of speech in his case. He wanted every bullshit bull-fight, cockfight, dogfight to go up in flames. He wanted the puppies in the labs to go for the throats of those sensible, maddeningly "reasonable" men and women who were only doing "humane" experiments, as they shot bullets into animals and mutilated them so that young ham-fisted surgeons could practice on them. He wanted everybody in the fucking shit army dead of colon cancer, he wanted all the rodeo stock to throw and break the red scaly-assed dumb necks of every shitheel moron cowboy on the circuit, he wanted every slimy-boxed whore at Barrie K Cosmetics suffocated in her own putrescent filth for the cruelties their lab assholes inflicted on animals, he wanted to take the offspring of the cunts watching every donkey baseball game and petting zoo and cheapskate-run mall pet shop and slit their whelps open while the bitches watched—and that was when he was in a good mood.

When he was in a dark killing mood—as he was now—well, by Christ, you'd better run silent and deep. Whoever crosses his path now he plants. To observe his actions you'd see nothing untoward. The man in his fishing clothes waddles out into the street and unlocks his ride, heaves his bulk in, and the driver's side of the vehicle now rides dangerously low on its springs as he starts the car and eases on down Bunker, turning at the next corner and disappearing from view.

The car is tucked away out of sight and he is puffing and blowing as he ascends the stairs of an adjacent building. Three flights later, his strong heart pounding like a jackhammer, he waits until he has his breath back, and easily penetrates the locked door that leads to the roof. Carefully and slowly he eases out onto the roof, keeping close to the air ducts, chimneys, and walls.

There are people visible on the adjoining rooftop. His computer logs "eight Caucasian males," then he sees a female, then another. Then an eleventh person who appears to be a young male. In his data storage bank he realizes that he automatically filed away the intelligence that there were no bikes on the street. He scans below as best he can and sees nothing—no passers-by to speak of. He sees neither bicycles nor motorcycles. He sees something that does not enrage him so much as freeze him inside.

An animal is thrown from the roof of the building; he hears the shouts and the noise as he momentarily files the image, realizing that the sounds of popping firecrackers he'd heard while inside the slum building were small arms. A dog. Airborne. Gunfire. Hoots and laughter. Inside his mind he has recorded the memory of a shout to "pull"—their game. They have seen skeet-shooting; this is their joke—their firing range. Killing stray cats and dogs for sport. He does not let rage come.

The first reaction is to get the SKS and take as many out as he can. No. They are a gang. There will be more to replace whomever he manages to exterminate. It occurs to him in passing that he wishes the biker gangs were more like the blacks. The crack dealers kill each other, while the white bikers are merely a general nuisance. He wishes all persons of all races would kill one another with equal enthusiasm and fervor; he is an equal-opportunity hater.

Now he sees *(a.) why no bikes*. This is their *play* place. They must have a club nearby. It is unlikely they would use their own haven for such fun and games as they prefer to draw no unnecessary heat—these outlaw gangs. Perhaps they cook crystal in the old building as well. This explains *(b.) why no guards*. No street kids. No beepers. No walkie-talkie units. His computer registers that he observed no *"jigger"* on the premises, "jigger" being D Seg slang for one who acts as lookout.

He closes the door to the roof and keeps the picture of the scene on freeze frame inside his head, and for a beat he allows enough of the red tide to come so that he can imagine clicking a full mag into the Chinese submachine gun (a crude copy of the Swiss weapon that he converted himself to "legal collectible" semiauto status), and selectively taking a few—but he thinks better of it.

Back downstairs, in his wheels, the huge killer circles the block until he sees street people. It takes him less than five minutes with his magnetic personality and acting ability to learn what he wants to know. He lays down a convincing screen of gab and draws the words in like a fisherman with a net, hauling in facts about the gang "doin' all that shootin' around the corner."

He has their identity now, their collective name, and he knows where they hang. When Chaingang Bunkowski has your name and address it does not bode well. The prognosis for your future is a gloomy one. You are in a world of deep shit.

He stops and retrieves a book and pen from his duffel and prints SVS/M in block letters, each letter perfect and without character, pressing hard with the writing instrument that indents each notation on the page.

Their name, he has learned, is Steel Vengeance. They regard themselves with a proud bravado they have not yet earned, but in time these errors shall be corrected.

Beneath their "recreational" address he writes the address of their meeting place of record. He will add their names and much more.

He thumbs past drawings: an M-3 firing unit duct-taped to a length of det cord.

A "smart bomb" activated by an ordinary kitchen food timer.

A recipe, for mixing powdered potassium chlorate with a modified Vaseline-base paste, that bakes a *very* nasty cake.

A device for starting an undetectable fire.

A place inside an ordinary home where a five-hundred-pound giant can hide and not be found—even by trained dogs.

A drawing of an impromptu fougasse bomb fired with an M-57, firing wire, and a fulminate of mercury blasting cap.

A powerful rocket launcher and projectile made from common hardware store materials and home appliance parts.

A lethal bomb made with nothing more difficult to procure than a shotgun shell, a nail, a cigar box, a spring, and an ordinary mousetrap.

The look on his huge, fat face was positively beatific as he devoured each drawing with his eyes. A sense of reverence filled him when he touched this tome, much as a Gideon Bible gives comfort to the soul of a weary traveler.

Chaingang Bunkowski had his own Bible of sorts. It was a very old Boorum & Pease Accounts Receivable Single Entry Ledger, blue with maroon corners, 272 pages. It was headed *Utility Escapes* and that is how he thought of it. The book had survived two prison incarcerations, one on death row, and had accompanied him on over a hundred excursions into murderous madness. It was much more than a book of escape plans, although it was certainly that. Over half the ledger was filled with meticulously rendered drawings, plans, diagrams, sketches, maps, schematics, blueprints for hideouts, evasion devices, mantraps, escape routes, dump sites, ready-made burial spots, and assorted doodles and cryptic signs decipherable only to the artist.

One reason why the book had not been permanently confiscated by authorities was that the head of the program responsible for Bunkowski's recruitment, Dr. Norman, had long ago prepared his own secret copy of the book, which he continued to study with the same fascination that one might examine the Rosetta Stone. He considered the pages to be the work journal of a genius of evil, and he regarded the sketches and jottings of his lunatic Leonardo as parts of a decoder. He had made certain that Chaingang would continue to add to his handbook of homicide, and so further Dr. Norman's own work.

In the ledger there were also names, addresses, newspaper

clippings, and tiny entries razored from various directories, books, and magazines. There were trial write-ups. (Judges were a favorite entry.) The district judge who fined the man a dollar for the death of several animals, quoting scripture as his higher authority, his name and address were recorded for payback—should an opportunity present itself.

The judge, defendant, and defense attorney in the recent matter of a tortured child whom his honor had returned to the care of the torturer were entered for retaliation. There was the stable owner who'd been caught whipping a horse to death for the third time, and the CEO of a large oil company. These were the names that Chaingang had memorized, sometimes complete with images, which he would scan in a kind of litany; familiar bedtime stories he liked to fantasize about. Men and women whom he hoped to take to the edge of whimpering, screaming madness before he let them die. In a way they were his prayers.

Bunkowski, possessor of a phenomenal eidetic memory unit, had no need for the ratty, soiled ledger which he continued to carry with him. But it pleased him. He would thumb past the dog-eared, yellowing pages, and the cutaway view of a wooden trap he'd once built in a catch-basin of the Chicago sewer system would fill him with nostalgia. Or the complex notes for a particularly insidious variation of a Malaysian whip would crinkle his face in a beaming smile as he remembered the pleasure of the first enemy he impaled on it. It was his Linus blanket.

He could open randomly to a small map that he'd once made driving through marshland and recall the pleasant hours spent at an old waterfront hideout, or see a place where he'd picnicked over the site of a mass grave of his own making, or recall with undisguised glee the planting of the shaped charges that once wiped out a squad of the little people. These were wonderfully pleasant memories. It was his family photo album. His vacation slides. His home movies.

Chaingang sometimes would hold the ledger without

opening it, not thinking of any particular entry, but just enjoying the knowledge that it represented countless kills, scores of escapes, dozens of times when he'd faced the monkey men and come away the victor. It was a survival manual. It reassured him.

Dr. Norman had been puzzled by six missing ledger pages. He knew the subject of his intense study so well, and Daniel was not one to allow blotched drawings, flawed map-making, or those sorts of accidents in something of such importance to him. Why had the pages been removed?

Daniel himself feigned ignorance of the matter, having claimed that from time to time when he'd been under extremes of duress the pages had been used to build fires, write messages on, and once—he admitted—when there was no toilet tissue available. Dr. Norman believed otherwise.

There was information on those pages—secret plans, perhaps—that Bunkowski did not want anyone else to see. That is what Dr. Norman thought. He was wrong.

The missing pages had been particular favorites of Chaingang's; pages that had warmed him time and again with hot recollections of steamy violence. Memory triggers and fantasy levers. Pages that in some way brought back the boiling pleasures of various crimes. The pages had been torn out in the heat of the moment and ingested.

They were gone, quite simply, because he had *eaten* them.

The ramshackle building that houses the biker club faces Fifteenth, squatting ominously between two slum tenement houses. A plethora of large street machines, Harleys for the most part, have crowded the small yard frontage spilling out into the street.

Midnight moonlight drenches the pavement. Probes for movement. Finds none. Blackens, bleeding into phantom silhouettes and pools of deep shadow. Quiet, untroubled, totally in harmony with the darkness and mood of menace, Death observes from the pocket of deepest impenetrableness. He has all the watcher's strengths: presentience, patience, concentration, and unswerving relentless hatred. His natural abilities number analytical acumen, logic by inference, observational reasoning skills, and other assorted gifts. His is an acquisitive/inquisitive mind. He wants to know.

How many? Who? Where? What are his options, parameters, hazards, vulnerabilities, escape routes? The one who thinks of himself as Death is master of the conclusionary processes: induction, eduction, reduction, deduction. The techniques are commonplace enough, but the processes— these are rare.

He has lowered his respiratory rate, not unlike the manner in which people can control their heartbeat rate by exercise. Death stills his vital signs by a kind of self-hypnosis, massive will, and the traditions that have become this killer's disciplines.

The single street light illuminates the clubhouse headquarters, its salient aspects being a street number above a filthy metal door and a painted sign reading SVS/M K.C. Chapter, near which two bikers loudly argue.

Death cares nothing of the names they choose: Steel Vengeance Scenic Motorbiking; Satan's Vipers and Sado/ Madmen; Silent—Vicious, Slaves/Masters; in his street conversations he's heard three names. In his head, they are the "dog and cat punks." Some of them wear their count proudly, in scraps of colored animal rags, or in cryptic notations on their skull-and-dagger colors. They are childish thugs and he will now eat their lunch and be done with them.

Death keeps his own mental count. Thirteen are present. Eleven inside the club and two in front. Seventeen names wait in the mind. One—temporarily gone—beyond even his reach for the moment. Imprisoned. Three are absent, and he will take them, too, very soon.

He waits. Something is ajar. His vibes are all he trusts, especially in such activities as these. Some loose end has taunted him since the killing field in Waterton, Missouri, where he constantly prickled from an eye in the sky, an invisible watcher somewhere beyond his scope. He found locator devices hidden in his clothing and custom-made 15EEEEE boots, and from that time he'd been able to shrug off the feeling. It had returned, inexplicably, an itching that had settled on the thick roll of muscle and fat at the back of his head. He forced his concentration past it and stepped out of the shadows.

"I'm gonna get me one of them damn things if—" one of the punks was saying when a steel chain link approximately the width of a coffee cup in diameter smashed his thoughts into jellied pulp.

As the other punk started to involuntarily react, his world was turned upside down.

It is an alien sensation for most two-hundred-pound men to find themselves suddenly dangling in the air, but that was only the half of it: something foul-smelling and awful and approximately a foot wide had picked him up by his face and shut off his breathing. This monstrous thing was connected to a mutant roughly as powerful as three or four of your average Kansas City Chiefs defensive linemen and it was pulling him down, holding him immobilized, suffocating him while he kicked and flailed about ineffectually.

He was not a man used to being terrified. The emotion was, in fact, new to him altogether. But an immense beast squeezing his face, mashing his lips and nose and eyes all into a grotesque parody of the adult who holds the child's cheeks tightly so the lips squeeze together, had taken away his air supply, his mobility, and his reason. The hand, with a grip so powerful it was tearing his flesh, crushing the bones in his face as it suffocated him, then suddenly released him and he sucked air in desperately.

But just as he did so the big ugly nightmare hauled up a mighty, reeking, toxic double-lungful of stale burritos, wild onions and garlic, bad tuna, and your basic terminal halitosis and belched this turd-breath into his mouth and nose as he inhaled, clamping that fist back in place and screwing the mouth and nose shut, asphyxiating, suffocating, strangling, and humiliating him all at once as he gagged to death on his own bad luck.

Chaingang watched him die, and then sealed the deal with steel, chainsnapping the man's head as he fell. He tucked the chain away and picked up the haversack. He armed it and threw it in the nearby open door, flinging himself down. The explosion was deafening.

His hearing was momentarily blocked by the concussive force of the satchel charge. He backed away, as he realized he was now completely deaf and—as he pulled wadded cotton from his ears—he would not be able to hear a police siren or a gunshot. He swallowed hard, but it was as if he were at the bottom of a very deep and silent well. His ears wouldn't clear, but something else was off—something in his remarkable life-support system had been screwed up, tampered with in some way. He turned and made a quick waddle for the nearest pocket of deep shadow, aware of unnamed and undefined tugs at his inner gyro.

Chaingang was a man for whom "future" was an incomprehensible and irrelevant abstract. He was a being totally in the now, and field expedience, homework, and battle tactics aside, reflective self-analysis was an insignificant part of his makeup. He had no special agenda, no game plan beyond the acquisition of food and revenge, and the assurance of his continued survival.

For all of that, he was capable of infrequent moments of introspection. He was subliminally aware, for example, that the destruction of the asshole bikers had been a rather removed and impersonal one. It bothered him—on principle—that he hadn't wanted to take time to rig a mass death for them that would be more suitably slow and ignominious.

But he realized that a hands-on confrontation with them would have been, in the end, unsatisfying. It had given him nothing to touch that biker out in front of their hole. Toying with them, torturing them, would have been pointless. Perhaps one animal or child abuser . . . sure; but such punks in great numbers were too overwhelmingly moronic to deal with. The dog-and-cat punks were so far down the food chain he considered them subhuman. They were beneath his contempt.

He also was acutely aware that this was also totally uncharacteristic of him—to analyze and pick at his own behavior. That bothered him because he knew his inner workings so well. Something was askew and it was something he couldn't identify. It rankled, put a big burr under his saddle, pinched the corner of his perceptions and pissed him off even more.

Then, too, there was the matter of his carelessness. He was now unable to monitor his actions properly. He'd had a charge wired to the back door but whether it had gone off or not . . . who knew? It was remotely possible he'd taken them all out with one haversack. He'd used too much high explosive, but he'd been irritated and didn't want to fool with them. He belched, swallowed, and still the deafness remained an annoying buzz inside his head. He was sure he'd have heard the other charge blow; he'd felt this one in his teeth.

Chaingang spat and recognized the salty taste. He'd probably bitten his tongue. A barking cough of laughter escaped. It sounded far away to him. This was intolerable. He turned and disappeared into the night.

Back inside his wheels, Chaingang took stock. He had used his last haversack. He had two pies left: three-and-a-half-pound antipersonnel weapons that could be fired from a variety of detonator modes. Each shaped charge contained a pound and a half of C-4 military explosive, an extremely reliable and stable plastique. He could, as they say, "write his name" with them. They were simple to point, prime, and fire. Electrical current blew a blasting cap and approximately seven hundred deadly stainless-steel ball bearings exploded outward in a sixty-degree blast pattern, each of the screaming projectiles looking to take names and dig deep graves. He loved and trusted his pies. Two were insufficient.

He had three grenades. A half dozen magazines and partials for the SMG. He needed that auction money and he needed to resupply. And he was fucking deaf, which irritated him to no end. His strange mind sorted pathways, payback methods, possibilities of extrinsic surveillance, all of these things on a subconscious scanning level.

Back in his temporary quarters, he rested and plotted. How would he arrange the final meeting with Miss Roach? He'd come up with an alternate way of running his traps if his hearing was still damaged in the morning.

Bunkowski slept soundly, and was delighted to have nothing more than a slight deafness when he awoke the next day. He phoned and Elaine Roach answered on the second ring.

"Hello?"

"Miss Roach, it's Tommy Norville."

"Oh, yes, sir!" She was always predictable to him and he was immediately reassured. The payoff would go smoothly.

"I wanted to check and see how much had come in so far?"

She told him in a long, laborious recounting about every nickel and dime that had come in response to the auction scam. He let her wind down and—not surprisingly—learned that "only a little over three thousand dollars more" had come in since the initial deposit in her account. Still, not at all shabby, and with the expenses deducted, he stood to clear a neat $12,500 on the venture. Adequate.

"I can't understand why none of the big bidders on Item number forty-one sent their money," she whined, obviously frightened that he was going to hold it against her and that their failure to remit was her doing.

"It's quite normal, Miss Roach. I too would be skeptical of such an item from an unheard-of company. Just wait until we've been around for a few months. Don't trouble yourself about these early results, they are precisely what I anticipated."

"Oh, I see." She was clearly relieved that she wasn't going to be held responsible. Much of her life had been a skirmish with blame and guilt.

"You did a fine job for me and we'll have a long and mutually pleasant association—just don't you worry!" he simpered, continuing to reassure her.

They chatted a bit more about business matters, and then he said casually, "Oh, Miss Roach, I almost forgot. I need to transfer some funds to a creenus account for faltrane, and here's what I would like for you to do . . ." He gave her the instructions to go down and withdraw all the Norville Galleries monies and take it home with her. He'd tell her where to send it in a few days. He did some double talk and used his gift of gab to convince her—over her objections— it would be all right to keep the large sum at her place. Yes, it would be his responsibility if it was stolen. No, she wouldn't have to hold the cash long. He instructed her to go get the cash "now," and that he'd be in touch soon.

The huge homosexual was there in the parking lot waiting for her when she came scurrying out of the bank, and he almost gave her a heart attack when he spoke to her from his vehicle.

"Miss Roach, it's *me!*"

"Oh!" she said with a start, clutching her handbag to her bosom, squinting to make sure it was her boss. "Hello!" It had almost given her a coronary when he spoke to her. She'd been hurrying for the safety of her car with the money in her purse, and she just knew she was going to be robbed. It was not all that incorrect a perception, as it turned out. He'd been waiting across the street from the bank, watching to see if she'd been under any surveillance. None that he could identify asserted itself, and he drove into the lot next to her car.

"Sorry to startle you. You sounded so worried on the phone I thought I'd go ahead and take it off your hands here and you would not have to mail it to me."

"Thank you, sir!" she said. "Do you want me to—er,

count it out now?" she asked, the white gloved hands with a death grip on the auction proceeds.

"Please," he said with a pout. "And may I suggest getting in the car first? We don't want prying eyes seeing that money, do we?"

"Oh, no, sir."

"You just don't know whom you can trust," he said, as she got in, agreeing with him and opening her handbag. First she counted the money into her own hands, then she counted it again into his. He watched her as she counted the bills, thinking how easily he could snap her neck—it would be like breaking a couple of pencils to him. Crunch! She'd be so dead. So easy. It was actually a shame he wasn't in some legitimate business, it occurred to him, as she was to his mind a *perfect* employee.

"Fifteen thousand nine hundred. Sixteen thousand. Sixteen thousand one hundred, sixteen thousand two hundred—" She counted the last of the bills into his enormous open hand.

"You're a good employee, Miss Roach. I want you to know I am pleased with your work."

It was as if he'd given her a thousand-dollar bonus. She lit up like a Christmas tree. Probably the first time anyone had been pleased with anything about her.

"Thank you, sir," she said with awe, then reverted to her normal downcast gaze, waiting for further instructions.

He peeled off a couple of hundreds and told her to take it, starting to say it was for all her extra work, but instinctively he knew not to do that.

"This is for petty cash, so be sure and keep an account of it," he said in a serious tone. She took the money with a curt nod. "That will be all until next month's auction, unless I should think of something and call in the meantime. Oh— just continue to deposit any remittances—and we'll settle up in a couple of weeks as we're doing now. All right?"

"Yes, sir," she said. She got out of the car with a final, nervous nod, and went to her own vehicle. They each pulled out of the bank lot, heading their separate ways. They would not meet again. Tommy Norville, in fact, ceased to exist, as did the Norville Galleries of nonexistent merchandise. The odd pieces bought for show had actually been resold to their original sellers—each at a loss. Chaingang Bunkowski's depleted war treasury had been restored. He was getting his hearing back. Last night had been a resounding success.

He bought a newspaper and looked for the stories on firebombings, a subject so near and dear to his heart.

11

Shooter Price came out of Kansas City Military Books in a dour mood. *Snipers and Silencers, Memoirs of a Sniper, Handbook for CounterSniper Teams, U.S. Marine Corps Scout/Sniper Training Manual, Sniping in the Carpathians, Police Sniper Handbook, Sharpshooters and Yeomanry;* same old stuff.

Two mall rats had come bopping out of the store next to the bookshop and looked at him speculatively and giggled at each other. They were fourteen, tops, dressed like typical slut mall rats, and he could see them whisper and stare holes at his crotch, and as they went by he heard one of them say something that sounded like "Where's Winston?" Whatever that meant.

He felt himself turn livid with bottled-up rage. Price was fuming. For a second, he wanted to go back and kick their asses, but the way that he felt an ass-kicking wouldn't do it. His "primary" had been staying up late and moving and he was tired of all the bullshit and he could feel himself snapping and didn't care.

What the hell did he have? He didn't have anybody who gave a shit whether he lived or died. He tried to count his blessings:

In Fort Worth he had his cars and his library. The books were worth maybe half a million at a conservative estimate. But they'd taken him ten million dollars worth of effort to run down in dusty bookshops from Lee's Summit to London: the finest library of books about snipers extant.

Hell, his 490-horse twin turbo F-40 was probably worth as much as the books on today's market. He'd found a degenerate gambler in Nevada who'd lost big time at the poker table and he'd transferred four hundred K to the man's account for the F-40 and a twelve-cylinder cherry "Redhead" with 430 miles on it, the latter Ferrari one that he'd driven a total of once, trading it off in a deal involving a ragtop XJ-S, a Silver Spirit, a Lamborghini Diablo, and a ton of cash. He had his parents' old Bentley Turbo R. All of these under Mylar in a private garage maintained by River Crest Executive Auto. Once a week, this kid ran a half a buck's worth of gas through each of 'em just to keep them ticking. For what? This is what his life amounted to at forty-one? It pissed him off so much he couldn't think straight. He was like a man about to plummet over Niagara Falls in a small canoe—he could feel himself being pulled over the edge yet he was powerless to fight the thing that was moving him forward.

It had started with the guy in the tavern parking lot, this release thing with the rifle—scoping out random targets. He'd seen Big Petey return to the place across the river, alerted first by the OMEGASTAR System, and then eyeballing him briefly through the scope as he did his thing. When Shooter saw the flames he knew it was Chaingang's work, even though he wasn't sure he'd heard the blast.

What a feeling of power he'd suddenly had, as he heard the sirens wailing in the night. There were sirens all the time, but he imagined these were ones responding to whatever Chaingang had just done. He thought about sniping the ambulances or cop cars, whatever he saw with a red ball. Maybe taking out some firemen.

The first target he saw through the scope was a figure moving up some stairs in front of a tenement. He squeezed one off and part of her disappeared. He swung SAVANT in a dizzying arc and spotted a lone figure in a faraway lot, loading or off-loading something, and he shot him. Swung halfway back, ejected the second case and reloaded. A man talking to a woman in a doorway. A challenge. He took the man out. Snicked the casing out. Slid another big hard APEX(X) in and got the woman, too—he could see her screaming through a window of the store where she and the man had been. What a blast! Four down in—what?—forty-five seconds, tops. It was better than the best sex he could remember.

He parked in back of an obvious dumping area and took the case, moving in the direction of cover. It was hot and humid and he felt like shit. He found a good place and opened up the fitted case and took his baby out and put her together.

"The system is sighted with the aid of the Laco 40X sniperscope," manufactured by Laco Optical, Inc., of Bettendorf, Iowa. A prismatic optical instrument utilizing forty-power magnification, the Laco lens of Magni-coat enhances the light-gathering capability of the weapon's sighting device to between ninety-eight and ninety-nine percent efficiency." He searched for the mall rats in his scope.

"The unit is controlled by the Eyepiece Focusing Collar, which is adjustable by manipulating collar in clockwise or counterclockwise rotation." Light glinted off a man's glasses and Shooter blew him away. *Snick!* Case out. Another big, hard round in place. Bolt closed.

"The Height-Adjustment Sleeve, which is manipulated in a similar rotation." BANG! The rifle thumped him as he squeezed her again, disappointed when the long-haired girl he'd scoped turned out to be a guy.

"The Image Intensifier, which is adjustable by accessing the Intensifier Port by means of an allen wrench and by manipulation of the Intensifier Wing Nut Control . . ." YEAH! A woman getting out of her car. Oh, shit—look at the bitches scatter. Snick. Load. Click.

"The Elevation Range Knob, which adjusts scope ele-

vation . . ." A boy on the run. Lead the mutha and . . .
Squeeze! Adios.

"Windage . . ." She was getting warm. He was heating his
bitch up good. Slid that old nasty expended shell out and put
a nice new cartridge in her hole. He could smell her juices.
Click. Good-looking black-haired baby doll in a sweater.
He'd give her a fucking Winston right here—*Choong!*

Ejected the shell. Reloaded slowly. Hell, he could do this
all day. What a fucking *rush! "The objective lens, which is
adjustable by manipulating the Adjustment Ring until scope
is focused, is adjusted only when parallax is present."* Big son
of a bitch about Chaingang's size. Let's see what he looks
like when you lay them crosshairs on that big belly and do
This! Lordy! What a mess.

Shooter pulled his face away from the scope. Took his
darlin' down and put her away, jogging back to the car. He
put her in the back seat and got in. It was hot inside. He
hated these wheels, even with the top down. To Price it was
just another disposable ride. He looked into the rearview
mirror and was surprised to see that one of his eyes had a
dark ring around it. His best girl had done up and given him
a shiner.

That night, Chaingang was working, trying to run down
his missing biker buddies from Steel Vengeance. Doing the
kind of tracing that keeps you on the telephone as you sort
trails and patterns. Price got antsy watching TV and took his
lady out for some night air.

He saw a guy walking down the street. Watched him
through the Laco without attaching it to the weapon. The
guy walked funny. He definitely needed to die.

*"To focus the scope continuously watch the target point
through the sniperscope, with the eye centered directly in the
eyepiece lens, keeping the crosshairs on the bull's-eye, and
moving your head slightly to the left. If the bull's-eye remains
centered repeat the procedure, moving your head slightly to
the right. If, when the head is moved slightly in either
direction, the bull's-eye appears to move out of center or
change position in any way, parallax is present."*

He nailed the center of the sighting hairs on the walking man's head. "Parallax *is the apparent displacement or movement of an object seen from two different points not on a straight line with the object." Squeeze!* Oooh.

Lieutenant John J. Llewelyn, of the Kansas City Metro Homicide Squad, skidded to a stop, killed the engine of his unmarked car, and got out of the vehicle leaving the door open.

There was tremendous glare from the flashing lights of other cop cars and an ambulance at the crime scene, and he shielded his eyes, a man always careful about protecting his vision, making mental notes of the salient aspects of what confronted him.

"Over here, John," Detective Sergeant Marlin Morris said.

"Who's got the handle on this?"

"Leo and T.J."

"Witnesses?" The Lieutenant and Sergeant went under a bright DO NOT CROSS tape.

"Lady over there." Morris gestured in the direction of a woman in animated conversation with two of his men. "Said she was coming out of this building over here, okay, and the guy blows up. Her words. 'He just blew up. It was awful. I thought something fell on him or hit him or something.' She said he was just somebody walking down the street."

"I.D. on the body?"

"Louis Sheves. Lives in Foley Park. Trying to reach a relative or neighbor, so far no luck."

They reached the body, which was surrounded by people. There was a crime photographer and another evidence tech doing pictures and measurements. The people from Kay Cee Memorial were obviously waiting for the police to finish. There was certainly no hurry. The victim was long gone. Literally. The lieutenant pulled back the cover from the remains.

"Holy Mother!" he said.

"Jesus!" Llewelyn heard another cop murmur. There was nothing left of the head. It had been almost completely torn from the body of the victim by whatever killed him. The force that had exploded the head had ripped it from the neck leaving only a hideous mess of ragged, bloody skin, bone, gristle, torn veins, and arteries, and a bit of spine stalk.

"Where's the man's head?" Llewelyn asked.

Nobody answered. They were standing in some of it. Dark blood had stained the filthy street all around the body. Llewelyn could imagine the witness screaming as this lifeless corpse pumped blood from the neck.

Blackened, oily blood was everywhere. On a nearby parked truck. On the splattered coat of the luckless woman who had experienced the bad fortune to be in Louis Sheves's proximity when he blew up, but had the good fortune to be missed by whatever hellish force had struck him. It was the sort of crime scene where you didn't want to think about the soles of your shoes.

"Lieutenant," one of Llewelyn's guys said.

"Leo. Where's the head?"

"We found some skull fragment and hair 'n' that, but"— he shrugged—"the rest of him's all over the street."

"M.E. done?"

"He said they can't tell us anything till they do an autopsy."

"What a surprise," the lieutenant said dryly.

"Witness see anybody? Vehicles? Anything?"

The detective was looking at his notebook, shaking his head. "She works in the building over there. She was coming out and he was walking down the street. 'There was kind of a noise like a baseball bat or something hitting and this man blew up. He just blew up. It was awful. I thought something fell on him or hit him, you know, like that. But I didn't see anything. He just exploded and I screamed and tried to cover myself. His body kind of went up in the air and came back down in the street.'"

"If the evidence techs are done I guess they can take him."

The homicide team moved aside as they covered what was left of the man and the people from Kay Cee Memorial began loading the remains on a gurney. "I want to talk to her," Llewelyn told his men, stepping over to the sidewalk.

"Yes, sir. We're trying to locate anybody else who might have seen it happen."

"Good." Llewelyn watched the emergency team roll what was left of the dead body over to the waiting ambulance, open the doors, and expertly slide the gurney in. The legs folded up under it as it went in the ambulance with its grisly load. That's the way he felt sometimes, as if his legs would fold up under his weight if he moved the wrong way.

Llewelyn was a prematurely balding, bedraggled-looking, thirty-seven-year-old career cop who suddenly felt one hundred and thirty-seven, and not without good cause. He had solid instincts, proven in combat and in the dicier halls of both military and civilian strivers. He could see his captaincy puddling and running down the nearest storm drain before his eyes if this thing got away from him. Oh, he thought, with an exhausted sigh, there was going to be a world of shit on this one. Twelve of the fucking hits—*and* the thirteen gang kids, which also smelled pro.

He ran a small "elite" unit that people fought to get on. One of his best investigators, Hilliard, pulled up and parked. They exchanged nods and she checked the scene over, speaking with T. J. Kass, the other one of the female dicks on his squad, then came over to where he was making notes.

"You talk to the witness yet, El Tee?" she asked him.

"Uh-uh." He shook his head. "Let's go." They went over to where the woman was beginning her tale of horror for the third or fourth time, telling them what she'd seen, what she thought she'd seen; telling them nothing.

12

Fort Meade, Maryland

The man reading a memorandum from his immediate superior in the Special Action section of SAUCOG's hierarchy shared something with the man whom he was about to call, the legendary Dr. Norman at Marion Federal Penitentiary. Neither of them knew the identity of M. R. Sieh, Jr., yet the conversation they would now have was a result of a memo he had received, subsequent to the latest datafax from NCIC, VI-CAP, and other data-gathering centers feeding their computers. When one of their field men had gone rogue, which in this instance meant he had escaped from prison, in 1987, a detective had followed a trail that led to the Special Action Unit's doorstep. No one had been amused.

The existence of the offender had been expunged from Whirlwind and other computers at that time, deleted but left as a trigger, to search, trace, and transfer back to the section any and all data about who might come looking. The trigger had various spurs. One of these had just been activated for the first time in more than six years.

122

Inside the control center, a pair of technicians finished their thorough investigation of the facility.

"Okay, folks," the sound man said, in the direction of a man seated at the central communications console. "We'll see you next month." Nobody acknowledged his comment or his wave. It was considered proper form to ignore them at all times. A professional habit. The men understood it. They wore Day-Glo yellow jackets bearing a stenciled admonition on the front and back:

ELECTRONIC SOUND SWEEP
IN PROGRESS
W * A * R * N * I * N * G!
DO NOT SPEAK TO ME OR
REFER TO MY PRESENCE IN ANY WAY

When the sound lock had been reactivated, he placed a secure call to the penitentiary, via double-scrambled hook-up. After a moment, he heard Dr. Norman's voice on the hotline.

"Hello?"

"Yes. I'm afraid our problem is worse instead of better. I'm looking at some tragic data. If this printout is correct the person in possession of SAVANT has killed eight men and four women, that we know of—in the last few days—with no guarantee the end is in sight. He has to be terminated, as you predicted."

"It won't be a problem."

"Our superiors will be relieved to hear that taking out a cunning professional executioner armed with a million-dollar weapon system is no problem." He said it without sarcasm.

"Not our problem, I should have said. We'll leave it to the individual most capable."

"What will you do to put this guy out of business?"

"With due respect, do you want to know details?"

"I think in this case—yes. I'll be asked for some of the operational details, I feel sure. What are your plans?"

"As I told you in our last conversation, I've been prepared for this contingency. A special communication has been constructed, which will be brought to the surveillance subject's attention. There is considerable history between the two assets, and subject's skills in such areas are unique. In time, he'll destroy the person who has the special weapon."

"Assuming he does that, what stops him from taking it and killing with it himself?"

"Well—" The doctor had to stifle a laugh at that one. "He neither likes nor trusts that type of weapon. It's much more likely that he'll destroy it along with the man, or damage it in some irreparable way. But as far as him sniping people— no. That wouldn't be his style at all."

"Um."

"Too, there's the matter of the implant. We'll continue to have him in our sights, and should it become necessary, we can simply put an end to him."

"What's to stop the sniper from using that same implant to track the target's whereabouts?"

"Nothing. But so far he's evidenced interest only in random kills of civilians. If he'd wanted to shoot our subject he's had hundreds of opportunities to do so. What we must do now is notify subject so that he can take certain precautions."

"You understand, Dr. Norman, I'm not personally questioning your methodology or tactics, but I'm going to be asked such things as—is this subject the only one you feel is competent to remove the person in question? And what sort of backup do we have, in the wings as it were, should things not work out as planned? Contingency plans? Backstops? Failsafes? That kind of thing."

"The most obvious aspect is that the OMEGASTAR tracker is a two-way unit. As he tracks subject, he too is under surveillance, in the sense that the control center monitors the locations of both the mobile tracker and the implant. So we have whatever backup we need from Clandestine Services, but the idea of utilizing the subject, to turn him back around, plays along a number of lines: first, there's the revenge aspect, subject is much attuned to that element; second, their past shared history will work to our advantage; third, there's subject's presentience. Should the person who is our SAVANT sniper decide to distance himself from the mobile tracker no one is better qualified to trail him than a man who has proven himself to be a stalker of unsurpassed efficiency. But rest assured that other measures have been taken."

"Excellent! Just a minor point—is there any chance that the subject, given his unique, er . . . personality, might ignore your attempt to communicate with him about the possible danger to him, and so on?"

"No. We'll be calling attention to the communication in a way that he'll find singularly disturbing."

"You mean with the dead animal? You mentioned to me something about roadkill?"

"Yes." The doctor had a distasteful expression. "This will disabuse subject of any notion he might entertain to, for whatever reason or whim, ignore our communication. It is a bit more subtle than it might appear. For all its crudity, he'll immediately pay attention to our message, but he will also grasp the implicit threat, albeit a nonchallenging one.

"He will be told the truth, without ornamentation: that there is only one reason he was permitted to be released from death row initially, that he has been a field experiment to give priceless insight into the behavior of one such as himself. That, when he was undergoing drugged hypnosis sessions, a device was surgically implanted in his brain to allow him to be monitored and followed; that while we understand he'll be enraged and wish to destroy us for this, that such a measure was the *only* way he would have been granted the freedom that he has. It will appeal marginally to his sense of logic. The implant, which he will despise, permits him to escape the confines of solitary and to do those things he does so willingly and so well."

"You are, I'm sure, aware of the incident with the motorcycle club that he blew up?"

"Of course."

"It seems to me, and forgive my continuing to play the devil's advocate here, but it seems unlikely such a man will willingly do your bidding. I should think his anger would preclude it. After all, the implant is a locator, not a control. What if he merely ignores both the message and the sniper?"

"When he is asked to extinguish this other asset, it will be made clear that the same person tried to assassinate him in Vietnam. That the target is at this moment trying to kill him. His survival instincts are astonishing. He'll be shown current photos of the sniper and schematics of the SAVANT weapon system, copies of the photos of some of its victims, and a piece of the OMEGASTAR unit that will not only allow him to track the sniper's moves but also educate him as to some of the mobile tracking capabilities we have. He is, in some ways, a true genius. I assure you he'll experience no difficulties in assimilating this data in all its implications, and he'll see that it is in his immediate best interests to destroy the target we give him."

"I know how high you are on the subject's proven abilities—and I'd be the last to quarrel with such an opinion—but from what I've heard, the sniper has a similarly impressive track record, and considering the fact he's armed with a long-range silent killing device that's without equal, and that he's able to monitor the subject's every move . . ." He let the question go unasked.

"It won't be a simple task. But think of it this way— imagine a batting contest between the greatest power hitters of all time: Joe DiMaggio, Hank Aaron, Babe Ruth, Mickey Mantle, and so forth. Who would win if they all entered a batting contest? You might argue that Ted Williams had the most perfect coiled-spring swing, or that Ruth had the greatest raw power, or that Joltin' Joe's numbers were the best, or that he was the most graceful natural athlete—and so on. You apply those kinds of criteria in hypothetical situations. But what if—just for the point of our discussion —we learn that King Kong has always enjoyed playing the game. We watch him at bat and he knocks them out of the park, and for a bat he uses a small tree." The man on the phone laughed at the analogy but Dr. Norman continued, in a serious tone. "And then you said to King Kong, 'King—only the one who wins this contest survives.' I would not wish to be Mr. DiMaggio or Mr. Ruth under those conditions. This is not a very carefully drawn parallel, but I guess what I'm asking you to understand is this: Whatever high technology we've given the man with the sniper rifle, I'm about to take away his most effective weapon. That has been secrecy. I am going to hand him to King Kong, one might say. And all the sophisticated electronics and weapons in the world will not counterbalance the subject's natural abilities and his drives. He is—in every sense of the phrase—a born killer. He's also the ultimate survivor." Then Norman said in a low whisper, "Truly, I would not want to be in the other man's shoes." And he meant it.

13

Kansas City, Missouri

Why don't we let this short cut grow out, Julie?" the hairdresser asked. "I've got a great cut in mind for your head."

"I like it like this, Sandra. It's nice 'n' short and I don't have to fool with it."

"You've got some natural curl in your hair. Do you know how many heads I cut would kill for some natural curl? My God, woman . . ."

"Whack it off," Julie said, laughing, knowing it bugged Sandra. Julie Hilliard was thirty-two and, like many women, had different looks at different times. She knew she could let it grow out a bit and Sandra would tease it to hell, and she'd put on a bunch of makeup, a ton of blush and lip gloss and mascara for miles, and some big dangly earrings, and smile with lots of teeth showing instead of her usual thin-lipped cop look, and she looked like an attractive woman. But Julie Hilliard was a cop, one of Kansas City's finest in a progressive shop that was staffed with more female dicks than any other homicide department in the country. She was also one of only two women on the prestigious Kansas City Metro

Homicide Squad, a slot that had taken her eleven kick-ass years of casemaking to attain. Homicide was what she lived, breathed, and ate. And her look was just fine, thank you.

"Not only that, this cut is all wrong for your face." Sandra had the scissors going but she was going to bitch about it all the same. "You've got terrific eyes, and you should spotlight them. This downplays them."

"The A-holes I deal with, they don't like my eyes anyway."

"Yeah, but God forbid you'd want to get married someday . . ."

"Oh, Lord."

"Meet a nice guy, settle down—"

"You sound like my mother, now."

"Well, I'm just saying . . . I could make you so much prettier. Check it out, perm those curls, eh? Layer through here, bevel the ends, keep it short back on your nape, but longer here on the sides and maybe streak it here, see? All you do is scrunch it. Shampoo, towel it off. Wham, bam, thank you, ma'am!"

"Whack it off," Julie Hilliard told her, looking into the mirror but seeing the bulletin board above Llewelyn's disaster-area of a desk.

"Well, at least let me spike it."

She finally took her freshly shorn head, and all the rest of her well-distributed 127 pounds, and got in her unmarked unit, returning to 1125 Locust. At headquarters, she immediately headed for the squad room. She nodded to people on the way up, and familiar faces in the hallways, but did not speak until she was inside the door marked Metropolitan Major Case Squad, which was the real name of the unit, but which nobody ever used.

Leo and T.J., the only other female detective on the squad, and the El Tee, were occupied elsewhere. Marlin Morris had been waiting for her so he could brief the three detectives present at one time. Michael Apodaca and his partner George Shremp, nicknamed "Abba-dabba" and "Jumbo" respectively by the other cops, and Julie Hilliard

—who normally worked alone—were the only dicks in the room. Sergeant Morris did not have to refer to notes.

"Honcho's with Leo 'n' T.J. They're working the fire-bombing. We've got thirteen people on Boyles. Rotating teams." Boyles was the name of the file on the "pro" hits, as they were perceived, beginning with the slaughter of a guy who appeared to have no ties to anyone, a colorless loner of a person, a part-time cabby, a twenty-three-year-old man named David Boyles. "That's not counting us. Right now we're going to concentrate on Mr. Dillon and see what we can break loose." He handed out a photocopy of a two-page report and a composite of twelve shooting victims' pictures. There was a second composite showing thirteen faces of young gang members killed in the firebombing/shooting incident. "I think an obvious possible tie is Tom Dillon to the bike gang. He coulda been dealing easy. He was a thief. Maybe he was selling or fencing stuff through the gang? Anyway let's look at everything. Show those pictures. See if anybody makes anybody." They knew what he meant.

Detective Sergeant Morris, a thirty-year-old lifer with a droopy semi-Fu mustache and thinning hair, a hardcore casemaker, talked about the weapon that had been used on some of the bikers outside their clubhouse, and discussed the reports on the various victims, speculating as to what had killed them. Julie Hilliard made notes as he spoke, realizing she was just doodling, really, as she saw she'd written *acceleration . . . explosive . . .* and *propellant* and had no idea what Morris was saying. She snapped back to life and listened to firearms and high-explosive talk.

"Neither the regional crime lab nor the FBI has anything yet?" Jumbo Shremp asked. She was thinking the same question.

"Huh-uh. Negative, so far."

"Some kind of rifle grenade," Shremp said. "That's what I think. Fits the pattern. A pro."

"Are we—" Julie heard her own voice. "Is anybody asking the military? This guy obviously has a back-ground—a military service record, right? Couldn't we put it on the computer and program it through to give us likely names on who has the expertise for all this stuff . . . uh, you know, capabilities. Demolition. Firearms. And then run those names against the vics? Would that work?"

"Yeah," Morris said. "That wouldn't take more than about ten million hours to program. No—it's probably the way to go." He shrugged. "But we gotta narrow this thing down first. You got too many guys in the services know this shit. We probably need to start trying to get some patterns here. I don't think this is random work. I think we're gonna find Dillon and some of the bikers tied together."

"I know one thing about the son of a bitch. He's hitting too close to home," Apodaca said.

"Yeah." Connally's was two blocks from the police headquarters.

14

A person can disintegrate in two seconds or they can fall apart over a period of months—even years. Shooter Price had appeared to implode, going off the deep end and killing a dozen times within the span of a few days, killing as he never had, randomly and without purpose. What had pushed him so far? Surely not one more rejection by a woman, or his inability to consummate the act of intercourse. Time, frustrations multiplied by time, the aging process, the cumulative effect of the last couple of months as he tracked a killer even crazier than himself—these were only some of the root causes of his falling apart.

This was, for whatever reason, some semblance of the old Bobby Price who awoke bright and early, feeling refreshed and rather guiltless, hitting the floor and beginning his normal regimen of calisthenics and isometric exercises.

He pulled on old clothes and went out to the car, put the top down, and drove to Hospital Hill Park. There was a place he'd seen where he could work unobserved.

He parked as close as he could to the site he'd found, and carried a new shovel to a place flanked by shrubbery. He stripped off his shirt and began digging, first scoring the earth in a large, fairly round circle, then making a smaller interior circle, which was not to be cut. He was digging earth with a vengeance, his powerful body glistening with sweat as he tossed full shovels of dirt around the hole. This would be a loose berm.

The center would be left as a gun post, a roughly cylindrical form around which he could move, but with a base for SAVANT to rest on her collapsible bipod, which he seldom used.

When Price had dug down a couple of feet, he made yet a third circle and started digging between the central cylinder and the outer edge of the hole. He dug far enough down that when he'd finally removed most of the dirt he had a large hole with a built-in seat that ran around the outermost edge of the gun pit. He could sit comfortably and sight the weapon at his leisure. The only problem was that the berm was up higher than the gun would be. He took a break, toweled off, and climbed out to fix the loose collar of dirt that surrounded the pit. When he was satisfied, he covered the pit with a large, but very lightweight bush net, and broke off long branches of leafy limbs from surrounding bushes and trees, which he used to drape between the gun post and the outside edge of the pit. When he'd finished, it was fairly well camouflaged.

While he dug, some of the same physical changes occurred in Bobby Price's biochemistry that once took place due to drug usage. When Shooter was doing cocaine, certain things happened when he sniffed lines: the white lady would jam the pump that regulated his system, overstimulating neurons, fucking with his brain, kicking him in the chest to get his heart started, floating in his synapses, jabbing his brain in the ass with massive paranoia and hard-charging psychoses. He was there again, but this time without the zip of the blow. One could see it in his eyes, and in his frenetic movements. Neurons were shooting at him inside his mind; lightning from a mental electrical storm was about to strike. Brain nerves fired and Shooter Price jerked as if his mind was exploding.

By the time he'd finished he was stoked with crazy

nervous energy. He got back in the car and drove around aimlessly. When a neon tavern sign caught his eye he stopped and parked.

He got out of the car and went in, instantly overwhelmed by the salty booze smell.

When he became accustomed to the darkened interior his gaze was drawn to a woman sitting alone at the bar. She was hard looking, but apart from the fact that she exuded a powerfully feral sexuality, something about her reached out for him. He walked over to her immediately, bending close enough that he wouldn't have to speak loudly to be heard over the music.

"Is it okay if I sit here?" he asked. The woman acted as if she hadn't heard him, ignoring the question. He sat down. Price was sure that he could smell her, an untamed animal scent that—together with the booze smells—was making him hot.

"My name's Bobby Price. Would you mind if I bought you a drink?" he asked her respectfully. Down at the end of the bar three stools from them, an office girl in a colored dress had breezed in and ordered a drink. She smiled at him invitingly but she wasn't what he wanted at all. He ignored the offer, and it was as if the woman next to him sensed it, and she grinned at him for the first time.

"I don't want another drink, but thanks." When she smiled, she looked a lot older, and he wondered if she didn't smile much—thinking it made wrinkles around her mouth or eyes. There were quite a few lines in her face, but he thought she was stunning.

"You're the loveliest woman I've seen in a long time," he whispered to her softly, "and I mean that in the nicest way. I hope you don't think I'm acting disrespectful."

She looked at him funny, cocking her head to see what was going on in his face. She looked back and seemed to be lost in thought for a second. Then she did something that almost made Bobby flip out right there at the bar. She reached over and slid her hand up under his cashmere sweater, and he felt long, sharp nails on his chest. People were all around but he wasn't aware of any stares. The bartender was too busy to watch and the people on either side of him were into their own conversations. She just stood there, playing with one of his nipples and suddenly she began to squeeze very hard.

"Ouch," he said before he could catch himself. Then he laughed nervously. She just smiled and kept squeezing. He felt so odd. Why was she doing this?

She just kept looking at him, reading him—as if his face were a book and his chest were Braille, and she had to pinch his tits to see the words form—and saying nothing. He felt like an idiot. He couldn't think of what to say. After several moments of pinching, she leaned over close and whispered something into his left ear.

"Do you know what Ben Hoa balls are?" That's what he *thought* she had said to him.

"I was stationed there during the war," he said. Her fingernails were still on his chest, but relaxed now. "That was a long time ago," he said. It was the funniest joke anyone had ever told her. She started laughing raucously, taking her hand out of his sweater and pounding on the bar. People looked over at them. He just kept smiling. The bartender said, "Tell me, too. I need a laugh." But she just ignored everybody. She laughed hard, finally stopping.

"What did I say?"

"Don't. Don't start me again. What did you say your name was, lover?" He started to answer. "Bobby. That was it." She slid that hand back under his sweater and he could feel the long fingernails stop at his left nipple, which already was sensitive from the squeezing she'd given it. "Bobby, I'll tell you what, old cowboy. You pay for these drinks and come with me, lover." She turned and was fucking gone.

He threw a twenty on the bar and was running to catch up.

"Hey—thank you, sir," he could hear the bartender say gratefully. Where was she?

He ran out of the dim interior and almost ran into her.

"You got a car?" she asked. She looked nearly fifty in the sunlight, and he thought she was the sexiest-looking woman he'd ever seen, including on TV and in the movies.

"Yeah. There." He pointed. Almost tongue-tied.

They got in the car and she sprawled out like she owned it. Her left hand glanced against the back of his neck and he said "where to" and she gave him her address.

Price started the car and pulled out, asking for directions and getting them. Her voice was cold and matter-of-fact. But her fingernails were playing with the hair at the back of his head.

He reached for her and she chilled him with her voice.

"You drive and don't be touching me till I want you to, okay?"

"Sure," he said, chagrined. After a few moments, he said, just to make conversation, "I don't even know your name."

"Listen. Here's the deal. You don't talk unless I fucking *want* you to talk, do you understand me?"

"Yeah, okay—but . . ." He was so confused by this woman, yet so totally drawn to her. "I . . ."

"You listen good, Bobby baby. We're gonna have a fucking ball. My name is Cindy Hildebrande. You know everything *about* me now, all right? You can call me Mama, okay?"

"Sure, okay." He smiled. Whatever you're into, he thought.

"Just drive, cowboy." He'd obviously done something to piss her off. He knew one thing. This old Cindy was going to be *dynamite* in the sack.

Kansas City, Kansas

There were four names in the Boorum & Pease Accounts Receivable Single Entry Ledger under SVS/M, and he regarded the names as unfinished business, to be dealt with in the harshest possible way.

Bunkowski no longer needed to open the pages to read the names inside his head:

Belleplaine, Rene (Tiny)
Cholia, Carlos Garcia (Kid Gloves, a.k.a. Cee-Gee)
Harrison, Donald (Donny)
Vale, Ashley Yaples (Bluto)

The third gangbanger, Donny Harrison, was doing hard time in the joint for second-degree murder.

He is aware that each of these punks holds a title in their now-almost-defunct organization: War Lord, Sergeant at Arms, President, Road Captain.

He has researched their real names, records, home and work addresses (a joke for the parole board's files), and all of this data he came by easily, with a few questions to street people, a few bureaucratic phone calls to the proper agencies. One could learn anything over a telephone with nothing more sophisticated than an official, curt tone and the proper-sounding jargon.

Chaingang wanted them all gone. He'd do these, and when the opportunity arose he'd whack the punk inside as well. Put an end to the line.

His mind sorted probabilities, tactics, strategic contingencies. He knew they were hunkered down in a trailer the gang kept north of town, and he was in his wheels, crossing the river, heading over the Intercity Viaduct bridge on the route that became Highway 24, turning left in the busy traffic on Winter Road, driving in the direction of Sugar Creek.

He knows what he would like to do to them, what would be fitting, and he has already taken certain steps toward that end. His computerlike brain probes for weak spots, exfiltration snags, and the myriad details of hazard assessment. He concludes that if something unforeseen happens he can improvise something. He does not see the three biker punks as a serious threat, but while he still regards them as buffoons, scum beneath contempt, Chaingang is conscious of the fact that his immediate goal is to punish.

He would take his time with the targets, and on a conscious level his logic was strong and uncompromising. His subconscious mindscreen, however, was scanning retrieval for something unrelated. Dr. Norman would have been fascinated to watch the beast's mental computer examine stored data:

Reclamation of X-velocity matériel from chemical compounds.
Big-bang mixtures from over-the-counter accessibles.
Improvised M18A1 antipersonnel mine detonation devices.
Construction and field usage of homemade munitions.
Chemistry, math, and the general sciences . . .

He also saw something with just the

EDGE
OF
HIS
MIND

and tried his best to stop it and look at it but to no avail. It had flashed by too quickly. Something akilter, out of place—jarringly so—an element he had "seen" with his presentience, perhaps, but not identified. A danger to him.

The harder he tried to lock on to it the farther it fled from his grasp, so he relaxed his mind and thought of pleasant scenes. Old killing fields and brutalized sex he'd enjoyed. Tried not to focus on the mindscreen's present to him—sometimes that worked.

Sterling Avenue caught his gaze from a street sign and he turned north into the flow of heavy traffic, driving defensively, but not overly slow—the model of a careful driver if you were behind him. (He was also capable of expert, fast driving. In his lifetime, he'd been stopped by various state cops a total of nineteen times. Once, in legal wheels, he'd taken and paid for a forty-six-dollar speeding violation. Seventeen times, in stolen vehicles, he'd talked the state rod into both tearing up or not starting a ticket, *and into killing the "wants/warrants" check!* He could have been an amazing confidence man had money interested him. Only once he'd been unable to dissuade the unlucky state highway patrolman with words, and had left him filling his front seat with blood.)

In a more receptive state, he realized that something was still seriously awry with his system. Each time he had this thought it seemed to center in the rolls of fat at the back of his huge tree-trunk of a neck, and shoot up the skull. He wondered if he'd had brain damage, or if perhaps he had some sort of brain tumor that was becoming malignant.

One thing he knew without question: Something was wrong. He knew his system like the inside of a ticking Swiss watch, from his thought processes to the regularity of his bowel movements. He was, for all his screaming abnormality and oversize bulk, a well-oiled human machine. He knew he was having "mental problems" of some kind. He was also certain that—by logical standards—he was not insane. Not by *his* criteria.

Bunkowski separated these mental problems into two parts: first, there was a vague torpor—as he thought of it; second, there were those physical manifestations that he could isolate as having begun sometime during his last period of drugged incarceration. When they'd prepared to let him out for the killing spree in Waterton, they had done something—either overdosed him in some form or struck him on the head while he was drugged. This was the hornet's nest, which was his way of thinking of the buzzing, dizzy sensation he had experienced a time or two since his release from the hole in Marion.

The torpor thing was what tugged at him. It was interfering with his day-to-day business, and affecting decisions.

Making him act weirdly in his own eyes. He was doing things that made no sense—giving Miss Roach two hundred dollars unnecessarily, for example. Why hadn't he simply buried Miss Roach and put her out of her misery? Very disturbing.

It wasn't torpor at all, when he thought about it. For one thing, he never seemed to be horny anymore. Not that he was such a randy goat to begin with—it's just that he had *normal* desires for sex, at least in his mind they were normal. Another thing he'd noticed besides his unusual celibacy was that he didn't seem to find killing so much fun anymore. Sure, it had been pleasant, doing the bikers in their clubhouse, but there had been no true exhilaration as he'd felt in the past, no genuine sense of satisfaction.

There was nothing good that would come of thinking along these lines, he decided, and jerked his mind off of the subject—or tried to. He saw a rib joint, decided he was hungry, and pulled in. But as he got out of the car he was quite shaken by the realization that the act of killing was not acting as a catharsis, if indeed it ever had. This knowledge did not keep the desire for revenge from rumbling inside his gut like physical hunger for food, but he knew it was a bad omen. He was tasting something he could never completely eat. Like a drug addict who gets off the first time like a skyrocket, and then spends his life searching again and again for the perfect high he experienced with his initial experiment. He'll never find it, and perhaps inside he knows he'll never recapture it—but addiction (if only to self-rewards) supersedes logic.

Was he condemned to go on killing and killing, forever searching for the big release that would bring him peace of mind? When he destroyed the bikers, would that give him relief? Was there satisfaction waiting for him in the steamy red geyser that would pump from Mrs. Nadine Garbella's severed neck? Or was the only satisfaction in slaking his bloodthirst and heart hunger?

The taste of an enemy's life force did sound good. In fact, the thought of sinking those shark teeth into the hot, coppery, salty meat of a nice fresh heart made him so hungry he felt positively lightheaded.

A waitress or hostess welcomed him, asked him if he wanted a table for one, and he had to nod—he couldn't speak, his mouth was salivating so badly.

"Would you like a menu?"

"No," he said, swallowing. "Bring me ribs. How many in a side?"

"A side is a dozen ribs."

"Bring me six sides."

"Right away, sir," she said with a smile, hurrying off in the direction of the kitchen.

Ribs, hot and mouth-watering, and smothered in famous Heart of America Barbecue Sauce, was what this place did. So for the folks who came in and ordered ribs and nothing else, who didn't sit schmoozing over appetizers or drinkies from the bar, there was almost no wait for the food. If you were a table of twelve drunks, or a table with a couple of crying kids, you really got fast service—they wanted you to eat and run. It was all of a minute and a half before Daniel Edward Flowers Bunkowski was presented with his six steaming sides of Heart of America barbecued beef ribs.

Picture the sight: Mavis Strayhorn of the Olathe Strayhorns, seated at the south side of table station eight, facing her husband, Herbert, whose back is to the door. Their dear friends of many years, Dora Lee and Monte Brown (Monte works at the bank), are at the east and west sides of the table, so when Mavis sees the thing and her mouth drops open they all look—naturally—and the three of them see the beast come waddling over and flop down right there beside them, bold as you please, talking in a big loud voice and ordering six sides of ribs. My God!

Monte snickers and says something across the table, longways, to Dora Lee, and Mavis gets the giggles, and Herbert Strayhorn says, "What? What's so funny?" in that dry voice of his. Monte says something else and the four of them laugh, and Herbert kind of turns and tries to get a peek at this vision, which just about convulses Monte and Dora

Lee, but which Mavis somehow manages to stifle. Pretty soon they go on about their business, and get back to eating their rib dinners.

The waitress who has his station hurries with the ribs, all seventy-two of them, a six-tier stack of delectable-smelling platters in hand, sits them on the table, and says, "Will there be anything else for you, sir?" But he can only shake his head slightly in response, or maybe that isn't even a shake—perhaps he is just moving that big head around in an involuntary physiological reaction to the smell of the barbecue. My God, he's *hungry* for *meat!* The waitress seems to sense danger and jerks her hands away the second the platters of ribs are on the table. She tears off a page from the pad she carries and places it surreptitiously at the far edge of the table, moving away from the station as quickly as she can, away from the implicit threat. Sharp teeth, brutal strength, fingers like steel cigars, knives that slice, forks with tines that pierce flesh—this table where the behemoth sits is like the dissecting table in a busy morgue.

The beast has no awareness of the waitress or the people around him, not at this moment. He is too busy eating, chewing, swallowing, too occupied now to speak or even nod as she thanks him in a faraway, fading voice. A faint red mist rises from the smoking, pungent meat as the beast tears at the ribs in a feeding rampage. How many writers have swiped the phrase "feeding frenzy" from *Jaws?* But that is what one sees—Chaingang over the ribs, crunching tooth against hard bone, devouring the food with ugly misshapen teeth meant to gnaw at chunks of flesh, cleaning each rib bone like a shark hitting bloody meat, or a starving carnivore over its kill. Ripping every speck of meat, gristle, fat, then sucking the tiny bones held in those huge, viselike paws. Methodical. Orderly and mad at once. Eating each beef rib in the same way, in a grisly, ghastly, gross spectacle of bestiality.

Picture what Mavis Strayhorn sees: the mountain of hard blubber and ugly muscle holds the rib just so, an expression on his dimpled face like an animal with its prey, taking the four sides of each rib in order, sucking the bone in a quick, wet, nasty slurp, throwing it onto the platter. Five, six, eight ribs. Gnaw. Suck. Slurp. Swallow. Gnaw. Suck. Slurp. Swallow. Cleaning the ribs bare. Eighteen. Nineteen. Twenty-six. Twenty-seven. The pile of bones beginning to resemble a carcass plucked by buzzards and stripped by maggots.

Not a scrap of edible food clings to a bone. The feeding machine is an efficient one and leaves nothing. Four fast ripping bites in each series, the loud sucking, the sound of the bone hitting the pile. The routine punctuated only by an occasional cracking sound as those sharp animal fangs penetrate bone.

Mavis and Dora Lee and Monte have stopped eating now. Herbert is still valiantly chewing away, their humble family platter sits between the four of them, untouched. Herbert keeps craning back to get a look at this palpably horrible thing that has brushed up against their orderly and clean lives of genteel normalcy.

The slob inhales the seventy-two Heart of America Barbecued ribs, "hickory smoked in our famous Heart of America Barbecue Sauce—hot or mild," and as he swallows the last of the meat wrested from the final naked rib he looses a gassy, wet, explosive belch that causes Mavis to begin to throw up—the nausea rises in her throat but she manages to catch it before it escapes and she swallows.

Herbert has turned and they're all watching this disgusting beast now, genuinely disturbed by his vomit-making presence. Grease and vestiges of sauce drip from his face as he languorously casts his eyes toward Mavis, appearing to notice the people beside him for the first time. He eyes Mavis's thigh, something pleasant to consider while dining. A lethargic, amusing consideration plays through his weird mind as he sucks a morsel from a tooth: belching again, wiping his greasy face, dropping the filthy napkin on the floor between them, standing heavily, shoving himself erect, undressing Mavis Strayhorn—not for sex—but for cooking. Imagining how she would taste, barbecued. Imagining the sweet taste of Barbecued Mavis, Heart of America style.

But now he was moving toward them, and for a second Mavis thought Herbert and Monte were going to stand up and try and *fight* with him, but the huge fat man smiled, an ear-to-ear parody of a human grin, and a deep basso profundo voice rumbled out of him, his eyes fixed on Mavis's chest.

"Look at the mouse," he said, pointing, almost touching her.

"Hey," Herbert said, his voice raspy and full of fear, "listen—"

There was a pin in the shape of a tiny gold mouse affixed to Mavis's sweater. His massive fingers were near her, and the smell of him was in her nose, rank and fearsome, like the scent of a cave animal cornered in its den, but he was doing the cornering. She looked down where the mouse pin had been. He was astonishingly dexterous with his big hands, he had a thief's touch, and he'd somehow removed the pin with the fingers of his right hand and was holding it for inspection.

"Say goodbye to the mouse," he said, and popped it in his mouth and swallowed the gold pin, turning and leaving in a swirl of poisonous body odor and barbecued meat smells.

"Somebody ought to call the police and report him, my God almighty—" Dora Lee Brown sputtered. Everyone sat there stunned, shaking their heads. Rooted to the spot.

What do you do in a circumstance such as this? Mavis Strayhorn of Olathe, Kansas, would be thirty-eight in September, and in all those years no one had *ever* eaten any of her jewelry before.

Cindy Hildebrande lived in a cheap tract house, in a neighborhood full of identical, tiny frame homes, all packed shoulder to shoulder in a blue-collar section of the city. She was no housekeeper. Bobby could see that right away. Stuff was strewn around, dishes were in a sink, and it was not the best smelling home he'd ever been in either.

Bobby Price was fastidious and the way she'd come on to him in the bar, the ride over, and now—the crummy home—had made him sort of nervous and jumpy. He wasn't sure about this deal anymore. But she soon turned him back around.

"Just stand there, pretty cowboy," she told him, "while I slip into something less comfortable." She went into a nearby room while he stood there, trying to keep from inhaling any more than necessary. He could hear her rummaging around in a closet, and when she came out she was wearing these fabulous boots, slick-looking thigh-high boots with spike heels, and she was carrying something.

"I'm ready to ride the range now, Bobby." She laughed, tossing her bleached blond hairdo around a little and making a face at him. Something about her was very sexy. She had a great way about her, he decided, tremendous style. "Know what this is, cowboy?"

"A quirt," he said.

"This is in case you're a bad boy to Mama. You're gonna behave, aren't you?" She brandished the thing like a large riding crop with a leather flail.

"Yeah. You bet."

"Take your clothes off." She towered over him with those big stiletto-heeled boots on. "You can leave your jock on—if you're wearing one."

"Sure." He smiled, pulling his sweater off. Eager to obey. "Aren't you going—" He started to ask her a question and she whipped him hard with the quirt—hard.

"*Jesus* Chr—" He rubbed himself where she'd caught him on the hip. This was no fun at all. She was a fucking nut case.

"I told you to talk when I ask you to talk and not before. Now get those little pants off, cowboy."

He obeyed in silence, his hip and leg burning like fire. She'd really let him have a stinging slap with the thing.

"Nice. You're a pretty one." She came over and played

with his nipples and pulled his head to her and kissed him hard on the mouth. Then she backed away and looked him over as if he were a piece of meat, standing there in his briefs with a reddening welt on the side of his hip where she'd whipped him. "You got a cute set of buns, Bobby. Come on in here for Mama," she said, taking his hard, muscled arm and pulling him down the hallway. But instead of taking him into the bedroom, she brought him into her tiny, filthy bathroom. He thought about just turning around and using his fist on this old bitch a few times. But something stopped him.

"This toilet of mine is so dirty I don't even want to shit in it," she said, roughly. "You understand me?"

"Yeah," he said. She got a toothbrush out from under the sink and handed it to him.

"You get down and clean this thing for me, cowboy. Make it real pretty for Mama—you do that?"

"Um." He didn't know what he wanted to do. He could just go pull his pants on and book, for one thing. But something made him want to see what she had in mind. He knelt down in front of the commode and started scrubbing with the toothbrush.

"Oh, shit. Yeah! That's it," she said softly in an urgent tone. "Go to it, you bitch. Clean my fucking toilet. Oh, do it." She was touching herself. "Don't look at me, you little whore!" she yelled at him, and he concentrated on cleaning the stained porcelain. "That's better, you sweet, sexy little cowboy bitch. You fuckin' . . . oh, uh-huh—yeah!" She was really getting off watching him scrub her potty. After a bit, she let him get up and they kissed, and she told him to lay the toothbrush down and wash his hands, and then come in to bed.

He didn't even want to touch the corroded faucets, or the nasty looking soap bar, or the scummy towels. Even the water from the tap looked dirty. He obeyed, however, and padded into the bedroom to find her seated in bed.

"Get over here," she commanded, spreading her legs a little. He tried to crawl between her legs and she shoved him away. "Not like that, Bobby. Get on your tummy for Mama." He moved. "Yeah. Right alongside me here. Um-hmm." He jumped when she touched him. He felt the briefs ripping. "There! Now I can see that pretty boy butt of yours." He felt the bedsprings move with her as she got something.

"See?" She held a box under his face and opened it. "Those are Ben Wa balls." Balls on a string. So? "From where you were stationed—eh?" He thought of the Ben Hoa airstrip where the spike team had once gone during a mission. He couldn't remember anything about the place but grunts, choppers, and fucking gooks. Too many moons ago. Everything was all mixed up now. Spike teams and spiked heels, Ben Hoa and Ben Wa balls. Too much that was weird.

"Oh!" he said.

"You know what these are for?"

"Huh—no. I-I don't know," he stammered. Her long fingers were touching him. Going up in him, forcing him open in back and pushing into him. The long cool fingernails that had pinched his chest.

"They're for a woman's pussy."

"Un."

"Uh-huh." She was rubbing one against him. "For your *pussy*, cowboy." She shoved a ball into him and he moaned and it just about drove her crazy. She started touching herself again, and he could feel his nipples harden. He was still sore there where she'd pinched him, and his hip and ass were sore.

"You cunt," she whispered to him, forcing another ball in.

Moaning in ecstasy, rubbing him, touching herself, reaching around and squeezing his nipples, then touching him down there.

"You fucking whore. You goddamn shit-ass dick-fucking tramp—" She was cruelly squeezing his balls, and his cock started getting hard. He couldn't help himself. He was getting a boner that was threatening to drill straight through the bed, with his nose full of her cheap perfume and the dirty bedspread and the sex of her. He'd never been so hot. "Go ahead, you little bastard fuck, go ahead and get that dick fucking hard and come all over my bed, you no-good son-of-a-bitching pussy-assed slut."

It was too much for him. He couldn't hold it.

"You cleaned the shit out of my toilet and now I'm treating you like a fucking pussy slave. Mama's cowboy *snatch*. And you're loving it, aren't you, pretty bitch?"

"Yeah."

"Answer me, goddamn it."

"Yes. *Yes.*"

"You're loving it to death, aren't you?"

"Oh, oh—yes!" She shoved the third ball up his exhaust pipe. Oh, God. He couldn't hold it back anymore. Not another second.

"Yes," she said, as the hot jism shot onto her fingers. "Now you can learn what's what, you fuck. Now you can find out what it's like to have real balls." And she started slowly pulling the smooth balls out of his butt, and he screamed with pleasure as he ejaculated. It felt as if he must have shot the load of loads, the king shit orgasm of the century, as the gut-tearing ultimate climax went ripping through him. He'd never known such total abandon and almost unbearable pleasure.

Her coarse tone cut into him as he lay jackknifed across her bed, nude, spent, almost unconscious in a kind of post-paroxysm of complete docility. If she'd told him to go back in and clean the rest of the house with her toothbrush he'd gladly have obeyed. He thought he was falling deeply in love with Cindy Hildebrande. He couldn't wait to buy her a fucking diamond or something outrageous.

"Come on. Let's go. I gotta get moving. Okay?" Her tone was the same as when he'd reached for her in the car. A man's command voice. A tough soldier's voice. A fucking D.I.'s voice. He didn't understand. Hadn't she liked it, too?"

"Cindy, wasn't it good—you know—for you, too?" he

asked her, genuinely perplexed at her sudden shift in attitude.

"Yeah. Sensational. Now I got to hit the bricks, doll. Come on. Get your clothes on. Let's go." Rushing him into his clothing, for crissakes. He pulled on slacks, the sweater, got his shoes back on. She was hustling him out the door almost as if she were bringing in the next shift. What was her trip?

"Man, you had me goin'," she said, conversationally, as she handed him his wallet, pager, keys, and pocket change. "I saw that pager—and I knew you weren't any fucking doctor. I thought maybe you were Vice." She laughed. He had no idea what she was talking about. She physically pushed him out the door. "I got my five hundred. I took it out of your wallet when I checked for I.D.," she said in a nonchalant tone. Just letting him know she'd been paid. His heart sank like a chunk of concrete.

She was a fucking *hooker*. He was a goddamned *john* to her. He laughed, by reflex, so that if any people were watching him they wouldn't know he was so upset. She'd conned him. *Played with him.* He snuffed back the tears at first, but then he let them come, streaming down his face as he got into the car, banging the wheel with his fist. He started the car up, but changed his mind, shifted into park, with the brake set. Got out and unlocked the trunk and took his baby out and put her together right there in the street. Fuck it. Snot running from his nose. Snuffling like a little kid. He blew his nose into the street and slid a big pointed APEX(X) into her. Lock and fucking load. Walked back across the street, spitting, blowing, clearing his throat. Trying to hold the tears back for later.

As always she saved him, pulled him out of the shit. The second he held her, professionalism took over, and the finest sniper alive became one with the unique killer in his arms.

"Cheekpiece, stock, shoulder rest, detent, oiler, adjustment port, spanner port, windage, elevation, parallax, receiver, recoil pad, base plate, grips, trigger housing group, action,

image enhancement control, safety, forward guard, bolt, bolt knob, bipod, anchors, objective adjustment, heat shield, Ultronics silencer and flash hider, sling connectors, forward grip, barrel adjustment, barrel—" His right leg kicked out and the door smashed open.

"Wait a goddamn minute—hold it!" He could hear her voice screaming from the bathroom. Water running in the shower. She came out with a towel in front of her and saw Shooter Price's killing face over the top of his baby's business end. That was the last Cindy Hildebrande would see or know. "What?" was forming on her lips when he squeezed one off. Inside the small hallway, it sounded like a telephone-pole guy wire tapped with a metal rod.

Pwiiing! A metallic thwock that wasn't as loud as the sound that parts of Cindy made splattering off the hallway walls. He was covered in stuff, and so was his darlin'.

Nasty! He'd never done anybody up close with the weapon. He'd had no damned idea in the world it would take them apart like that. It was one thing to see the results at a mile away or whatever. But the power of her up close was fucking awesome.

He found a couple of rags and got her wiped off, and then cleaned himself up as best he could, wrapped the rags in another rag and carried his weapon and rag bundle out to the car. There was nobody watching him—that he saw, anyway—and he loaded her into the trunk, put the rags in a box to be thrown away, got in, and started the car.

It was amazing how much better he felt. He flipped the toggle on the OMEGASTAR and saw that Big Petey was nice and quiet. He switched the pager over to OMNI DF, put it back on primary monitor, and drove down the street.

He was almost back to the motel, feeling good again, keeping time to the radio with his fingers on the wheel, a golden-oldies station playing "Hard for the Money," when the movement alarm sounded on the DeMon.

He killed the audio and pulled over, checking the OMNI.

The primary target was in motion. He felt like working. Why not? He pulled back out and headed north.

The big boy was moving fast. He unfolded a Kansas City map. What the hell was out this way, he wondered, besides the county line? Well, one thing for sure, he couldn't go too far or he'd be in the fucking Missouri River.

15

Chaingang loved to cruise the strange, darkening burbs of the heartland in the hours following sunset, watching sensors kick the arc lights on, feeling his own vital signs quicken with the coming of the night. He thought of it as sightseeing and he could drive aimlessly through suburban tract developments as one chauffered one's family to see the Christmas lights on a snowy December's eve.

It was invariably fascinating to him, an excursion to slowly negotiate the clean, traffic-free streets, musing about the monkeys who lived inside their overpriced, boxy ranch homes with two-car garages, red-bricked Colonials, and fake Tudors with swing sets and swimming pools in the back yard.

Of an evening the twinkling amber lights would glow from their windows like yellow cats' eyes, portals to mysterious worlds of taxpaying, workaday dads whose preoccupations were with the trivialities of sitcoms and tended lawns. Aliens, they seemed to him, with their absurd play morals and ridiculously structured lives of regimented and duplicitous familial love. Who *were* these monkeys? Where did they come from—they were everywhere now, snapping pictures, chattering; brainless simians who lived behind five-hundred-dollar doors in impeccably decorated Sears showrooms.

They pulled him, you see, with their quiet residential streets and tended shrubbery. He felt the magnet of vulnerable humanity drawing him. How easily he could penetrate their portals, slice through the cozy pseudo-safety of their bolted, locked doors. The weight of his massive killing chain became a serious presence as he thought about how he might enter their lives and turn their worlds into sudden hellish shitstorms of pain. . . .

He flows with the traffic on Sterling, past Norledge, Gill, Chicago, veering northeast now around Mound Grove Cemetery in the direction of Mill Creek Park and a point beyond. Sees the neatly stacked series of firewood logs—a half-dozen racks of wood, perhaps—which appear to have been lined with a plumb bob. Perfectly symmetrical lives play out their days and nights inside. Next door, the house is dark. Maybe up close you'd hear the sonorous sound of ever-present television from within. A "security door" stretches his face into the wide, beaming dimpled radiance that is his most dangerous smile. Pass, his instinct warns him, and he forgets these houses. But then at the next block, midway, he is inexplicably pulled by the hearts that beat inside a home that glows with lights.

Something about this dwelling screams at him. *Victim!* it shrieks, on a level he cannot pinpoint. If only time permitted. He has so many to do, so little time to do them in. It is impossible to be bored in such a rich and alien world: the phantom empire of Lemuria or Muritania; west of the pillars of Herakles; south of Middle Earth; a thousand million fathoms below the surface of sunken Atlantis; in the subworld towers of topaz; Daniel glides through serpent-infested, monster-haunted seas in search of monkeyfish.

He is nearing the place where they live now and his concentration kicks into third gear. He passes a huge truck stop, and the names on the fronts of the eighteen-wheeler giants type on his mental processor: Freightliner, International Transtar, GMC, Peterbilt. He sees the street sign. Parks. Gets things from his duffel and melts into the shadows.

The DeMon glows like a blue-eyed devil in the darkness of the car interior. Shooter flips the LocLok keys to "3," "ext," and "Trans," hits the intrusion-detector alarm switch, the OMNI DF mobile tracker, and opens the hood of the motion pager switch, flipping the toggle to the ON position, and selecting SILENT on the pager.

He parks and examines his surroundings: a small, blue-collar industrial pocket on the edge of hilly Sugar Creek. Giesler's Country Store and Gas. "REG $1.01," Stritt Spraying-Seeding and Soil Evaluation. A plant nursery. Mount Ely Auto Body Repair. The immediate surroundings, for some reason, are called Mount Ely, locally. He takes the weapon case and moves across the road and into the tall weeds. Stops. Turns and checks for watching eyes.

Traffic passes: a beige Ford Ranger with a camper, a gray van chrome-stripped in gleaming flashes of silver that glint in the headlights, a beat-up pickup with two boys in the front—he turns and moves deeper into the weeds. Across from him, down a slope and beside a gravel road, he recognizes Big Petey's ride. He sees the familiar form of his favorite behemoth waddle out of the shadows with something on a rope—or so it appears.

Men, tethered to one another with something—a long rope maybe. Three guys. He puts his eye to the Laco and sees their surly faces. Moves over to Chaingang and his practiced fingers find the bolt knob of SAVANT, and he snicks it back. Loads his lady's mouth with a shiny hard killer. Closes her up tight. Chaingang is smack in the crosshairs.

One has heard the phrase "itchy trigger finger"? Shooter has an itchy trigger side—the whole right side of his body trembles to execute this fat target of opportunity. His brain advises his right hand to squeeze just as Bunkowski is behind a truck. He will get him. There will be another opportunity soon and he'll pencil the big fucker out. Fuck it!

"Get him in there. Help him or I'll kill you. *Do it!*" Chaingang ordered. He held a submachine gun with a silencer, wrapped in brown butcher paper and tied in white string like a big fucking salami, and they'd already found out he was serious. The weapon, which looked like a toy in his massive arms, had just shot a round into Mr. Cholia's leg.

"I can't get up there, motherfucker, you shot me in the le—" *Bam.* Cholia fell against the tailgate with another round in him. This one in his head.

"Son of a—"

"You fuckin'—"

"Move him *now* or you go down!" Chaingang didn't care if the whole neighborhood saw and heard what was happening. They loaded the biker into the bed of the pickup. Belleplaine and Vale were handcuffed in thick bailing wire, and the three of them had been lashed together loosely with a fifty-foot electrical extension cord.

"Excellent," Chaingang said, leaning over the side to give each man an expert tap, just enough of a chainsnap to put them out, a blow designed to silence but not to kill. He was already sorry he'd been impatient with the dead one. These cat-and-dog pukes were starting to irritate him. He shivered as he got in the pickup, ignoring his own ride. "Somebody just stepped on your grave, Mr. Cholia," he said, over his right shoulder, keying the ignition with the biker's key. Echoing the engine noise with the barking thing that was as close as he came to the sound of laughter. It would be pleasant to take these punks off the count. The contemplation of his next act kept him smiling all the way to the kill zone, which was a secluded field adjacent to the highway, only the turnrow visible from the traffic's perspective. There was in fact a slight knoll to this part of the community, which is how it had come to be known as Mount Ely. He thought it was fitting.

There were three large landscape timbers, and three

creosoted poles. He had purchased the poles and had stolen the timbers, back when he first hit on this idea, and once he'd selected an appropriate setting, he hid the timbers and poles in deep bush, selected for its preponderance of thorny wild rose and poison ivy. He was impervious to both.

They waited for him now, along with his digger, which took him all of ten minutes to use. He could dig and tamp in a large wooden cross in two to three minutes, tops, the hole digger biting earth with a vengeance, the soft dirt flying as a quarter-ton rhino pounded the sharp blades in and bit another monstrous chaw from the ground.

The crosses took only seconds to spike together with ten-penny nails. Messrs. Cholia, Belleplaine, and Vale also took no more than seconds to spike together, that is to the crosses, using—again—your ordinary hardware-store crucifixion nail. *Pow. Pow.* This is for doggie. *Pow. Pow.* Nice Mr. Hoggie. *Pow. Pow.* This is for kitty—right through your titty. Oh, this was going to *smart* when they came around. Well, that's life—eh? Life can be hard. The biker life. Doggone.

Then he was gone, back to the trailer, to get his legal wheels and move on down the road. Happy as a big fat clam. Knowing when those punks came to they'd be in a fucking world of serious pain.

But it was not to be. Shooter couldn't see shit in the headlight glare and he was a man to whom eyesight was everything. Maybe he was getting too old for this work? Bullshit. It was that fucking hooker that had messed up his night, damn the cunt to hell and back, which is where she probably was right now. He wrenched his mind back to his target, the blip on the screen of the OMNI, and flipped the unit back to the auto-track position, keeping a very loose tail on them.

Where—oh, *there's* that fucker. Always down the damned turnrows and gravel shit. Why didn't he just whack these assholes out and go on to the next gig? Always a big fucking production. Always he had to slice and dice and shit. What a fucked-up guy Big Petey was. Oh, well, you couldn't help but love the sum'bitch. I mean—shit, he thought, nobody who had killed that many folks could be *all* bad.

He parked and a rustbucket of a VW blew by him doing ninety-and-change. "Get some, Bugs," he whispered. Probably got a Porsche in the bitch. His mind was full of four-barrel carbs and ratios as he carried SAVANT to a place where he could take care of bidness. He needed to get hisself a cool set of wheels and then settle down and find him a good woman. And he needed to fuckin' wax a few more assholes, is what he needed. Screw it down on the fuckers.

He couldn't see shit and the bugs were biting and bang, pop, wham, what's the big guy doing down there—building a house for crissakes? He carries his lady and eases around where he can see something and—*holy fucking shit!*—Chaingang has got the fuckers up on sticks.

Three of the bastards on poles. He took his piece out and put her together and eyeballed the scene. *Jesus.* They were up on crosses. He'd gone and crucified them!

"The SHERFSAVANT's mil dot duplex reticle in the Laco unit provides extended range-finding capability." Where was the big boy? *"Extended ranges are determined by a simple mathematical method called 'the 666 formula.' This formula compares the perceived size of the target visually, through the 40X sniperscope, as measured in mils, to the actual approximate height of the target, as expressed in yards."* He wanted to see Big Petey waddle his huge, vast yards of fat ass into the scope's crosshairs.

"The computation is made by first sighting the target through the Laco. 1 mil on the scope reticle is equal to one actual yard at one thousand yards distance." He computed the shot. The shot to Chaingang's head. He'd blow that ugly gangbang up real good. But where was he? In the fucking shadows, jerking off, he supposed.

"The formula for the computation of extended range is: *Actual height of target in yards multiplied by 1,000 over perceived height of target in mills. The* 666 formula *computes as follows: If a human target is believed to be approximately six feet (two yards), tall, and is perceived as having a height of three mil through the scope, express numerically as 2 x 1000 divided by 3 equals 666.666 yards. (100 meters, a hectometer, equals 109.36 yards. 1000 meters, a kilometer, equals 0.62 miles.)"* Just as he recited the numbers 666.666, he saw the men clearly. A cloud moved past the moon, and in the added light SAVANT picked up the detail of their chests. It was a heartless crucifixion. He heard the truck rumble off and whirled in the hopes of seeing it and taking a shot but Chaingang was gone again, the fat cocksucker. Damn!

Way to go, stud. He chewed himself out, using the word what's-her-name from the bookstore had used that first time in bed. She kept calling him a stud and he couldn't get hard for the fucking bitch and then she kept on using it, so stupid she thought she could coax him into a woody. Jeezus Q. Jimminies. It kicked his ass just to think about what bitches had put him through from his perverted cunt of a nanny on.

"Corpus Domini nostri Jesu Christ custodiat animan tuam (Thump!) in vitum aeternam." (Click. Load. Squeeze. *Twomp!*) A-fucking-men, asswipes. (Click.) Goombye, farewell, adios from your friendly neighborhood city morgue. You stab 'em . . . we slab 'em. And we guarantee *our* work.

16

The famous reporter held the microphone directly under John J. Llewelyn's proboscis. The light was bright in the lieutenant's eyes, and the presence of both mike and camera made him nervous. He could imagine how his bald forehead would catch the light and glare like a cueball on TV. He tried in vain to recall the famed investigative journalist's name.

"So you feel the persecution of the L.A. police chief is unfair, is that what you're saying?"

"Look. I don't know the details of what's going on out there but you take any industry where the guy at the top is responsible for the actions of thousands of men . . ." He was finding it so difficult to concentrate with that microphone shoved in his face. "Some guy runs a big plant, and there's fifteen thousand employees, and fifteen hundred cases of pilfering, I mean—do you fire the top guy because he allowed pilfering? Do you go on a witch hunt and—"

"So you're calling the brouhaha in California a *witch hunt?*"

"I didn't say that." They could always twist your words. "I know we do our best here. I can't speak for other people in other departments outside the Kansas City area. We do a good job, I think."

"You never worry about your detectives beating someone up?"

"Our detectives spend their day beating on doors, not beating on citizens."

"Get up."

"Pardon me?"

"I said get up."

"Hey!"

"You're dreaming." His wife was touching his shoulders, gently trying to get him awake. The light was blindingly bright in his eyes.

"Jesus, turn the damn light out. What the hell—" He was still brain dead.

"John, honey, *wake up.* It's the phone."

He came out of the dream and took the phone from her hand, having to wipe his eyes to see if he was holding it upside down and if the switch was moved over. He pulled the antenna out and coughed into the mouthpiece, then realized she'd put it in the ON position already.

"Hello?" he said, in a sleep-fogged voice.

"John, I'm sorry, bud. Hated to wake you." Brown, from the night tour.

"S'okay."

"I was gonna wait but *(whirr)* . . . said . . . wanted you to . . . *(whirr)* to call." Llewelyn got up with the cellular phone and moved.

"Shit!" He'd slid the button to OFF as he held it, still half asleep. He pushed it back to ON and somehow Brown was still there. "Sorry. I couldn't hear you."

"Can you hear me okay?"

"Yeah, now. What time is it, anyway?"

"Five fifty-five. You wanna grab a quick cup and call me back in five? It ain't that urgent. Let you wake up a bit?"

"No. S'okay. Go ahead."

"Okay. Guy in a light plane, coming from K.C. International, dude we know, used to be PIO for Civil Air Patrol and so on, he's coming low over the river out by Mount Ely, just as the sun's coming up, 'kay? He says he sees bodies on crosses. Just like in the Bible—all right? Three dudes on crosses. He thinks it's some kind of prank." The words slice down past the sleep, cutting deeply, making something stand up on his skin, electrifying the hairs, prickling his skin. "He goes around and checks it out closer. Crucified, John. Three bodies look like men—headless men. He's pretty shook up. Said he damn near crashed into a power line going low for a closer look."

"You talked to him?" Llewelyn's mind was not receiving information.

"I talked to him myself. I said, 'Are you sure it isn't dummies?' 'No,' he says, 'it could be a hoax, but it looked like decapitated men.' Three of them on these crosses. They had to be fairly large crosses he'd see them from a plane, I tell him. He says he flies low like that whenever he comes to Mount Ely, he likes the view over the river. The sun is coming up in the background over the horizon, big red sunrise, and there are these bodies in the middle of an empty field. Captain says for you to come in when you can—er, forthwith. Meet him at the crime scene?"

"Tell him I'll be right there."

The sky was full of July sunshine, titanium silver clouds against great slabs of Cézanne blue and Matisse gray, the blue beginning to deepen as the sun rose higher.

The one in the middle had been put in place upside down. It was bad. Three of them. Nailed to poles and yardarms fashioned into crosses. They found a common Western Auto tool, an orange wrench with its grease crayoned *29.95* still in place. Dotted with the same dried blood as had coagulated in pools under the crucified, mutilated victims. Blood on a bright length of extension cord and pieces of wire, which would end up in evidence bags marked LIGATURES. I.D.s on two of the three. Heads completely gone. Two of them with the chest cavities opened up. Doer had taken the hearts. There were wounds that appeared to be bullet holes in the one whose heart had not been ripped out. No shell casings. Bits of exploded humanity all around. Insects having a field day. In the field.

Lieutenant Llewelyn needed a strong drink. He needed Special Agent Glenfiddich to get over there and pour him a tall one. The captain had fiddle-farted around and "supervised" the evidence techs and securing of the scene, grooming Llewelyn for serious barrel time. He did everything but stencil SCAPEGOAT on his forehead. John had, in turn, Marlin Morris soon at his side, and was trying to get the stencil transferred. Morris in his turn would pass it on. On a case like this, it came down heavy, hard, and each time rank passed it down it smelled a bit worse. This one was only halfway to grunt level and it already stunk to high heaven.

There were all kinds of people rolling on this one from Clay to Jackson County sheriff's homicide units, the entire metro squad, and the lot of them were commissioned as field examiners. Every dick in the Crimes Against Persons Unit was, for that matter. There was a wealth of talent crawling all over this nasty puppy, and pretty much just grabbing ass.

Julie Hilliard got the nod from her crew sergeant and came over to where Morris was taking notes and snapping Polaroids.

"Do we know anything? I mean—besides the biker gang tie-in?"

"Well." He sighed heavily, looking at the mess. "These three are not going to tell us much."

Yeah, she thought. Right. They're pretty much confirmed kills, too, huh? She watched a tech make a cast of tire-tread marks.

This was one of the scenes she called *hurters*. After you'd been on a bunch of these it hurt you. It hurt your chances to recapture a strong belief in the hereafter. This was another of those crime scenes that makes a tiny voice inside whisper, "Hell is here. You've *seen* hell, baby."

Something more terrible than Steel Vengeance had done this to three violent, deadly streetfighters, binding them in baling wire and electrical cord, nailing them to wooden crosses . . . ripping hearts out . . . blowing heads off.

This was one of the moments when horror becomes a relative quality, and cops are nudged by the assertion that there are no fundamental truths. At such times, reality and fantasy blur, become indistinguishable, as that which exists and that which is illusion merge. Reality and imagined reality swirl disconnected around the black magnetic hole at the hub of a centerless void. One senses that one exists, at least for that horrific moment, in a universe without a heart.

Chaingang knew something was wrong when he saw the darkened home as he pulled into the driveway. An unobtrusively located, perfectly ordinary-looking small rental property in Overland Park, which he'd been using as a safe house. No broken windows. No lights on. But something elbowed him sharply. Danger. The presence of others. He was instantly wary, moving away from the car and into deep shadow, the killing chain in his powerful right hand, ready to lash out at whatever moved. He waited for a long time, letting the protective darkness circumfuse and protect him.

Slowly, he moved back to the wheels and slid the suppressed SMG from his duffel bag, easing the bolt back and putting a ready round up the spout. He eased toward the back, listening, hearing nothing, carefully unlocking the back door and pushing it open without entering.

The first thing he saw was blood. Just a few drops. He flashed on his old dream. The hunter's dream. The stalk of a wounded enemy. The blood trail. The dream in which the target and the hunter exchange perspectives. Was this what the dream had meant to warn him of? He was not a man who thought in metaphors or symbols. Blood trails were blood trails.

There was an explosion of insight the moment he saw the animal affixed to the wall. A common Didelphis Virginiana, a lowly opossum, dead and mounted under a red banner. Pogo the possum, nailed to the living-room wall with his hardware nails, and across the wall, carefully printed in the animal's blood, *D A N I E L*. An envelope nailed to the wall beside it.

He froze. Accepted nothing for what it appeared. Stilled himself, forcing his vital signs to slow. Slowing, stilling, quieting his pulsing life source, calming himself. Gun up, finger on the trigger. He ignored the dead animal and eased through the house in search of intruders, although his heart wasn't in it. This already answered too many nagging questions.

They'd suckered him. It stung for a moment but his rage pushed it down. There was danger: thick; moist; in the air; as real as humidity. They'd been watching him all along somehow. But how? Why hadn't he seen the signs? The monkeys were never that good.

Nobody in the house and no sign of damage beyond the wall. He did not open the envelope but first examined the possum, which had a tractor-trailer-size tire tread through its middle. Roadkill, he noted. He saw no surprises, and he removed the nails and threw it into the back yard.

Chaingang wet some paper towels and made an initial attempt to clean the wall. He did the best he could, put the bloody towels in a grocery sack, took it out in back, and burned it. Still he did not touch the envelope.

He had become proficient at killing with nothing more lethal-appearing than a thick, Manila mailing container. But it was not a hidden bomb that caused him to pause. It was the hidden truth. He was not anxious to learn the bad news, which he knew would explain the out-of-sync personality shifts he'd undergone, the weird "normalcy" that he found so repugnant, the buzzing and the torpor that began in a roll of fat at the back of his neck, and that kept him from being all that he could be.

With a heavy grunt he took the thing and opened it and read. It was from his friend Dr. Norman, the prison doctor from Illinois. He read it as an out-of-body experience, watching himself read the pages of infuriating monkeyspeak. *"Surveillance . . . brain implant . . . monitored at all times . . . every movement is known . . . no way to escape*

... *Robert Tinnon Price/a.k.a./Shooter.*" Photographs of the sniper in the 1960s, and a recent shot of an average-looking man with psycho eyes and a blondish buzzcut on top. A jock. Smallish. Wiry. He recalled the man from his spike-team days gone by. *"Attempted to terminate you when mission was aborted . . . special weapon . . . motion detector and locator . . . tracking device . . . intends to assassinate you unless you destroy him first."* Schematics and pictures of a strange-looking rifle with futuristic configuration and woodsy camouflage finish. Scope. Silencer. *"Effective up to two miles."* A dossier on the murder victims. Price was killing on *his* turf. He'd rip the little pissant limb from limb. He'd even spoiled his tableau at Mount Ely.

The dossier advised him to *"open closet door by front door."* A small version of the mobile tracker had been delivered for his convenience, the message concluded. He opened the door and found the thing, boiling mad the more it all sunk in. Those fucks, tampering with his *brain.* On one level, he was planning to turn Shooter into gristle; on another, he was promising himself that someday he'd eat Dr. Norman's heart for this unforgivable act. The notion that he had an implant, the towering humiliation of it, was almost more than he could bear. Thoughts of the biker in prison, and of dearest foster mommy Nadine Garbella, were now a million miles away. First things first.

He was a man who lived in the moment. True enough, Chaingang espoused the "plan hard, fight easy" militaristic dictum, but as far as analyzing the future, the grand scheme of things, his idea of planning didn't extend much beyond the boundaries of trench tactics necessary for his survival. Had he been motivated to examine his battle strategy, his long-range goals, he'd have probably found them extremely limited. On some level, he knew he would ultimately have to arrange a fitting demise for Dr. Norman, after—that is— he'd somehow negotiated the removal of this implant device. But battle plans . . . ? He wasn't interested. There was never a creature more truly situational than Chaingang.

This, however, was an encroachment, an invasion beyond

anything even he had experienced. Chaingang, the ultimate survivalist, took as much of the problem as he could immediately chew and digest, and the rest he simply stored. But where—in most persons—the information would have lain dormant, his autopiloted brain set about to deal with this danger to him, to resolve a seemingly unsolvable problem.

While the beast dealt with immediate details, his computer ingested, sorted, retrieved, and began to build a long-range order of battle—something hitherto alien to him—the climax of which was two-pronged. He would have to figure out a way to force Dr. Norman to shepherd the removal of the implant, and then he had to be totally eradicated, since he represented such an invasive and loathsome threat.

On the conscious plane of the banal, Bunkowski considered the initial problems, as he loaded the tracker unit into the back seat of his ride, packing it tightly beside the big duffel, and roared away from the safe house for the last time.

How does one correct an inflamed pustule? One squeezes it until it pops. He drove, unerringly, in the direction of Bobby "Shooter" Price, to squeeze and be rid of this festering pimple. But it would not be enough to simply squeeze the lifejuice from the doctor, nor would the eating of his heart be sufficient.

The mindscreen offered his subconscious words of the surrealist Dali, whose description of popping blackheads seemed uniquely apt:

"All those aerodynamic, gelatinous . . . massive salivary" experiences, involving "exuberant and sticky viscera" . . . the "apparitions *aerodynamiques des êtres-objets*" . . . Dali's favorite expression: "There is nothing that cannot be eaten . . ." Ah, to eat everything! All awareness "transformed into gourmandism . . . awareness of reality by means of the jaws." The dioscuric and aesthetic cannibalism, cosmically extended: "the wish to know devours me, but I devour that wish."

Mad as a hatter or the one sane man in an insane universe, Dali had—alone—sensed the dualism of eating and death that transcended the mortuary ritual of tribal funereal consumption. He intuited the reality of cannibalism.

Dr. Norman, too, may have sensed the connection in his paternal playacting, those tender moments when he strove to inculcate his beloved Daniel with the notion that he—Norman—would ensure his marvelous creation's safety and immortality. He would have given anything to be Daniel's literal maker, to be God, or, failing that, to be Chaingang's biological father.

As Dali wrote in *How I Put My Father to Gastronomical Use,* "the consecrated wafer of the paternal communion . . . became a sublime and delectable representation of my father . . . Thus I had the possibility of tasting my father . . . in small succulent mouthfuls." There was but one final solution. Dr. Norman must be allowed to become his own transcendent dream.

Chaingang had to dispose of him by eating him. Not just the heart, but all of him, so that nothing remained. He would eat his clothing as well. Everything. When he was finished there would be nothing left but perhaps a pair of eyeglasses and a name tag!

The thought boiled inside him, bubbled over into his innards with volcanic heat, warming him with pleasure and purpose. For the first time in his life, so far as he could remember, Chaingang had a real goal.

17

Trask had no trouble simulating illness on the second day he called in sick. He phoned Flynn to let him know how ill he was and Jerri Laymon spoke with him.

"Sean's out for a couple of hours, Vic. Do you want me to have him call you?"

"Not unless he needs to speak with me, Jerri," he rasped into the phone.

"You sound awful."

"It sounds worse than it is."

"Well, get some rest and I'll tell everybody, okay?" she said. He thanked the Mystery Tramp and broke the connection. He *was* ill. He'd had almost no sleep during a headachy period when he was coming down with a cold, and the lack of sleep had done him in. He had the odd feeling of being in a great mood, jubilant in fact, and sick as a dog simultaneously. He socked the vitamin C down, popped aspirins, and worked.

He knew what he had to do and it was making him nuts to think how much had to come together just right to make this sweetheart really happen. He had the inside track on one of the great beats of the year. It coursed through his innards like molten lava—he could taste the richness of it. *Gang war!* He'd hit on a secret that maybe even the cops hadn't found. He was positive of it. Every time he tried to test his theory it "proved" against the known facts. And he was in the process of weaving it into the very guts of his massive presentation on "American Violence."

On the face of it, the discovery didn't appear to be much of anything. Everyone knew that drugs were the cause of most violence nowadays. What he'd found, however, was a secret beyond chilling—it was so frightening he hadn't completely sorted out the ramifications of it, and he couldn't without official cooperation.

He'd found what he was certain was evidence of a secret race war being waged under Kansas City's nose—*without* the cops' knowledge! It scared the hell out of him.

Victor Trask's apartment was papered in faces, biographies, background checks, newspaper clippings, photocopies of maps, magazine stories, and his own notes. Looking up from his desk this is what he saw:

The face of the young cabbie, David Boyles. Lived in the 700 block of Truman Road. Secretive. A loner. A weird kid of a man who identified with the De Niro part in *Taxi Driver*. His friends—such as he had—were casual ones who knew he liked to smoke a little hash, snort some blow, party quietly, and—if you were a bud, he'd deal you some stuff for a profit. Trask was an expert investigative guy when he really went on trail, and all you had to say was "I'm preparing a show for 'Inside America,'" and people would talk. They were conditioned to personal questions such as Flynn routinely asked on the air, and most persons would open up to radio or TV people in a way that even cops had trouble matching.

When you were talking to somebody "off the record," or on "deep background," it was truly amazing what they'd reveal. Tax scams, black-sheep confessions, drug usage, there wasn't much they wouldn't reveal about their own pasts, and they'd tell you everything about the next guy. People, basically, liked to gossip.

From mustached, dark-eyed closet dealer David Boyles,

an arrow ran to the other side of the room where wild-haired twenty-four-year-old Steve Yoe's picture adorned another sheet of notes. There was a tie between the two of them. Yoe was an artist for Anderson Design Group, and his own drug record had come to Trask's attention. His connection at one time was "a guy who drove a cab." So Vic knew he was on solid ground.

He didn't know how Jim Myers, Laura Miskell, Annie Granger, Gerald Smotherman, Henrietta Bleum, or Bub Foley fit into the mix yet. But twenty-three-year-old Brad Springmayer, a sheet-metal worker at Mid-America Products, Inc.; thirty-one-year-old waitress Mae Ellen Dukodevsky; and Robbie Allen Scovill all had acquaintances who'd inferred that a puff of reefer or a little hash oil was not out of the question. Bernie Salzman, a pre-med student who had been killed mysteriously just before the big firebombing, had once figured in a three-person scandal at one of the hospitals in which drug thefts had been suspected. Drugs flowed through so many of these names you couldn't help but see the commonality.

Trask had a face for nearly every clipping he'd collected: "Man Admits Murdering Daughter's Husbands," "Kansas Man Charged in Gun Battle," "Woman Shot in Robbery," "Man Charged in Wife's Death," "Woman Pleads Not Guilty to Murder"—dozens of clippings that at first did not appear related to drugs in any remote way. They stared back at him from the wall, between the genial, fatherly face of James Wrightson, Sr., the manager of Missouri Farm Machinery, who was shot and killed in a "drive-by" according to one source, and the sullen, pretty countenance of Monica Foster, twenty-eight, the woman who'd been a fifth-grade teacher at Priester Elementary before she'd been blasted apart. There was another common quality all the victims had.

The Steel Vengeance Scenic Motoring Club members, the forty-three-year-old housewife married to a carpet store manager, the guy who worked at Truesdale's, the woman who'd been decapitated in her home, all these victims of mysterious shootings and even the three headless, mutilated bodies found north of Sugar Creek—they all shared the same thing. There was not a black face among them.

To find a black person who had died violently in Kansas City, Missouri, excepting a thirty-nine-year-old stabbing victim, one Marcus Little, you had to go back over a month. The recent spate of shootings, bombings, and the mob-style executions culminating with the crucifixions on Mount Ely, had claimed non-black victims. Even the three Hispanics and one Asian who had died in recent fatalities were light-skinned. The black man who'd died of his stab wounds had been killed in a drug-related incident.

Drugs and *Race* were the common threads woven through this tangled blanket of violent crime. Somebody had stepped on a gangbanger's turf, and a drug lord—perhaps one far away—had decided to wage a small war against the non-African-Americans involved.

To be sure, there were holes in this rough blanket. For example, the killing of Henrietta Bleum, seventy, a widowed woman, appeared on the face of it to make no sense. Then Trask discovered she had a grandson involved in dealing. There were a couple of others who seemed to be totally without ties to drugs, even by friends, coworkers, or relatives—but in time, these names would give up their secrets as well. All these killings were tied together, Trask thought.

His confidence was only bolstered by what he learned about Louis Sheves, an unemployed street guy, and a crook—perhaps even a hit man—by the name of Tom Dillon, both of whom had lived on the fringes of organized crime. The more Trask looked at this thing the clearer the picture became. Dope and gangs. Biker thugs cooking up lethal narcotics. Small-time drug guys, and the users/dealers who were their connections. It all fit together like a jigsaw. If the black gangbangers were an offshoot of the big clubs on the West Coast, or in league with the Colombian cartels, the seriousness of the ordnance also was self-explanatory. Either way, they would have access to rifle grenades, bombs, and the sort of individuals who could wield them expertly.

There were some problems in putting this whole bag of disparate parts together. First, he had to keep it absolutely his secret until he was ready to present it, complete and wrapped in pretty ribbon, to the radio station. If *anybody* found out what he was working on, this would no longer be a Vic Trask project. He'd have lost both his beat and his shot—which he saw as once-in-a-lifetime. Second, he had to go to the cops. If he was right, they had to be told about what he'd found. He thought it was quite possible, however far-fetched others might think it appeared on the surface, that he'd uncovered something the cops hadn't. His desire and his ego were cooking on that high a burner.

First things first: prepare for work. He had to have a presentation that would appear to preoccupy him, a seemingly rich skein of interwoven subjects that did not touch on this subject matter. His "stealables," he called them.

This divided into subsets such as the Factlet stuff. He had a collection of them:

"The *Independence, Missourian* reports that fifty-seven percent of Americans surveyed would support a tax-funded government program to shelter and care for the homeless." Flynn could almost do a show around such a fact.

"Did you know that when stamps get stuck together by accident you can put them in the freezer for a few hours and they'll usually come unstuck?" He had tons of that kind of stuff. Some of it was of little value, but he was looking for quantity not quality. He wanted bulk for show. And there was wheat with the chaff.

He had some good topics researched. Barb couldn't steal all of them, surely. He had a slant on the ban of rock concerts, and a series of likely booker-interview subjects that began with the Who concert deaths, and ranged from a local ACLU guy to the spokesman for Guns N' Roses—about an incident at a Missouri concert date.

There was a show on local broadcasting that Flynn, and

for that matter Trask himself, would get off doing: a lot of data on the station that was being sued in a libel matter, they were appealing a multimillion-dollar judgment; the anchor at "4" who was celebrating twenty-five years on the air—he had a great slant on why he'd turned L.A. down twice; the scandal with the morning team who had talked their newsman into reporting a fake UFO sighting—all kinds of neat interview possibilities.

Then in with the goodies, he'd salted the notes with stories that he hoped Barb would steal. The KPERS show, about an investigation into the Kansas Public Employees Retirement System, an exposé on white-collar crime, an interview with a guy in the Kansas attorney general's office that he knew would semi-suck, a big story on a judge who'd dismissed speeding tickets that was tied to ambiguous outmoded laws and "lost" ordinances, which would be about as much fun to research as gum surgery.

He had a large, graphic presentation that looked so good he thought it would work as a show in spite of having been conceived to be swiped, a thing on the five planes found in formation, wing-to-wing, on the ocean floor, that appeared identical to the famous, missing "Flight 19." All the planes had been Navy Avengers, and one of the numbers on the war planes matched the unit that had lost a squadron in 1945 (a story that hadn't done anything to dispel the "Bermuda Triangle" myth). He'd tied that all into a famous local story about a woman who had proof her husband, an MIA in Vietnam since 1970, had recently been seen. "Missing In Action" had Sean Flynn written all over it—he knew he'd build something with it.

Then there were the pure spikes. Tantalizing show titles he'd simply pulled out of thin air and his imagination:

Fatal Attractions
Up the Academy
So Long, Mr. Farmer
Bounty Hunters—Above the Law?
Closing Costs, the Real Story

High-Tech, Two-Edged Sword of the 21st Century
Closing the Porn Shops
Honorable Men in Politics—Are There Any?

He'd crossed out "Men in Politics" and substituted "Politicians."

Laser Surgery
The New Retirement
Politically Correct, Buzzwords and Censorship
Outsmarting the IRS
Last of the Pioneers
Elvis Imitators—The Dark Side
Back to the Middle East? Post-Victory Questions
Religious Sex
Palimony
The Next Energy Crisis
Payola's Resurgence in the Music Business
Dubious Cures
Dinosaurs
Health Care—"Going Up?"

On and on. He put his stack of "stealables" and related visuals to take to work aside, and concentrated on his real thesis, on American violence. Trask's précis was headed "Causes of Increased Numbers of Violent Crimes." Based on the report prepared in part by the Kansas City Metropolitan Police Department, the Missouri Health Department, and the Department of Justice, its primary elements were listed as follows:

Cause: Abject poverty, unemployment, lack of hope.
Solution: Government work programs, community-wide welfare projects targeting the lowest economic strata and the homeless, education about job-finding, education about alcohol, drug, and other substance abuse, more programs for substance abusers.

Cause: Ghetto slums.

Solution: Planning of urban housing codes and enlightened federal, state, and city housing authority decision-making, prevention of neighborhood deterioration by stricter enforcement of existing codes, prevention of deterioration by grass-roots citizens groups, formation of neighborhood crime-prevention organizations, more funding for police, more targeting of high-crime areas for patrol by law enforcement agencies, more undercover units in high-crime areas, more crack-house raids, more drug sweeps and streetcorner-dealer-level busts, more gangbanger sweeps, more DEA units.

Cause: Abuse of children, females, elderly.

Solution: Education, more enlightened foster-parent systems, community programs for abusers and local PSA-campaigns aimed at increasing communication skills among abusers, toll-free "help" hotlines (1-800 numbers), more shelters and shelter guidance, increased funding for counseling.

It looked hopeless when you imagined how much that kind of funding would translate into increased taxes. Perhaps the way to go about it would be to isolate certain areas of vested-interest lobbies—not defense spending, as that was too big a ratings tune-out. But the vested interests now controlled the U.S. Congress. There was an angle there. He wanted the solutions to completely resolve, at least theoretically, the thorny dilemmas which the series of programs on violence would imply if not categorically state.

If Kansas City was under the gun, as he believed, in the midst of a horrible series of homicides orchestrated out of racial hatred, and as retribution against encroachment on a drug mob's territory, what would the white population do? He envisioned a white response, a backlash to the response, and these widening out into all-out racial war. If Trask wasn't very careful about every move he made he could imagine himself touching off a powder keg!

He thought of another swipable note and jotted it down: *"The maddening waste, abuse of perqs, and financial mismanagement by the House and Senate—did this earn them each a raise?"* Then he decided that wasn't necessarily stealable and put it in a stack of "iffy angles." It had been jarred loose by his thinking on the lobbies, and maybe it belonged in some kind of sidebar to his précis. Trask made another note to go through the "iffy angles" pile and sort out those things that might have some relevance to possible solutions. He made a list of interview subjects: four blacks; an Asian; an Israeli man who was particularly articulate; two whites. He jotted a note for himself to make a *"list of suitable Congresspersons worth interv'g."*

Trask saw a scrap of note he'd made headed "B.R. Sez Station Bugged." He lifted his phone from the cradle and hit numbers. In a few seconds a young, chirpy woman's voice announced "Z-60" in his ear.

"May I speak with Buzz Reid, please?"

"Buzz Reid?" she said, in the voice operators always use when they're unsure if such a person works there, or in fact exists. "Um—just a moment, please." Another voice came on the line.

"Reid."

"Hey. It's me—Trask."

"You got a cold or somethin'?"

"Somethin'. Hey. About our recent talk. Any chance you could give me another chance to pick your brain about the same topic?"

"I charge."

"Oh-oh. How much? I'm poorfolks."

"At least a cuppa Java."

"Okay. I might be able to scrape that up. Same place?"

"Nah. You at the other place?" He meant the radio station.

"No. Home."

"That's better. You know where the fountains are? The ones *we* like?"

"You mean—" Trask thought he meant downtown.

"The *old* tasty fountains," Reid said to him, in the kind of codephrase an old colleague would remember. They had once talked at great length about great fountain sodas "just like they used to make." Only this one small greasy spoon still made them—or so they had agreed.

"Ah! The fountains of our youth."

"That's the place."

"Yeah." It was a few minutes away. "When?"

Reid gave him a time, and Victor Trask thanked him, hung up the phone, and headed for the bathroom. The thought of burgling KCM had loosened his thirty-six-year-old wimpy bowels.

18

Marion, Illinois

Dr. Norman had a large stack of mail waiting for him when he returned to his office. He sorted through it quickly, not opening the envelopes, which he was in the habit of slitting himself, going through the obvious offers, junk mail, and work-related communications from various sectors of the scientific, penal, or other government agencies with whom he had contact. He was used to a great deal of mail, and much of it was discarded.

There were three packages, one of which immediately froze him the second he saw the address. A crudely sealed envelope, which appeared to have been run over by a truck, had been addressed with a black Magic Marker, the writer using overly hard strokes, mushing the tip down as he pressed his marks into the paper, making block letters. The handwriting immediately identified the sender. He looked at the address, afraid—it was only natural—wondering if the contents would hurt him physically in some way. The address was this: *"DR. NORMAN, Ph.D., Marion Federal Penetentiary (sic), U.S. Prison System, Marion, Illinois."* Daniel did not have enough information to address the package correctly, and since he'd never been permitted to receive mail during the periods when he was incarcerated, he did not know the exact address of the place where he'd spent several years of his life.

Should he get some bomb-squad personnel to open it for him? That was ridiculous. If Daniel was going to send him a mail bomb he'd do it much more cleverly than this. No—this was not going to be a bomb. He brushed aside the packages from Justice and NSC, gently touching Daniel's envelope. It was not hard. He lifted it. Relatively light.

Norman got a metal box and placed the package in it very carefully, trying to decide whether or not to X-ray it. It had already passed through the prison detector. Of course, that in itself was no guarantee of anything. Daniel could have something in here that would be sufficiently ingenious to appear innocuous and still inflict a terrible death on the unwary. Dr. Norman could imagine him turning to one of the secret pages he'd torn from his ledger, building a small contraption that would scratch the recipient in such a way as to infect that unlucky person with an HIV-positive blood specimen. He'd know a thousand ways to maim, kill, burn, slice, explode, infect, poison, blind, or otherwise incapacitate the target with something as ordinary as a hastily sealed envelope.

Logic won out. Dr. Norman slit the envelope open, wearing face-shield and gloves, holding it behind an impromptu screen, just in case he'd misjudged Daniel's sense of humor.

A plastic bag, the kitchen type, sealed with duct tape. There had barely been time for Daniel to react to the dossier and he would, of course, be enraged by the implant. He would not forgive Dr. Norman for the liberties they'd had to take with him, but there was nothing to be done about that now. What Daniel had sent him was his way of responding —letting him know that he'd be coming for him in due time. The moment he saw it he knew precisely what it was, and scientific detachment notwithstanding, it had the desired effect. Seeing the object was like being cursed by one's own son. Norman put the bag down and went to his desk. The message had hit him hard.

He picked up the classified directory and punched in a number over his sanitized landline. In the operations section of a unit known as Clandestine Services, a secure phone rang and was answered by a warrant officer. Norman established bona fides and made his request.

"I need a team to locate and isolate a female Caucasian who was last believed to reside in Kansas City, Kansas. She is probably in her late sixties or early seventies. The name she went by was Nadine Garbella." He spelled it, and gave an address on Bunker. He was reading from Daniel Edward Flowers Bunkowski's dossier. "If this woman is still alive, it is vital she be found and taken immediately to a safe location. It is also imperative I then be notified the moment that is accomplished. If there are any encumbrances, get in touch with me as soon as possible."

Inside the bag, browned with blood, was the heart from a small animal. Dr. Norman fully understood the nature of the insult, and its attendant implicit threat. The heart of the dead opossum spoke volumes.

19

Okay, Buzz. I think I get the idea. And I could get all that stuff—you know—without a problem?"

"Go over a few blocks to Radio Shack, man. Get everything you need to build a great bug." He shook his head. "Get your earplug or headset, your connectors, your listening unit, monitor, recording unit, everything you'd need to be in business."

"I didn't know it was so easy to record private conversations."

"For all we know *this* could be recorded. The guy who owns it is worried one of his waitresses is running setups, okay? People eating steaks and lobster and paying half their tab. The waitress and the customers are both ripping him off. Happens." He shrugged again. "He thinks the cook's in on it. So he bugs a few of the booths and tables. We could be on tape right now. You called the station—for all we know *that's* on tape. It's absurdly easy to record conversations."

"But you wouldn't use the, uh, jammer thing."

"No. See—that tells them you're hip to being recorded.

181

Hell, if somebody is bugging you, get smart. Get even. Bug *them."* The thin, wiry man took a noisy sip of coffee. "Fuck 'em all, down with everything, and up with the ladies' dresses."

Trask laughed quietly and unfolded a twelve-by-eighteen-inch sheet of art paper he'd been working on—a rough layout of the radio station. "Recognize it?"

Reid just stared for a minute.

"KCM."

"Yeah. I see it. There's the front doors. What's all that shit?" Reid pointed.

"That's the second floor—see—upstairs?"

"Um."

"Wow, Buzz. You mean you don't think I'm too great an artist, eh? Man, I'm hurt."

"I wouldn't give up your other job yet."

"Okay. Anyway, let's say you wanted to do what we had discussed? How would you do it? You got a twenty-four-hour security guy right here."

"Okay. That's easy. You come in to work. Do your thing. Go home. But you forget something. You go back—all right? This is about three-thirty-five A.M. There are fewer employees between three-thirty A.M. and four-thirty than at any other time. Right?"

"Yeah."

"You come back. 'I forgot something, damn it,' you say as you bullshit with the guard. I assume you bullshit back and forth, right?"

"Not really. They just wave you on in. We don't talk that much back and forth."

"Okay. You go in. Walk back, go in the elevator. Get off on the second floor, and you go right back to Engineering. Now the last time I was there they had monitor cameras here, here, and here." Reid made dots in the foyer, in the elevator, and across from the programming department in the hallway.

"As far as I can recall—yeah. I think those are the ones I'd go past on the way to Engineering."

"There aren't any cameras back there. You'd open the door across from Purchasing with a key I would make a copy of for you. You unlock the Engineering Supply door. You close it behind you and lock it."

Trask sneezed. "Sorry about that." He blew his nose.

"You close and lock the door. You try not to sneeze real loud." They both laughed. "You unlock the cabinets against the west wall with a key—as before, I make a copy of for you. You pull out the shit on the floor, stack it neatly in a row, and pull the floor hatch out. If it's locked, you'll take a prybar or whatever—you'll get it open. No big deal. You'll see a ladder. You'll carefully climb down. There's a little ledge just a few feet away. You'll have a flashlight—and get the kind with a ring you can attach a cord to and *tie* this thing to you so it can't be dropped. Make sure your batteries are new. Okay, you still with me?"

"Uh-huh." Trask felt as if he were in dire need of a half hour on the po-po. This could be a miracle discovery—want to be regular again? Move up to the ultimate laxative—contemplate burglary!

"You're standing on the ledge now right back of the heating ducts, the pipes are in front and back, electrical cables, air conditioning, and what you do now is—"

It was way too much for him. He'd known it to begin with but the idea kept appealing to him. What a payoff to the violence-theme series, to have proof of his own employer's intrusions against the staff. He didn't have a clear way to tie it in yet, but something along the lines of psychological battering might work. Wasn't this a kind of force being exerted against the worker ants?

He listened to Buzz tell him how simple it would be to remove, bulk erase, or simply rewind and sabotage the six security camcorders with the remote unit. Photograph the room, take examples of illegally taped phone conversations and bugged offices, and go back up the ladder, replacing hatchways and locking doors.

"'Course—" he heard Reid tell him by way of a disclaimer in case he was caught or captured, "I'm not sure how you neutralize a hidden security monitor, but I don't see 'em being that smart or whatever. I think you'd have some trouble bypassing an alarm system, too, so if they got an alarm set you might trip that. But they're probably too fuckin' cheap for that. With those two exceptions, it would go smoothly. It would all be a lot easier than it sounds."

"Man, I gotta tell you." Vic Trask smiled. "There's no fucking way. I'd love to do it. They deserve it. But halfway through your thing there, I felt my balls shrink to approximately the size of frozen peas. Okay? I just don't think so. Thanks anyway, buddy."

"Fine. Okay. Just go to the Shack, or go to Bob's Electronics and get what you need. Bug 'em back. Get your proof thataway."

"Yeah. Write down what I need to get and show me how it connects together." He folded the large piece of art paper so Reid could write on the back.

They shot the breeze a while longer and Trask thanked him and they said their farewells.

Less than two hours later he was back in his apartment sitting on the john, sipping O.J., munching aspirin, and wondering what to do next. On the table in the next room, in a Bob's Electronics bag, were a few small packages that had kicked a great big hole in the middle of his checkbook. But he now had the ability to secretly record private conversations.

Trask went back to the station the next afternoon with roughly the same feeling of happiness one has on the way to an IRS audit or triple-bypass surgery. Gloom descended over him the moment he came through the big showy double doors, clip-clopped down the impressive first-floor foyer past Security and the front desk, and hit the UP button on the elevator. It took some discipline not to look up at the camcorders, but he made it upstairs. Monica Heartbreak said nice things to him, cooed solicitously, and he started feeling a bit better.

But just as he rounded the corner by Louie Kidder's office

he ran into the dour Babaloo Metzger, who greeted him in typical fashion.

"Welcome back. Come on, we've got a production meeting." He never got to open his office door, take a leak, or plant a bug in Barb Rose's potted plant—just "hi, how are ya, let's go."

His distaff nemesis was out on assignment. Metzger, Laymon at his side, and Flynn distanced from them by the length of the Programming Conference Room table, kicked around concepts.

"Got anything for the hole?" Flynn asked. It was his turn. He slid a pile of papers over to The Man. Sean Flynn was in his customary garb, dress shirt open at the throat, silk tie pulled loose, trousers of an expensive business suit on, looking very serious and somewhat pissed.

Flynn read for a moment and spoke. "I like the media thing. The post–Gulf War coverage through Somalia to present day. I like some of this. Let's clean it up and do something with it. But you don't have a slant yet." He went back to the pile, reading a few lines as he shook his head.

"The Big Bang. It may have killed all the dinosaurs and it's going to smash into the earth again. Giant meteorites on the way. . . . Tie it in to the Jurassic Age theories. . . . Palimony . . . Love Gone Sour . . . from Marvin to Martina . . ."

Flynn was again getting that look he got when he was pissed off. He'd started losing it with the media thing, but he had it back, a serious, worried expression on his face, as he rubbed his forehead and eyebrows with the fingers of his right hand.

"Out of Gas Again? Solar power, electric cars, gasohol— the fuel of the future." Flynn looked up at the Mystery Tramp. "Jerri, make a note to check on state vehicles using the gasohol mix, I'll understand what it means.

"Yes, we have Joe Bananas." Was he really the boss of bosses? Is Big-Time Payola Back? Dubious Cures for Terminal Diseases. The Deficit and the Coming Catastrophe. The Other Sex, What Men and Women Want from Each Other.

"Vic?" Flynn looked at Trask directly. "You know what killed the dinosaurs?"

Trask saw it coming but he shook his head no.

"Forget the meteorite business. I'll tell you what killed the dinosaurs . . . ennui. They were bored to death."

Gee, Sean, he thought, smiling on the outside, does that mean you don't like my ideas so far?

Trask, ensconced in the snug privacy of the tiny cubicle he called an office, sorted through a pile of news clippings and wire service copy, culling the stuff that was going to go inside his pocket. He took two write-ups on the "crucifixion/mutilation killings," and some miscellaneous stories on violent crimes. Made a few telephone calls just to get on the books, in case his phone was being monitored, and went through the motions of typing up some Factlets for Flynn.

When he could do so with a reasonable measure of impunity, he got up and walked out of the office, turning right past the talent lounge, and again in the direction of the programming foyer. He was pleased to see the hallway empty, so raging was his professional paranoia. Monica Heartbreak was occupied, and he was able to make it to the elevator without having to exchange pleasantries, much less explain why he was leaving so early.

Outside he found a public phone and dialed the police, asking for the Homicide unit.

"Apodaca, Homicide," came a terse male voice, succinct to the point of being unclear. It sounded like "bakka-dakka-ahm-side." Each concise syllable spat out and bitten off as if the man had said it ten thousand times and to say it once more would poison teeth, lips, tongue, and roof of mouth. It threw Trask, who was nervous and shaky, off so badly he couldn't remember Julie's last name for a second. "Bakka-dakka-ahm-side" had knocked it right out of his mind.

"Is—uh—may I speak to Julia, you have a detective by that name?"

"A detective named Julia?"

"Julie," Trask corrected, his mind an absolute blank.

"Detective Julie Hilliard," the desk officer volunteered in that suspicious tone cops have.

"That's the one. Is she in, please?"

"I'll see. Just a second."

"Thanks."

In a moment the voice came back on the line.

"She's not here right now. She'll be back in a half hour or so, I believe. Would you like to leave word?"

"I'll call her back. Thanks."

"Could I say who's calling?"

"Thanks. I'll call back." Trask hung up abruptly before the cop could pressure him to leave his name. The last thing he wanted was Julie Hilliard to call up KCM and ask for him. He could see the pink message form on the spike: *Mr. Trask,* it would say, *call Hilliard at Police HQ.* No. He didn't think so. Trask walked to the parking lot, got his car, and headed home.

He pictured how the conversation would go, tried to imagine what he'd say to her. Would she snarl "Hilliard, Homicide" into the line like the other dicks? Probably. The woman had a way of wearing her cop identity as if it were a shield, which, in a way, he supposed it was.

Trask knew some of the guys at KCPD fairly well, others just as familiar faces. He wasn't sure why he hit on Julie, except that they shared some history between them—not good history—but at least something. She didn't care for Trask at all, and she'd not been one of his favorite people either, but this was business. Hers, presumably, as well as his.

There was some heavy baggage between them. Vic's ex-wife and Julie Hilliard had been close buddies years ago, and she and Vic had not been at all close under the best of circumstances.

Once, when his ex had become fed up with him for the umpteenth time, it was to Julie's apartment she'd gone.

There'd been the usual angry words. Many a tear had fallen. He barely remembered the incident, but feit sure Julie would.

His ex was now living in Aurora, Colorado, married to a rich podiatrist, and was the mother of three "used kids," as someone had put it. Their beautiful daughter, Kit—short for Kitty—had detested "the proctologist," as she insisted on calling her new stepfather, and all siblings attached thereto. She blamed Victor, her dad, for every second she'd had to spend under the man's roof.

Kit, who was cursed in that every day she looked more and more like a beautiful and worldly woman, had become wilder and tougher to control. Now, at fifteen, she was living with her second live-in lover and was a year out of the nest. Gorgeous, smart, she was a champion skier, and barely spoke to either parent, but seemed to have the greatest animosity for Vic. He had written his family off, he realized. It killed him that he no longer even thought about his daughter, and he knew this made him an asshole, but he was what he was. If you wrote him off, he wrote you off. He was sure Julie Hilliard would know all this.

After a half hour had gone by he called and got her on the phone. She was coolly professional and agreed to meet him, but couldn't get away for a couple of hours. He told her no problem and they decided on a downtown restaurant. He was evasive when she tried to ask what it was about, and she didn't press the matter.

Julie was unnerved a bit by the call. She wondered if the daughter had got into trouble. Probably not. If she was a runaway it wouldn't have been Vic Trask who called her. She hoped nothing had happened to Jasmine, her friend of years gone by, but pushed it out of her thoughts and concentrated on the meeting.

The metro squad was in the conference room, away from prying eyes. Unlike what films and TV shows often depict, the K.C. Metro Homicide Squad room was not covered in maps with push pins showing all the murder locations. As a matter of fact, there was little that a civilian could see. The ongoing investigations were contained inside the file folders and attaché cases of the investigating detectives, or they were kept in locked file drawers behind closed office doors.

Llewelyn was doing a chalk talk inside the conference room, and it would be scrubbed off with wet erasers when they left that particular enclosure. A homicide investigation, especially one like this, was a very confidential matter.

"Boyles," he said, and the word tasted bad in the lieutenant's mouth, like a disease. He said it as one would say "trichinosis." An unpleasant, distasteful matter, for a career guy who was seeing his ambitious job plans get sacrificed.

Julie Hilliard opened the file labeled BOYLES HOMS.

"Hildebrande," he said, writing the name on the upper right of the blackboard in hurriedly printed letters. "See the notes on disintegration of brain matter." He circled her name. "Two immediate ties." He wrote *PROS* above her name and said it, pronouncing it *"pross."* He drew a squeaky chalk arrow to the name Tom Dillon. Another to the long, thin rectangle containing the first thirteen victims of the SVS/M club. He wrote *RIF GRENDS* and drew another squeaky emphasis line beneath it.

"Ms. Hildebrande was a *pross.* On at least one occasion, she was arrested propositioning a vice guy in Connelly's Pub. Tom Dillon was into prostitution, Hildebrande's specialty was freak action, the Steel Vengeance outfit were freaks." He circled the three Mount Ely kills. "One, two, fifteen, eighteen victims connect in two ways, weaponry and possible motive." He drew a sloppy line running from Dillon to Hildebrande to the SVS/M rectangle to the Mount Ely names.

"So where does that leave us with Boyles? We've connected over half to prostitution. Are these johns? Are these people witnesses to something? Is this a sex freak blowing people apart with rifle grenades? The FBI laboratory confirms the regional lab findings. A disintegrating-type fragmentation device or projectile. Frags? Rifle grenades? Firebomb devices of some kind? Whatever the killer is using, one thing is certain—it's a military weapon. This guy has munition chops out the kazootsky. He knows firebombs, submachine guns—you name it."

"El Tee, are you saying this is one guy?" Hilliard asked.

"That's it. The Mount Ely homicides link all the kills together. The same weapon that took off the biker's heads when they were on the crosses did all the others. He may have used some sort of modified frag to firebomb their club headquarters. Those are the only two times he used his machine gun. And the only time he took several down who were in one place. Although here"—Llewelyn pointed to a series of half a dozen homicides linked together in a continuous line—"he did all these victims within ten minutes or so. That's firing his weapon over a space of two miles or more. Makes you wonder how he lined them up, or if he did line them up in some way."

"Didn't those have to be random?" Shremp asked.

"It's possible, but it's also possible this guy wanted them to look random. Look here: Number five, Ms. Dukodevsky. Had a couple of things for suspected child abuse. A drug charge. Number six, Mr. Watson. Got him once for possession. Maybe he was into something kinky, too. Number seven, Mr. Yoe. Young guy who was a suspected part-time dealer. Looks like he might be gay. This is a freak doing these killings. I figure it's one guy, who has weapons and munitions capabilities to the max. Probably a former soldier. When we can nail the motive that ties all these kills together we can go for him." Llewelyn swallowed a yawn. He was used to hard work and long hours. A bottomless in-tray full of paperwork without end. A never-ceasing flood of crises, large and small. A parade of witnesses, victims and their family and friends, suspects, endless details, ringing phones and calls you had to make. Doors. The ten million doors you had to pound on, the shoe leather you had to wear out. But this case was something else. It was the sort of investigation that would steal more than your time. It would take your job if you let it.

"You got to find somebody who saw something. All these

homicides and not one damn witness. Why? Get out there and find that person who'll tell us what they saw. The biker-gang thing must have looked like World War Three out in the street—find one of your informants and shake some info out of 'em. Every hour goes by we get colder on these victims. Remember that the first order of business here is containment. Don't let this son of a bitch get out on the street. Boyles, the case itself, does not exist. There is nothing so far in the papers or on TV where anybody has linked the two biker scenes to the others. Anybody gets fancy about witness reports, you sit on it. Anybody says—okay that 'mysterious fatality' where the fifth-grade teacher and that other guy had their heads blown off—is the perpetrator's firearm matched up to the heads that were blown off here?" He pointed to the Mount Ely crosses. "Stonewall. You can categorically state there are no such findings. The lab work is *verboten* territory. Stress that the biker thing was internecine warfare with a rival gang—or whatever. These thirteen and these three were horrible, violent homicides. The mutilation and crucifixion stuff—which God knows how all this information leaks out—but just take the position this was the rival gang trying to cover their tracks and make the crime scene appear to be a ritual deal. No. Don't even say that. Just admit that the two incidents were connected to each other but are *not* connected to any other recent homicides. If you have to, you can point to the increased national statistics in homicides—Kansas City is just part of the national picture—blah, blah. You know how to do all that. All right?" Everyone nodded.

"Informants. That's your key. They could solve this one for us. Freaks. We want to know about freaks, maybe some guy really into pain. Kind of a joker who would seek out Ms. Hildebrande or the sort of working girl who frequents Connelly's. Concentrate especially on Indiana Avenue, east of downtown, Thirty-first to Thirty-sixth and Main, 'chickenhawk alley.'" He meant the area around Tenth and Cherry. "Let's go nail this asshole."

* * *

"Hi, stranger," Trask said, when Julie Hilliard strode up to him in the downtown beanery.

"Hi, Vic," she said, and they had that awkward moment when two persons meet in public and can't quite decide whether to hug or kiss. They touched each other in tentative embracing handshakes, and pecked in the air like California society matrons at a fund-raising gala.

She didn't think Trask had aged a day, but was mildly surprised to see him in such sloppy attire. He wore faded jeans and an open shirt. She supposed people dressed in a more businesslike fashion working for a radio station. His lined face with the pitted, acne-scarred cheeks appeared the same. He had a craggy look that—combined with his go-to-hell air—gave him the appearance of someone much younger than his thirty-six years.

"You haven't changed a bit," he said. She was fairly tall—five feet six or seven, he guessed—slim and trim at a muscular 130, tops. She had wiry brunette hair and fair skin. He knew she'd spent her entire working life, at age thirty-two or thereabouts, as a homicide cop. Her profile would never adorn the cover of a woman's magazine. Her mouth was overly wide, the upper lip not as full as the lower one, and her fashionably mannish hair, curve-concealing outfit, and "dyke boots"—as he thought of them—made an immediate statement. To Trask, sexist pig that he was, the statement was somewhere between an advertisement for the lesbian lifestyle and a defiant "don't worry about my appearance, bozo" kind of proclamation. Either way, she always managed to goad him.

"I was about to say the same thing about you." You still dress like a loser, she thought. His shoes were scuffed and there was a little hayseed scoop in back of his shirt collar when they slid into a booth. Everything she recalled about him was negative. But at least in her memory he dressed like an adult. She thought he looked like he'd been doing yard work.

"What's it been—five years?"

"Every bit of that," she said. She wanted to ask about Jasmine and Kitty, but she swallowed the thought.

"I'm sure you wonder why I got you down here. First, it's nothing to do with the past. Nothing about Kit—or Jazz—I, uh, haven't heard from them in a long time. Kit's left home and living with a guy, but that's neither here nor there." She was staring a couple of holes through him, and not making the meeting any easier. He plunged on. "I'm still researching for KCM; I'm senior researcher for 'Inside America.' And I have been working on some recent homicides."

Christ almighty, she thought, I believed this was something serious and this asshole wants to interview me. "I don't mean to cut you short, but I don't do press interviews at all, Vic. I have a firm policy on that. We have a press—"

"No. I understand. This isn't about an interview. Hear me out a second." Already she'd pissed him off. "I think I may have inadvertently stumbled on some information the police may not have. It may be bullshit, but I want you to take a look at some of my findings. Also, I'm trying to put together news material for the show that ties all this together, and if I help the police I want to feel like my material will be treated in confidence. I don't want to be scooped because I'm coming forward with information I've uncovered, you know?" He was smiling as if he thought he'd told a joke. She just raised her eyebrows and continued to stare holes in him. She had steady, wide-set, piercing eyes, and she made him uncomfortable as hell.

"What is it you think you've found?"

"Okay," he said, bringing out some large, folded pieces of twelve-by-eighteen-inch Strathmore artist paper. There were photos of homicide victims, which she saw that he'd cut from newspapers mostly. Crime-scene shots. Polaroids. Faces and places linked together with arrows. Charts. Trask's neatly typed summaries and bios of the decedents. He'd been a busy boy, she'd give him that. "See?" he said, showing her more.

"So what is it you think you've discovered?"

"The connecting motive behind all this violence. Do you see anything unusual about all these faces?"

"Nope. Not really."

"There aren't any blacks."

"Yeah. So?"

"I think . . . I know I've hit on something here. You've got a gang of drug dealers who've been killing mostly whites, people encroaching on their territory probably. It ties the killings of the motorcycle gang into all these people. You've got all these mysterious deaths and shootings and drive-by murders . . . it's obvious, when you study it, that the one thing that links all these homicides together is drugs. And the M.O. is usually the same—right? So my conclusion is this: a black drug cartel has hired an assassin to begin executing non-African-Americans who are dealing drugs. And—"

"Can I be straight with you—I mean, without you taking offense? You've seen too much television. It's that simple." She couldn't help it. She laughed in his face.

"No, I know what I'm saying. I'm not talking TV fantasies here—there are too many killings in a short period of time." He shook his head. Fuck her and her tough diesel dyke attitude. "And you didn't let me finish what I'd found."

"Sorry. Go ahead."

"Thanks." Patronizing bitch. "If it isn't an assassin hired by a drug gang, then the alternative is that we've got one of the worst serial murderers of all time killing people right and left. Am I right?"

She laughed again in spite of herself. He looked so serious. With his charts and amateur detective bullshit.

"Too much TV, Vic. It's nothing to be ashamed of. We run into it all the time. You've taken stories about certain homicides and made a neat scenario like a television show, and there's nothing to it. Sorry." She smiled.

"What do you mean certain homicides? I've taken every

violent homicide in the Kansas City area within the last four weeks—and there's *one* black in the lot."

"First, the stories you clip out of the paper or that you get from the press room at headquarters are only a portion of what actually goes down. Number one: not everything is released to the press for dissemination, surely you know that?" The chill was thick in the air between them like a layer of frost on a windowpane.

"You're saying—"

"I'm saying you don't show Jeffrey Hawkins, or James Copeland, or DaVelle Yates, or Tyrone Phelbs, or Manuel Calderon—just off the top of my head—and none of them are white, and each is a violent death that occurred in the last few weeks in Jackson County alone. You get out into Clay, and Platte, or Cass County—"

"Hawkins—and these other killings—how come they never made the news?"

"Homicides are frequently kept confidential, depending on the nature of the investigation. I thought you were aware of that—being in the business as long as you have."

"I'll bet Adam David would be surprised to learn he's not being given access to all the news. I never heard of such a thing."

"I'm giving you background information—strictly off the record—and expect you to treat it that way. We know each other. If I thought you'd act irresponsibly, or put it on the radio, I wouldn't even be talking to you. But that's the truth of it. Some investigations are of a nature that preclude the dispensing of those stories to the press while the cases are being made." She looked up as a waitress came to take their order.

"Would you folks like something?"

"Just coffee."

"Nothing. Can't stay," she said.

"One black coffee, please."

They sat mutely waiting while the waitress brought him a cup, poured, and asked if there'd be anything else. He told her no and she left. The two of them were taking up a booth for the price of a cup of coffee, and the waitress was doubtful the guy would even leave a tip.

"These aren't gangbanger shootings. They're random incidents, Vic. Believe me."

"I know if they're not drug related it's gotta be the work of a serial killer. Got to be." He had his teeth in this story and he wasn't giving up.

"Hawkins was shot in the projects Friday night. Small caliber pistol to the back of the head. We're working a black suspect," she whispered to him, wondering if he was wearing a wire. She'd have to have the El Tee put a "copper-stopper," a deletion order, in his information bottle when she went back to the shop. She didn't want to hear all this bullshit voice-tracked in the six o'clock newscast. "All this is strictly confidential and sensitive, not to be repeated, okay? But I'm just showing you. Yates took a shotgun blast in the face. Blew the kid's head off, darn near. We know who did it. Calderon and Phelbs were both stabbing victims and we're looking for the doer. Again, the person is known to us. You just happened to research some homicides in an unusually busy time frame and when, coincidentally, some of the homicides involving blacks were ongoing or sensitive investigations. Understand?"

"The killings are all drug related, though." He tried to hang in, as somehow he saw his entire theme show concept eroding if she shot him down on the serial theory.

"Vic, all homicides are either over drugs or money or women—I mean going back for years and in every major city in the country."

"Maybe so but . . ." He couldn't think. Jesus! "What about your ballistics department? Isn't it true that all the so-called random shootings are with the same two or three weapons?" He was fishing.

"First, it isn't a ballistics department, okay? Ballistics refers to the trajectory of projectiles." That patronizing ha-ha voice of hers was making him nuts. "The department is Firearms and Toolmakers and, no, the random violence is just that. There is no common link with respect to forensics or lab findings, or match-ups on bullets and so forth. There's just a lot of violent crime going on—not just Kansas City. I know the statistics for other large population areas are much worse. No—"

"You guys never talk about serial murders anyway, right? You wouldn't tell me if it was a serial killer, would you?" He had her on that one.

"Well," she said, breathing deeply, "I'm sure you're aware that the policy of the department is not to identify serial homicides during investigations because of obvious reasons. We know that such publicity very often fuels more killings, or if not feeding and stimulating the ego of the killer or killers, it can also create copycats."

"Is that what you have here—copycat killers?"

"No," she said with a pinched-up face, really selling it to him. "These homicides aren't related in M.O. or any other way. Every one is a different story."

"Okay, what about the biker gang and the three who got crucified? Those are tied together—everybody knows that."

"You know I can't talk about specific details on that one. That's still ongoing." He took a sip of his coffee and she used that second to slide out from the booth. "Gotta run. Believe me," she said, "you're off on the wrong track."

"Thanks for your time."

"No problem," she said, and with a curt nod was gone.

She hadn't even bothered to read his background stuff. He knew things about David Boyles and some of the others that he was sure the guy's casual buddies hadn't told the cops. They hated cops. But she didn't want to hear it. She couldn't be bothered. He'd go over her head. To the chief of detectives. He paid his check, left a dollar tip, surprising the waitress, and went out to his car.

The El Tee was gone when Hilliard returned to the squad bay, and she was wading through paperwork when Victor Trask's voice startled her.

"Long time no see." He was standing at her desk.

"Yeah, really." She made no effort to keep the irritation out of her tone.

"I forgot to give this to you—and you were in a hurry, so it didn't dawn on me until you'd left." He handed her one of the copies of the page on HOMICIDE VICTIMS WITH BACKGROUNDS AS DRUG DEALERS. She looked at it and was mildly surprised at the information.

"How did you get this?"

"Interviews with the decedent's acquaintances. People will tell reporters and researchers things they won't always tell cops."

"Um." She appeared stone-faced as usual. "Well, I'll see this gets passed along, okay. Thanks."

"You didn't have that information, did you?"

"I really couldn't say," she said. "Was that it?"

"Yeah." He turned and started out the door, cursing her mentally. There were three men and Hilliard in the squad room. Each working at a desk. He saw computer terminals and files everywhere, but little else. He could hear a telephone ringing. As he walked out of the metro squad section, he passed a closed office door with a lieutenant's name on it. He tried the knob and peeked in, prepared to say, "Oh—I thought this was the way out" or some dumb thing. "I can't read English." Something. Nobody at the desk. Trask did something with a piece of equipment about the size of a large push pin, and turned, leaving, and a man filled the doorway.

"Can I help you?"

Trask just about let it go in his pants. "No." He laughed, as if this fellow had just told him the funniest joke in the world. "I took a wrong turn." He stepped back into the hallway feeling the man's eyes burn into him. "Which way to get back downstairs?"

"Right there to your right. You here on business, sir?" There was an official edge to the man's voice.

"I'm an old friend of Hilliard's," Trask said. Big smile. He waved as he turned away. "Thanks."

"Uh-huh."

Trask kept going, waiting to hear the command to stop, but none came. His bed was made and there'd be no unmaking it now. The bug from Bob's Electronics was stuck under a shelf in Lieutenant John J. Llewelyn's office—for whatever that was worth.

Outside on the street, he bought a couple of papers. In one of them he saw the headline "Police Deny Mysterious Slayings Related to Sixteen Gang Killings." Clearly he hadn't been the first person to go fishing in this particular stagnant pond.

"Hey, Snooze," Sean Flynn called out from fifty feet away, as Trask rounded the turn to Production and Programming back inside KCM. Flynn, obviously in a good mood, was coming from the conference room. He only used his nicknames when he was in a good mood, which was— fortunately or unfortunately—almost never.

"Yo."

"Got a hole next week. Whatcha working on?"

"Right now?" Trask was ready for him this time.

"No. Not right now. What were you working on last February? Yeah, right now," Flynn said brightly.

"Telecommunications for the deaf. I've got a whole thing on the technology, the various devices, the way the operators work, the backgrounder—I've got staff and management types lined up. There's an eight-hundred number tie-in. A thing about prejudice against the deaf—they don't like the phrase 'hearing impaired,' by the way—and I, uh—"

"That's good. What else?"

"I got a thing on how parents, students, and media people have been acting as a pressure group, trying to get the U.S. Education Department to change its position on releasing crime reports at colleges and universities."

"Borrrrrrr-ing!"

"No. Wrong! Wrong, O mighty Flynn of the night. I got a bitchin' hot interview set with this gal who edits the student

199

newspaper. She took 'em to court and won. It's perfect for you—the ant kicks the elephant's ass, so to speak."

"That is good. You're right. It's unboring as hell. I take it back. I stand chastised. Work that up. Like maybe three examples—each with a guest."

Sure.

"One other thing," Trask said, "I know what really killed the dinosaurs."

Flynn's handsome puss broke into a big smile. "Yeah? What's that?"

"They died trying to find a parking space."

20

Bobby Price had slept on the floor of a deserted office and woke up stiff in most of his joints, no pun intended. He could not force more than one push-up out of his muscular bod, so gripped he was by a languorous, listless, languid, lovely, lethargic lassitude. He was up on those hard, extended arms, toes erect, frozen in midpush, thinking of lazy words that began with *L*: lazy, languishing, lambasted, lard-assed, latency. *Latent*—couldn't that suggest dormant? He was latent. A fucking latent. This lonesome longhorn, this lithe and lank lad was lamentably limp in the lap. Was he a motherfucking latent? Lordy, lordy, lock and load.

The shooter was a neuter, nude and unscrewed, and he had a need to see folks bleed. Bobby Boy had gone bye-bye yesterday evening, and a deliveryman in white coveralls had conned his way into the Kansas City Convention Center, pushing a large, heavy white box (marked FRAGILE) on a dolly. Bullshitting his way in with a big, foxy grin, getting into the building's knickers, finding a floor with nobody home, finding a place that was just the right space.

The deliveryman's costume was on the floor next to the box and the dolly. Hello, dolly, how's your box? He had the case open, his lady screwed together, his tool kit out. He decided to pull his clothes on—the carpet had left his skin with an itchy feel. He needed a hot bath, and a long shower. He felt unclean, and the stink of chemicals from the carpeting was strong in the room. *Nanny, li'l Bobby don't feel so good today. Tan I stay home fwom school, pwease?*

He used the glass cutter and popped a good-size chunk of glass out, with some effort, keeping low and close to the corner. *"Red Rock Match Grade Ammunition is available in two classifications of sniper rounds: Super-Hard-on and Anti-Pussy."* He forced his mind back into the groove. *"Super-Hardened ARmor-penetrating Projectile, High Explosive cartridges."* He loaded a SHARP-HEX round into his sweet baby. Eye to the Laco. Careful to keep the tip of the silencer and flash attachment nearly flush with the glass. Far below, he saw a man driving a shiny new car and he blew the fucking thing to kingdom come.

"They consist of an incendiary detonator, a high explosive charge, a super-hard-on tungsten-carbide penetrator . . ." He snicked the spent shell case out onto the stinking carpet and slid an APEX(X) into her. Eyeballed the Laco. Red Nissan it looked like. Bus. Dizzying pan of vision. Woman in white shirt in front of a self-service gas station pumping her gas. A young girl getting out of her car. Why not? *Squeeeeze.* Ooh, grue.

Businessman in shirt and tie. Watch him die. Yeah! Reload. Paunchy man in green shirt, blue cap—time for your nap . . . surprise!

Keep this up all fuckin' day. Man on cherrypicker, two guys beside a truck but they move and spoil the shot. Billboards for the Missouri lottery and the virtues of diesel. Man walking. Squeeze . . . blood in the trees.

Load and look. Another dizzy arc as he searches for targets. Creme Pontiac Grand-Am. Distant image of a kid on a bike—a good two miles away. He sees a man and woman coming out of a building. Hallmark Greeting Cards, Inc. Imagines them talking about Hallmark signing Shaquille O'Neal of the Orlando Magic; the woman—she's into basketball players, the guy—he writes those sentimental verses inside cards. Roses are red, crosshairs on your head, here comes the lead . . . now you're dead. Hold still Sam, *alakazam* . . . wham, bam! Guts and jam.

To Shooter, at this moment, those who'd warned Columbus of a flat earth were dead right. It was flat, and the end of the world was marked by the horizon line in the far distance. Squinting into the 40X sighting scope, rubbing a sleep cinder from the left corner of his right eye with a thumb, he was amused to feel himself trembling.

The sun had come up the color of blood: a bright red fireball rising in the dark gray beyond the flat edge of the world. Blood red against gray. Far down below him, over a three-and-a-half- to four-mile radius, people were screaming, sobbing, hollering, becoming panic-stricken, telling other people what they'd seen or thought they'd seen, calling the police, calling for the doctor, calling for the nurse, calling for a lady with an alligator purse. But none of this was why he was trembling.

He saw a sign of movement near the locus of his focus and the word *lollygag* came back into his head after thirty years. He could recall nasty Nanny telling him "not to lollygag." Lollygag? He couldn't spell the fucking thing—but it was another lazy *L* word. Lollygag!

In Fort Worth, you heard folks talk about how they was gonna "sashay" over to so-and-so. He hadn't heard the word *sashay* in a hundred years. Sashay, lollygag, traipse. Traipse! There was a dandy. He hadn't traipsed in a coon's age. Traipse? He hadn't traipsed in a month of Sundays. He felt himself jerk, watching for the bright flashes from the mortar tubes. *Shit!* This was gooder'n sex. But he looked back to rub his eye again and saw all the empty brass on the floor and it snapped him into action.

He took his honey apart and put her back in the fitted case, and began to strap the whole shebang onto the dolly. He was out of there.

Chaingang had started to go roaring after Shooter Price to find him and kill him, but he'd immediately felt his governor stemming the hot tide of fury before it washed over him beyond the point of return. His legal wheels, the precious previously owned Oldsmobile, was a perfectly street-clean ride with sanitized, checkable title. The endless unnecessary aggravation he'd put himself through replacing the vehicle initially stopped him. He needed to take a car that he could dump after he was through with Shooter. Trade his Olds for something a bit more upscale. The implant kept intruding on every plan he made.

In theory, it was extremely difficult to engineer surprises for Dr. Norman, since he had an access to monitors that detailed Daniel's movements. But there were other ways to handle things: third parties, for example, who could be easily manipulated into doing his bidding. He needed to think, plan, and—when he'd done his homework—act.

First stop was the Kansas City Public Library, main branch. A glorious place full of tasty treats for the epicurean information addict. He took Dr. Norman's thoughtfully detailed dossier, replete with schematics, and dressed in his finery, he spent the morning researching. There was the matter of the OMEGASTAR mobile tracker, which he knew could be defeated, and the implant, about which he had no such confidence.

The overlarge fellow was an obvious student of some sort, the reference librarian observed. Clearly intelligent. It just showed you—you couldn't judge a book by its cover. But up in the hidden stacks, the quality of mansuetude and academic devotion was shrugged off, momentarily, while Chaingang licked a diagram, found it irresistibly delicious, and began eating it. It was a sight the gentle librarian would never have forgotten—Chaingang ripping a page from a library book and chomping down on it with those ugly, yellow fangs of his. My God! Such a thing had no possible earthly explanation. It fell outside of one's acceptance cone. Perhaps somewhere in the universe—beyond Mars, a few black holes away—maybe there they ate books. It just wasn't *done* here.

He was still hungry when he finished at the library,

and—driving in the direction of a nearby mall—he spotted a fruitseller set up on a busy sidestreet. He pulled over and bought a half peck of Heartland Orchard Red Hearts. "Fancy sweet yellow flesh" had caught his eye. They were great for canning, the crate assured him, and he thought of his pleasant days spent in the home of a woman named Mrs. Irby, whose extensive canned goods he'd once ravaged.

As he thought of her, he demolished the fresh peaches, his system crying to him for more fruit, and he vanished them in a continual, wet sucking. His huge hands would grab a peach and he'd appear to swallow it whole, a three-part noise accompanying the ingesting of the fruit and skin, and the spitting of the pit: *slurrrp-fwahp-ptttht! Slurrrp-fwahp-ptttht!* He sucked them down, inhaling the delicious meat, biting into their bloody hearts, slurping them down with juice running from his chin, sucking peaches, spitting pits, wiping the sticky blood from his face with the back of a huge hairy paw. He noticed someone watching him from across the way—an old man—and he spit a peach pit at him, plopping back in his ride with a groan. Twenty-one peach pits littered the sidestreet. So much for his appetizer. Now he needed to go get some red meat. Chaingang's hunger rumbled in his massive gut like summer thunder. He mashed the radio dial, trying to take his mind off food, and some monkey man was raving about "the game next weekend in Arrowhead Stadium." He smashed the noise off, hating the monkeys for their childish fascination with the trivial and mundane.

He could not go back to the unsafe house and he was weary of motels and hotels. He needed isolation. He needed many things—Dr. Norman, chemistry, math, and the general sciences. He let his mind scan freely, allowing anything to come to the fore as he digested and rechewed his mental cud.

You must understand that Chaingang Bunkowski, in moments such as these, cannot drive through Hardee's and order a dozen mushroom-and-Swiss burgers and hope to satisfy the craving inside. The need for a human heart was so strong he almost stopped and took one at random, but whatever remained of his good sense prevailed.

His strange mind scanned a world of languages as he drove, searching for acceptable desolation—if not wilderness—remembering Assamese, Breton, Baluchi, Catalan, Dutch, Faeroese, German, Haitian Creole, Icelandic, Judeo-Spanish, Konkani, Hashmiri, Kafiri, Khowar, Kurish —or was it Kurdish? Had he forgotten Frisian? Irish Gaelic? He thought about implants and how little he'd gleaned as he subconsciously scanned Marathi, Nepali, Ossec, Oriya, Punjabi, Portuguese—he was vaguely irritated at these lapses—Persian, Rhaeto-Romanic, Rajasthani, Scottish Gaelic, Sardinian, Slovene—what about Sanskrit? Tajiki, Urdu, Venetic, Welsh, Wendish, X-lac-tian, Ukrainian, Yiddish, Zanzkritian. He played games with himself, seeing the image of a spotted dog named Duke that one of the guards at Marion owned. Dalmation?

He would kill someone and eat their heart and take their car and then he'd get something for dessert, and there were nearly twelve million medical implants in living North American surgical patients: he sorted through the diagrams of screws, plates, wires, pins, joints, lenses, valves, silicone tits, and collagened lips. He thought of chewed peach hearts, mangled maniocs, calabashed cassavas, squashed spurge, ruptured rootstock, somatic mutation of peach pit, necrotized nectarines. . . .

From nowhere, inside his mind, he pictured blood geysers streaming from Mrs. Nadine Garbage-belly's severed lifestreams. Old Faithful spewing from that neck as the ticker pounded. Half a million human monkeys had pacemakers implanted in their shithouse skins. He saw fake surveillance monitors; barking dogs; sensor-controlled lights; magnetic switches; electric eyes; window foil; closed-circuit cameras; sound, movement, and heat-sensing detectors; infrared ray receivers; Chaingang could bypass them all. From Ma 'n' Pa kitchen-table business alarms to the underground repeater station hookups for Ma Bell, Holmes, national ComSec ops, Newton Secure Systems, Brinks, Pinks, tiddlywinks. *Tagalog!* Another forgotten language.

How-who-why-when-where did he learn about Irish Gaelic, peach pits, Newton Secure Systems, and silicone tits? He learned them the old-fashioned way: at the "lie-berry," very often. He learned from eating libraries full of books on chemistry, math, and the general sciences, reading the books, sinking them down into the deep, fat wrinkles in that remarkably weirdly eidetic memory and eating the best parts.

That same gray matter mass fires a warning shot and he slows, brakes, pulls into a mall. A fairly busy shopping complex that he loves the instant he sees it. It pounds at him, screaming the *V*-words he loves so much: vulnerability and victim. He sees victims everywhere he looks. He can victimize a mall, for God's sake—take it down from one end to the other with any luck at all. But that is for later. What stopped him is a toy store. He parks, lurches out of the Olds, and waddles across the hot parking area.

"Hi," a friendly salesgirl says, "may we help you, please?" He does not like her tone. He makes a poem to her inside his head as he looks for the toys he needs.

I wanna meet you, defeat you, eat you. Learn you, churn you, burn you. Overpower you, deflower you, devour you. Chain you, brain you, drain you. He spots a toy robot thing.

Robyn Brock has worked here for two years come November, and this is the first time the person has not *answered* her. It is insulting and confusing and she is frightened in some way she cannot understand. Oh! It dawns on her. He is hard of hearing. She walks up to his immense back and touches him lightly on the arm, spinning this beast around and mouthing in an exaggerated way so he can read her fucking lips, "Can I help you with something?"

Five hundred pounds descends on her instep and she screams in pain. Nearly eight hundred dollars' worth of well-designed and cleverly boxed plastic junk cascades from the shelves.

"Oh. I've hurt my back," the man moans in his sissy voice.

"Don't try to get up," she says, doing her best to wiggle out from under him. "I'll go get help." She tries to walk, wondering if her foot has been broken.

"No!" His voice freezes her in her tracks. "Never mind. I'm going to go. I'll go get off my feet. I'm sure I'll be all right."

"What happened?" All she can think of is the huge lawsuit against the store.

"You just threw me off my balance—I don't know—I slipped. My fault." He began to mince his way out of the store, almost limping. His right ankle was weak and he sometimes limped when he was tired, so it was quite easy to fake.

Back in his wheels, he watched her, after having repaired the stacks of fallen toys, taken her shoe off, and inspected her sore foot. A barking cough of amusement escaped his gut as he turned his attention to the three items he'd shoplifted. Two of them were worthless and he pitched them out of the window into the parking lot, but one was going to do.

The robot, designed to move along a black line drawn on white paper, was guided by a photo interrupter. It was the eye and the preassembled printed circuit board he wanted. The thing was only seventy-five dollars, but she'd irritated him.

He had other stops to make and when he'd assembled all of his purchases he drove to a nearby spot that was sufficiently secluded and began unloading items from the trunk. He carried his digger, a poncho half, and his fighting bowie knife. In the small thicket of trees and bushes that backed against the mall, he began digging. It only took him a few minutes, as he didn't go too deeply. When he was finished, he used the outer berm of displaced dirt to pack down two edges of the poncho cover, and with his big knife hacked down a couple of heavy tree limbs to weight the other sides. In his pocket was an aerosol spray which he used to cover the entire area. It was a scent that was extremely offensive to dogs. He didn't want this grave tampered with.

Chaingang returned to the parking lot and cruised, watching for easy targets. He saw an older woman in a silver Lincoln Continental Mark VI and followed her, pulling into the slot near her. He watched her get out and almost made a move but the warning system kept him off. She had too much savvy in her movements. Something. He had to get those strong victim vibes or he'd usually pass. This time he passed. A lucky woman who was shopping for a bridal shower, who wore too much perfume, and used too much spray on her hair—a fortunate gal who moved as if she knew what she was about would not go to meet her maker. Not today.

He cruised slowly out of the lot, looking for mall cops in unmarked cars. Perhaps that is what drew him to these shopping complexes. The ones that felt empty of prying eyes titillated him. He cruised slowly, staying away from the shopping area for a while, driving leisurely as he looked for a sweet victim.

The Olds rolled past a carpet store, a small paint shop where he'd recently made a purchase, a framing company, a large supermarket, a cleaning establishment, a photo kiosk, a religious bookseller, a woman's clothing shop, a mall restaurant, any number of potential targets.

She was driving a new red Buick and he wanted to trade up anyway. There was no question she'd do nicely. Attractive. Although that was not a factor. He'd read up on his condition. Perhaps the implant had touched near whatever stimulates such responses to sexual impulses. His sex drive might have been short-circuited. Or it might be that he was merely off his feed, in the same way a recently divorced or otherwise separated person will not have that immediate desire for a while. It was nothing to be worried about. Rape, after all, was such a piddling violation when compared to taking an involuntary organ donation.

Red was in her twenties. He had parked across from her and had been careful to scope out the presence of any possible observers.

"Hi! 'Scuse me a second?" Still in his nice clothing, but not as faggy now. Booming voice all hail-fellow, hearty, maturity, and purpose. "I've got a problem." He certainly did.

"See this?" It looked like a folded map. "Would you have any idea how to gradis Thornbill from hocken flanner? Can you go right across or is that no longer cut through?"

"Pardon me?" Indeed.

"See?" Forcing her eyes to that damned map. Meanwhile, he looks all around, rubbernecking, positioning himself just so. Blocking off any other possible observer, his huge meaty slab of a back shielding the action from his weakest point of cover. "Thornbill." He points. The huge finger draws her eyes.

In a situation such as this one, comfortingly in full sign of people, broad daylight, and a busy mall, how worried does one get? After all, nothing's going to happen to you.

But if you scream, he tells you he is going to shoot, and these words are funny at first because he is so comical and they are the words to TV and movie scenes seen and remembered, but the Colt Woodsman he has tucked into the map does not look like a toy, and he is not playacting. All those fictional crime shows have educated you. You know a silencer when you see one—that's the long thing on the end of the pistol . . . and if it was a piece of hacksawed pipe with a bushing on the end, how could you be expected to detect that?

The point is you move. He is obviously afraid of nothing and you are very much afraid. You don't wish to die— someday, maybe, but not today. You beg. He doesn't like this and now you are in a moment of extreme pain and on the floorboard of your own car. Not unconscious but very near. The mundane and commonplace seem so important, suddenly, so you file away the fact that the monstrous apparition is moving your seat backward, sliding it and clicking it into place, then rummaging around, finding your car keys, touching you. Your purse is gone. You drift, mercifully, into blackness.

Chaingang drives away in the smooth-riding Buick, experimenting constantly to get the seat back. There isn't enough room for his gut. Piece of crap!

The toadstool world is filled with midgets, small-minded dwarf monkeys for whom all clothing, furniture, and vehicles are designed.

His Olds sits locked and legal in the mall lot with 150 other sets of wheels. Has anyone observed and, if they did, what did they really see?

His warning system is not blinking at him. Well, perhaps a nudge, but only a very vague, general sense of discomfort. He finds the grave site. Pulls her out. Gets his bowie knife.

Three deep cuts. What he calls "the Y," the autopsy Y. Two from the titties to the center and then straight down. Much blood and he's in such a hurry he has his good clothes on. He strips, comes back to the body, stepping in the bloody mud and ripping the heart from this monkey woman and sinking his teeth into it. Oh, my goodness, that tastes good. She is rich and sweet.

Eileen Todd, twenty-six, an employee of Gale's Print Galleria, drives her parents' Buick, he learns from the contents of her purse. He covers her corpse with dirt, using her ripped clothing remnants to clean himself as best he can. In his pants pockets are small premoistened towels, which he also uses.

He sprays the grave again, scatters rocks around, and heaves his quarter-ton back into the red car. He knows this thing costs over twenty thousand dollars, list price—how can it not be roomier? Tsk, tsk! A world designed for scaled-down Lilliputians, it was. He had thought about wiring a couple of shotguns under the hood and making it into a war wagon but he was too bummed out by this car. He was disappointed. He'd been all set to trade for a Buick. Surely there must be something on wheels built for a man and not a fucking monkey?

He decided he'd feel better if he'd go kill that little faggot sissy Bobby Price. Drove back and loaded the duffel, with mobile tracker unit inside, secured the Olds again, and took off in the direction of the white blip. Already he was getting more used to the position of the wheel. There was no question about it, he decided. He was a real GM man.

He had the tracker up on the dash and the passenger seat of the Buick was covered in papers: the Kansas City map enlargement, the SAVANT and OMEGASTAR specs, Shooter's dossier and current likeness, all of which had been duly memorized, but remained there for inspiration. The goonybird face of tightly wound, psychotic Shooter staring at nothing from a street-van surveillance picture, no doubt. Shooter's mouth open, speaking to someone, looking like a jock on his way to the tennis court. Chaingang remembered that Price came up to his bellybutton—the little midget piece of trash. He'd kill him and pinch off his pusshead right there in the fucking street. . . . He found this car intolerable.

Chaingang was parked at a stop sign, waiting in the traffic, experimenting with the seat and the air conditioning. He had it on sixty degrees—cold. Somebody was walking between the cars. If it was one of those bagrags who wash windshields, Chaingang would pull out the .22 and drill the monkey just for practice.

"Paper!" the guy was screaming. Chaingang hit the button that lowered the window, after a few misses, and told the monkey to give him one. Gave him pocket change. Flipped through the wrong section first, then turned it and saw a small front-page headline: Six More Killings, Police Admit Serial Killer. That little fucking shit! Killing on *his* ground. Who the fuck did he think he was? Someone honked in back of him and he started shifting into reverse to ram them, but then better judgment pulled his sleeve. He had to stay on track and take care of this.

In that moment, he saw through a window in his rage—he was a different person. Celibate! Losing his temper when it could hurt him. He was behaving uncharacteristically. It

sobered him and he bit down on his thoughts about the
implant, screaming out of the line of parked cars in the
direction of Shooter Price, tearing around a beige
Oldsmobile and a white Dodge Caravan, driving around a
muscle car as if it weren't there, the white blip growing
larger and stronger in the center of the OMNI device.

He was locked down now. Concentrating fiercely, with all
his energy on the act of destruction, slicing through traffic—
five hundred pounds mashed down on the gas pedal,
floorboarding it through teenagers and retirees alike, around
a kid in a Pontiac Bonneville, a woman in a brown Chrysler
LeBaron, a kid in an old Roadrunner, a couple in a Jap
thing—zooming out of nowhere to loom larger than life in
Price's mirror.

Shooter had been tracking *him*, he was going to whack Big
Petey with his baby, who was in her case in the seat in back
of him, and he'd been parked on a side street, but when he
saw the blip—the blimp-size blip—coming nearer, he
turned the car to follow him and take a shot, but suddenly
Chaingang was on his ass, driving a different set of wheels,
roaring down on him with a vengeance, and he was scared
almost to the point of going sane.

He saw the car come out of nowhere, moving way too
fast—he knew cars—they were gonna hit. He floored the
accelerator and shot out into traffic and some poor devil in
an Ace Trucking Company job smashed into the little M30
with a resounding crunch of chrome, metal, fiberglass,
plastic, shit, and shinola. Shooter grabbing SAVANT and
shagging ass as the glass—already cracked—shattered under a hail of lead.

Shooter just went—*fuck* the mobile tracker—and he was
running fast—zigging through honking motorists, zag-
ging away from the hail of terminal saturnism—that's your
basic Beaumont–Port Arthur lead poisoning—splattering
around him. There wasn't but two things Shooter Price
could do besides pull a trigger and both of 'em was run, and
he flat out ran for his crazy life as Chaingang Bunkowski

stood flat-footed, next to a wrecked M30 and an Ace who'd been in the wrong place, glass all around his fat ass, oblivious to the wail of distant sirens, a Chinese copy of a submachine gun cradled in his arms as he cursed his slowness and ran one more magazine through the pipe just for luck.

Bat-batta-bat-bambambam; popping rounds came across the traffic in the direction of disappearing Shooter, the felt-padded bolt clattering as the weapon blew smoking cartridge cases into the broken glass and car parts.

He had to make himself squeeze back into the car and get in the wind. After all, as his dearest mommy used to say, there was a time and a place for everything.

He made a U-turn, swung around, reached into his duffel and plucked out one of his remaining grenades, and after determining that it didn't have a file-notched spoon (the way his luck was going he'd blow his fat ass up with a short-fused frag!), he took the pin out and tossed it into the M30 convertible, tromped the gas, and watched it blow in the Buick's rearview mirror.

Some days were like that. No matter what you did you just couldn't get arrested.

21

Victor Trask was supposedly out taping bites for a piece on miscegenation for "Inside America." He was inside his car, taping hallway conversation from a parked car in the eleven-hundred block of Locust, scared all the while he'd be busted and thrown in jail for illegally recording the cops, and getting zip for his chances.

The logistics alone of such a thing were beyond him. He'd not used a voice-activated recorder, so when he couldn't personally monitor he'd had to go back and skim-check hours of random tape, hoping to catch a tiny fish in this enormous sea.

He'd caught nothing but a worse cold, which was now, he thought, settling in as a virulent strain of summer flu. What had he learned? A man—the lieutenant who occupied the bugged office, presumably—had a real hard-on for the Jackson County medical examiner. He was addicted to mixed metaphors. He spent his day on the phone or away from his desk; the long, confidential talks he'd imagined overhearing were nonexistent in this office. What Victor did hear was a bunch of career-related shit about how Sergeant so-and-so should get people to solve their own problems instead of coming to him, and a lot of platitudes about work delegation, keeping options open, prioritizing tasks, and stuff he'd obviously picked up on at a seminar. He kept talking about his "Masters in Advanced Death Investigations," "Project Assignments in Criminalistic Factfinding," and various other subjects that sounded as if they should be in capital letters. He heard nothing about blacks, drugs, serial killings, lab findings, or anything of relevance.

What he finally mined—the lone nugget—came from a headache-inducing monitor of a hallway conversation that he could only halfway hear. It was a maddening thing, like listening to a loud conversation taking place in an adjacent room where you hear isolated audible phrases but can't make out the overall conversation. A man and woman, not Hilliard, were speaking discursively and a third voice shouted something about a weapon. The word perked up his ears. The chatter moved away from the microphone, and he rewound the tape and listened to it again, not on the tiny earpiece but at full volume on playback, and he was able to discern ". . . got some more . . . (INAUDIBLE) how many or anything but it's the same weapon. Estimate the thing has a range of one and three quarter miles and he . . ." (INAUDIBLE.)

He was too excited to listen further. He turned the engine on, rolled up his windows, and headed back toward the station. He'd gone a couple of blocks—he was very nauseated—and he felt as if his sinuses were so stopped up his head would explode. That was the thought Trask would remember thinking when he saw . . . someone's . . . head . . . explode!

Had he fallen into some terrible time-warp daymare brought out by his worsening flu? The gorge rose in him and he barely got the driver's-side door open in time. There were car horns, trucks honking, and a cab nearly clipped him as he swung to the curb and lurched out onto the sidewalk to be sick again. People were going ape shit. Across the street, they were already converging around a man's headless torso.

He managed to get across the street, his mind racing. Should he phone it in and do a report? That would normally be his reaction—he'd call the news room, record an on-the-scene sound bite. He tried to assimilate what he'd seen as he pushed into the swarm of milling onlookers. People were in total confusion, some of them crying, one woman screaming like a banshee. A siren was loud in his stuffed ears. He coughed, almost gagged again, spat into the gutter, blew his nose. He was a mess.

It had been beyond his immediate powers of description. He'd seen the head . . . just go. Dematerialize! There was no question it was real—awful human matter had left splashes across the storefront behind the man, as well as the sidewalk where his decapitated corpse fell. The shirt, the white shirt the man had been wearing, was now red. The sidewalk was blackish red with his spilled blood.

Trask was wasting time. He stumbled back through the mindless traffic, flung himself into the car and keyed the ignition. He headed back to the station again, violating a "termination clause" contract rule and parking in VIP Sales parking. He burst through the front doors, his face like death warmed over, past Security and the front desk, not waiting for the elevator, taking the stairs two at a time.

He walked into Flynn's reception area, ignoring Jerri Laymon, barging into Flynn's office without so much as a glancing knock.

"I got the big one," Trask blurted out. He was puffing, blowing, winded from his run up the stairs and the brisk jog, nearly exhausted from the flu bug and drained by what he'd just seen. On top of all that, he was almost on the verge of tears. Inexplicably, for a screw-up whose career—such as it was—had become his focus of concentration, Trask had been emotionally twisted by the awful murder he'd just seen. Someone had been killed seconds ago in the most gruesome way and here he was running to cash in on the man's death. Was there nothing to him of any substance? "I've just seen one of the murders take place—not four blocks away." He pointed with a limp finger, working to keep from crashing physically. "I saw a guy get his head blown right off his shoulders—it was the most godawful mess you can imagine . . . it's a serial killer. He's behind all the mysterious deaths, including the biker-gang homicides and, moreover, I've got you two months of shows back-logged and, well, I'll tell you about those later." He sucked in oxygen. "Right now we gotta get to work on tonight's show. You gotta kill it so we can go with the thing on all the murders. I got it all, the whole nine, chapter and verse. Everything. Deep background with somebody who even knows about the weapon that's doing all these people. Inside cop stuff. I got a thing from a homicide detective who alleges that there are killings the public doesn't know about." Fuck Hilliard. "Coverups. You'll have the exclusive story."

"Excuse me," the Mystery Tramp said in her sultry voice, and Trask turned, annoyed. She was looking at Flynn, who hadn't moved or raised so much as an eyebrow since he burst into the man's office. She held a dainty fist to her ear in the sign for telephone call. "I didn't want to buzz you. It's that call you'd been waiting for."

"Right," Flynn said. "I'm sorry, Vic," he added politely, "I've got to take this. Could you just wait—excuse me for a couple minutes—I'll, uh . . . just give me two minutes, could you?"

"Sure." Trask went outside and sat in one of the expensive chairs Flynn's "Inside America" guests often waited in. They used Jerri Laymon's office for a kind of "green room" when there was more than a single guest to appear on the show. The chairs were better than what he had in his apartment. He waited for four or five minutes, getting antsy, wondering if VIP Sales would get on his case for parking downstairs. Fuck Sales, he decided. Finally the Mystery Tramp's phone buzzed.

"Okay," she said, "you can go back in."

"Thank you," he said, going back into the office.

"Sorry about that. Now . . ." Flynn sorted through a pile of notes on his desk. "Here's the deal. I commend you. You get an A for effort, but the problem is—I don't know what you've been doing lately, or how you got on this serial-killer deal, or what went down between you and the cops, but they got a call downstairs from the police. They, in turn, talked to Chase, myself, and Adam David. The investigation is off-limits 'till further notice,' so far as media is concerned. We've promised not to touch it. There was also some concern that you were probing a racial angle that the cops thought could be inflammatory in the community, potentially, and a lot of other stuff about you having overstepped your bounds as a reporter."

"That's bullshit. I did my homework, which is more than the fucking cops did."

"I don't dispute that, Vic. I'm certain you have. But, you know, our hands are tied. You blew it, man. You should have come to me and let me—or Babaloo—or even Adam—work with you to develop a lead and go on the air with it. If you'd done that, we could have put it on the radio first, and if they'd insisted further mentions be deleted, we'd have been forced to comply, naturally. But we'd have had it on. This way, what might have been a scoop—I'm saying, assuming this stuff you've dug up has some basis in fact—would at least have found its way to the air. Now KCM is out of the ballgame. By your playing The Lone Ranger, you see what you've done? You've effectively managed to put a gag order on the people who are paying your salary." Trask was hearing it and not believing it.

"I don't even know how to respond to that. I just saw a fucking murder. I'm sick. I've been working around the clock on all these violence theme shows. I've got a ton of solid research that will win you a fucking Peabody, man, it's so strong—everything tied together with hard facts and interview subjects. Solid gold stuff, Sean. And we've got an eyewitness beat on the worst serial homicide case in Kansas City's history and you're telling me we can't use it?"

"That's it. You've screwed yourself, Vic. You should have done this with the team. You know how we work by the numbers. If it isn't a team effort, it isn't us. That's what you've always done in the past. Why—when you had what might have been a hellacious beat—would you jeopardize all that and go it alone? What was the point?"

"I knew you weren't that happy with what I was producing for you. I had the insight on this great violence piece and everything I turned up fit the conclusions I had reached. I was seeing my stuff get lifted by other staff members."

"You mean Barb—that one fucking story? It was a coincidence, baby. You just got paranoid is all." Flynn's smile was infuriating.

"I may be paranoid, man, but she had every goddamn piece of a story that I'd researched, and it was too many coincidences. I knew damn well she had tapped my phone somehow."

"You've been working too hard or your cold is getting to your head. I mean it. You're just not thinking clearly. Why the hell would Rose tap your phone? Like she doesn't have enough to do with her own assignments? Is your stuff that much hotter than hers? Come on."

"She wouldn't have to tap my phone. Everybody knows —since day one—this place is bugged. I've heard there are mikes in the offices and shit . . ." He was tired and ill. At this point he just wanted to go home and sleep for two weeks. "I've had engineers tell me that stuff is videotaped, and the phone calls are monitored down in Security. I've always heard that shit."

"Um, Vic . . . you really believe that? You think I'd work in a place where they tapped their employees' phone lines? Jesus."

"You might not know about it," Trask verbally shrugged in a lame voice. He sneezed and coughed.

"Get Bill Higgins for me," Flynn said into the telephone. "Thanks."

Trask looked down at his shoes. He was really fucking up. The whole thing was becoming too much for him. The buzzing phone sounded like a snake striking. He felt watery inside.

"Hi. Thanks. Yeah—are you real busy at the moment? I want to reassure one of my people—a valued employee who thinks his phone may have been tapped or his office bugged.

Could we have some of your time? I appreciate it. Yeah. If you could."

"He's coming up. Just forget all that stuff about Barb, man. She's not out to get you."

"Everybody always said, you know, she and Babaloo . . ." He let it go. This thing was lost.

"Babaloo is old enough to be her father, for one thing. They're friends. They go way back—from Memphis— they've been a team for a long time. I can assure you they don't have anything going. Not like you're inferring. Vic— what can I tell you?"

There was a brief period when no one spoke. Trask could hear music, talk, ringing phones, faraway conversations, the Mystery Tramp typing. "Hi," he heard.

"Hello." Inspector Higgins of the Yard. Another mustached, receding hairline type. "Hi."

"Hi."

"Bill—Vic has concerns. He feels a phone call may have been bugged. Maybe a mike in his office. He worries about rumors he's heard about KCM having a policy involving the monitoring of conversations—things like that. I thought perhaps you'd set his mind to rest."

"Sure. Do my best." Higgins had such a warm, trustworthy smile. They hadn't exchanged fifteen words in all the time Trask had been with the station, but he instantly liked and trusted the man—suddenly. Perhaps because he seemed so open.

"It's bullshit, I guess," Trask said. Defeated. "I've always heard that—you know—there were hidden mikes."

"Not bullshit at all," Higgins said. "When I came here there were units in all the office intercoms. The general manager back in the old days—I don't have to tell you— had a penchant for eavesdropping. He had it fixed so that all the office intercoms doubled as microphones. In theory, they were always on, and all he had to do was flip a selector switch and he could listen to any office from downstairs. We had all those mikes removed."

"Everybody said—you've heard, I'm sure—that you guys tape everything with the camcorders and stuff . . ." He was no longer even bothering to form complete sentences so incoherent were his thoughts.

"The camcorders are for your protection. Programs such as Sean's are often controversial or provocative in nature and—even the newscasts—will sometimes be capable of generating a degree of anger in the listener. You know, I'm sure, about the dangerous lunatic fringe of any large audience, be it radio or television or whatever. This is why stations like KCM have to have security staffs. We're not watching you, we're trying to keep you safe. I'd be glad to take you down right now and show you how we operate." All of this in the friendliest, most open manner.

It ended up that Trask, Flynn, and Higgins had to troop downstairs en masse and take the fifty-cent guided tour of Internal Security. Somehow Trask made it through the rest of the afternoon and early evening without collapsing, even if half his time was spent on the throne in the men's potty. By nightfall, he was home—violently ill—and within twelve hours he was getting flu shots, albeit too late. Mercifully, he was dead to the world and missed the next couple of editions of the local papers and the various electronic media newscasts. The news would have only made him sicker as he'd have had to watch others slide the pieces of his jigsaw together for him.

22

Shooter Price, SAVANT in his arms, had managed to escape unscathed. It filled him with self-confidence, to have so easily evaded an attack by an adversary as cunning and deadly as Chaingang. Those fucking shitheels had used his own tracker to locate him. But he had fooled them! He was alive and well, with his incredible weapon and plenty of rounds for her hungry maw, and he would show all of them what payback meant—starting with that fucking hippo.

Back in Illinois, Dr. Norman did not think of Daniel as a hippo so much as a huge, angry bear. He shuddered as he read of the killings, and of the attempt to get their sniper. Like maddened polar bears who have invaded the same huge ice flow, they were now circling each other in the dance of death. One, armed with a sniper weapon without equal, the other with presentience to warn him of danger; each seemingly invulnerable to attack from the other. But Norman knew, as he read the account, precisely what the outcome would be. He knew that there was no living human who could go up against Daniel and live. And he understood the prison wisdom that stated "Chaingang has nothing but his hatred." He was sure that the knowledge of the implant had only amplified that, if anything.

Bunkowski, the man, was precisely the reverse of Danny, the little boy. In Chaingang's world, he rules and you are the victim. The cons always said there were three codes inside: the penal code by which the prison operated, the inmate code by which cons coexisted behind bars, and the survival code. The last code transcended the others, the one that Chaingang practiced as a religion.

In Kansas City, Missouri, it was another day. The dawn had come up gray and wet-looking. Shooter felt tough and privileged. He did a few half-hearted push-ups, but his thoughts were elsewhere. He showered, shaved, and dressed with some care, dressing for success.

Price wore sandwashed bronze linen slacks from Côte d'Ivoire, a metallicized anaconda Western-style belt with verdigris-patina buckle by Mark Cross, and a River Crest Pro Shop pullover in mulled claret. He pulled on pale yellow silk socks from Neimann's, and antique gold, woven ostrich quill skimmers. The sniper as fashion plate. It wouldn't matter. He was going down in the pit, under full camouflage.

Shooter in Missouri and Dr. Norman in Illinois both began their morning with the same news. Neither man happened to turn on their respective television sets. Each read, with divergent reactions, the substantially identical accounts of the previous day's violence. One from local law-enforcement agencies' reports to the various data-collection terminals such as NCIC and VI-CAP. The other from the Kansas City papers.

"Six More Killed in Bloody Massacre" was the headline of the *Star,* and Bobby Price smiled when he read the stories under the subhead "Police Confirm Mass Killer on Rampage."

A lone gunman is believed responsible for six murders and one attempted murder in midtown Kansas City, Thursday, as the spate of bloody homicides continued, pushing the city's violent death record to an all-time high. In what were termed sniper killings, a man that witnesses called huge, over six feet tall, weighing between 350 and 400 pounds, is thought to have taken six more lives using a long-distance rifle of some type. Lieutenant John J. Llewelyn of the Kansas City Homicide Division of the Crimes Against Persons Unit said that he is believed to be using some kind of high-explosive projectiles such as rifle grenades.

Llewelyn confirmed that the killer's weapons and methods appear to match those employed in twenty-nine recent slayings. He's probably got automatic weapons, grenades, and is familiar with various explosives.

Kansas City Homicide has called in a special department of the FBI for assistance with the case, which may or may not be drug-related. The shootings and firebombings that resulted in thirteen dead in an attack on a biker gang's headquarters, and the grisly ritual mutilation and murder of three other bikers at Mount Ely, have lead to speculation that drug dealers may be involved with the slayings. The biker-gang members had a history of drug arrests, both for possession and distribution of drugs like crystal meth.

Fatally wounded Thursday were Mark Berkemper, forty-two, a professor at State Business College; a Jane Doe of approximately twenty-six years of age, Dick Thompson, thirty-three, an advertising consultant with Saveth-Blackman-Grant; E. L. Campbell, twenty-six, a driver for a lawn center; George D. Unwin, fifty-seven, U.S. Army, Ret.; and Phyllis Guthrie, thirty-eight, a clerk employed by the Kansas City Housing Authority. Neither the Kansas City Police nor the FBI would comment further as to any possible connection between these killings and what were called random murders. The deaths brought

to 173 the number of homicides in the city since
January 1.

Price laughed at the crude police composite sketch that
was prominent in both papers. The eyes and mouth were all
wrong. Gangbang was even fatter and uglier than the
drawing. He read the other account in which *he* was
described as a "motorist."

"The so-called Crucifixion Killer," the caption under the
drawing began, "as described by witnesses to a high-speed
car chase that ended in gunplay in midtown Kansas City
Thursday."

After killing at least six more persons with what are
believed to be rifle grenades, the giant-size mass
murderer attempted to shoot another motorist, who
was able to elude him after the killer first tried to ram
his car, then fired at him as he fled on foot.

Shortly after the car chase, the escaping motorist's
car was struck by a truck, in the vicinity of 28th and
The Paseo. At this point, the killer fired approximately fifty rounds from a silenced machine gun, failing to
hit the fleeing motorist. The driver of the truck was
not injured.

Witnesses told police that the huge man, who wore
a dark blue shirt and green trousers, then threw a
grenade into the motorist's empty vehicle, and sped
away in a late-model red car. No one was injured in
either the attempted shooting or subsequent explosion.

Shell casings found in the vicinity may be tied into
the recent biker-gang slayings as well. Detective Sergeant Marlin Morris told reporters the abandoned
car's registration is being checked to determine the
motorist's identity."

If Chaingang wanted to find him, he thought he'd make it
as easy for him as he could. He'd bring the fat piece of shit

out in the open and blow him into a million pieces of rendered lard.

He called a cab and asked to be driven to a car-rental agency. After he'd fixed himself up with a ride, he loaded his best girl and drove to the concealed sniper hide near Hospital Hill Park.

Oddly, he thought, it made him hot to consider how much power he had at this moment, assembling the weapon in his camouflaged gun pit. The cops wanted him, SAUCOG wanted him, fucking Chaingang wanted him, but he was like The Invisible Man—untouchable, unseeable, and all-powerful. What a turn-on! He could do any damned thing his heart desired and get away with it. Who was left to stop him?

"This round is particularly effective against vehicles, buildings, walls, barricades, and other hard targets." He loaded a SHARP-HEX round into the breech.

"Red Rock Match Grade ammunition . . ." His mind went blank. He felt a wave of nausea that came over him and vanished as quickly as it had lapped up against his senses. He peered into the Laco scope.

He saw a youth in a black car, maybe a Trans-Am, gone now behind a truck. A black man wearing a dark jacket; a fellow in work uniform, standing on the bumper of a trailer truck. Another peered under an open hood. He moved to other visions: a couple of people talking on the street; a nurse; the crimson of a sweatshirt on a jogger attracts him like a red flag waved at a bull, and as he focuses he spots a movement near a cement mixer. A man steps out and Price flings him into the air from a mile and a half away. "Way to *get* some!" What was once a man has now become paint, and it drips from the blasted belly of the cement mixer. The exploded man has become a red-and-silver streak. They sound like comic-book superheroes to Shooter: The Exploded Man and The Red and Silver Streak, in this adventure-filled issue of Gangbang Comics!

He loads an antipersonnel round and peers into the 40X scope. A used-car salesman stands with a prospective customer under a row of pennants in front of a dealership. A woman walks to her car flanked by a Safeway bagboy. Shooter lets the crosshairs touch him. Keeps moving. Passes over a maintenance man in shirt and jeans, working beside the roadway.

"I exorcise thee, unclean spirit . . . tremble, O Satan, enemy of the faith, thou foe of mankind who hast brought death to the world." He sees the chocolate-over-beige prefab of an armed forces recruitment center. He sees a uniform and squeezes. He prays for Chaingang to find him now. *"In nomina patris . . ."* His mind wanders.

"The removable accessory vault, located in the butt of the stock, forward of the shoulder recoil pad, is accessed by removal of the butt base plate, and by releasing the serrated latch detent which is housed in the upper edge of the recessed butt chamber. Slide the base plate forward and grasp the lip inside the base plate, pulling the accessory vault down and out."

"That's how I get into your butt," he whispers into the black hole of his own madness.

The implant was all but forgotten for the moment. It was less than a sublevel awareness, excepting those moments when he felt a fleeting tingle of alien discomfort somewhere between the giant roll of fat at the back of his immense neck and the top of his scarred, hard skull. He would take these ones who needed killing step by step: Mr. Price, Mrs. Garbella, Dr. Norman—his sissy *friend.* The concept that Norman would be monitoring his movements on a distant electronic screen could have upset his gyro, and he would not let that happen again. He was doing Dr. Norman's bidding, on his team for the moment, and their immediate goals were not antithetical.

Chaingang knew that he would prevail over the sniper with his miracle gun, all else being equal. But it was vital to act with celerity now, since Shooter Price was obviously far over the edge, and the police were under the impression that he—Daniel—was the sniper. One more preposterously intolerable event in a chain, which he would now begin to break.

There was no real wilderness anymore. Not this close to urban civilization. You could still find rough, raw chunks of empty space, but not true isolation. There was always the chance of running into somebody. It was no longer possible to get back of beyond—vestiges of humanity appeared everywhere. He hated them so, the stupid monkey men on this planet of dumb apes. He loathed their loud noises, happy laughter, and blank faces full of self-assuredness and herd mentality. He longed for the cleansing of isolation.

He had found a momentary pocket of quiet, where he could plan, plot, prepare—soak up the stillness and solitary joy of seclusion. The monkeys were far away.

The building was stone, a small rectangular structure approximately the size of a small tool shed. Solidly made, but for the roofing, which he had easily restored. The railroad spur that had once existed through these woods was long gone and Mother Nature had reclaimed the bed on which the tracks had rested. Thick near-impenetrable woods surrounded him.

There were others in these woods, but he sensed no monkeys at the moment; rather, there were roving packs of dogs, wild mongrels he imagined, coyotes and their cousins, coyotelike hunters, whose signs and conversation he'd seen and heard nearby. Deer. Other small animals. Humanity had been limited to a single light plane flying over the distant treeline. It was perfect for him.

He felt alone and rather safe in his cozy hideaway, and was pleased he'd discovered it without undue exertion. He found such places by logic, processes of education/deduction, luck, vibes, and something transcending intuition but akin to it. These places pulled him.

Neither vehicles nor mantracks touched the surrounding woods near his small stone sanctuary. No hoof or boot prints gathered water in 15EEEEE super-extra-wide heel marks. No sign of human life hung twisting in a bush or tree limb, to place his safety in possible jeopardy.

If you knew where to walk and were extremely cautious, you could go a few hundred meters and find the red Buick sedan registered to the late Eileen Todd's parents. It resided under a car tarp, inside a rotting barn that hadn't been used for anything in many years. The barn was decorated in rusting POSTED NO TRESPASSING and KEEP OUT warning signs. Obviously private property. Again, the structure had been restored by its latest occupant. If you dared you could breach his security system and find the vehicle, camouflaged, hidden inside. But you would have cause to regret such a discovery.

You would have every reason—though probably not the time—to rue the day your woodsy picnic had led you to this ancient shell of a barn.

The vehicle inside had been hidden by someone who had studied demolition the way others study for the bar, or study medicine—a postgrad student with a doctorate in explosives and concealment. Your untimely discovery would transform you, noisily, into a wet shower of unidentifiable red offal.

High explosive, not purchased with his ill-fated auction profits, but recently purloined, is wired to a short-fused frag, but with the ordinary M-26 fuse replaced with a 308-G, the so-called ADD or Anti-Disturbance Device. There were other tremor-sensitive security treats now waiting in these environs, guarding his back door—as it were—from the unlucky meandering monkey.

He has the big map out in front of him, covered in lightly drawn circles. A huge circle surrounds the immediate Kansas City, Missouri, area where Robert "Shooter" Price has chosen to die. The heart of his killing zone has been computed, measured, marked. A series of concentric rings make a pleasantly uniform design as they encircle this heart's edges.

Each of the smaller circles is divided by two lines bisecting each ring's diameter. Each reticulation has the appearance of the crosswires inside a sniperscope. The circular patterns are areas where Price has killed or where he might kill next. Every sector or quadrant of the reticle marks has a grid designation. These grid designations are graded.

Chaingang Bunkowski and Shooter Price once hunted together, at least in theory, as part of the same spike team. Bunkowski recalls the little punk's arrogance. He knows precisely how he will behave now. Without the mobile tracking technology to depend on, he will have no recourse but to try to entrap his enemy. Price will know he cannot hope to find him in a dense population area such as this.

Unless he would have a photograph, or would contact the police and various reporters to correct the poor likeness authorities are using in trying to I.D. him, only his size presents a problem. He does not think Shooter will provide the police or media with such help. He is an arrogant twerp who will think he and his powerful rifle will be enough to accomplish Chaingang's demise. This belief will kill him.

The zones with the best or highest grades of likelihood are now to be analyzed by his mental computer. Chaingang knows old Kansas City, and to a great extent, he has been able to familiarize himself with the new aspects of the town—the tall buildings, the new structures of note, the streets and sprawling population areas that have only existed in recent years.

He was through here during a killing spree some three years prior to his most recent release from prison, and even in that time he sees industrial parks, freeway changes, and large construction projects that were not there before. And always, it seems, the monkey men work on their ridiculous highways.

Diminutive Shooter, for all his misplaced confidence, has a certain degree of experience in these matters. He will know that the moronic cops will be dutifully watching the taller buildings, water towers, overpasses, and similarly obvious vantages. He will be reticent to utilize such areas, except as possible entrapment sites.

On the other hand, Shooter appears to have gone even more gunny-fruit than he was before, perhaps due to an abuse of controlled substances—Chaingang remembers a certain proclivity for pharmaceutical cocaine—or other atrophy of the mental faculties. In news accounts subsequent to the most recent snipings, there is mention of one of his sniper hideouts having been discovered, in an empty office within the Kansas City Convention Center. The actions of a person whose mind has snapped cannot be predicted.

The beast studies his map and open ledger, making notations, figuring probabilities, eliminating locations, refining his plan of attack. The word *Civilization* snakes across his mindscreen and he sees the adjectival root word and its forms, the noun and its variations, and the ironic definitions of the word. It slithers away from him, leaving him with the pleasure of his lonely thoughts of destruction.

Power will come with preparation. He tastes the power-hunger even more than the thirst for Price's spilled blood. In a coil nearby is a yard-length weight of tractor chain. A steel snake waiting to strike, to smash out and demolish, more deadly than any mamba. The chain is inches from his massive killing hand.

Eyes black as midnight, hard pig's eyes, set in a doughy face pale as dawn's light, stare unblinking at the pattern of circles. He tastes the coppery salt of his own mouth's fluids; sharp, misshapen teeth biting through the skin of his lip in fierce and determined concentration. Willing his mind to find the scent of the little faggot shit. Willing his hatred down into the mighty fingers shaped like thick sausages that reach out for the snake and clench it in a strangling vise of a deathgrip. He must get power—raw killing power. Plug into it. Make himself invulnerable in its shielding cloak.

Ice and fire. Bloodlust and the soul of a killing machine in one. Desire to deal death that fills him with heat, but in his monster's heart he is as cold as a shuddering winter chill. Deep inside he lets the rage catch, and the heat propels him out, pushing him toward the monkeys to slake whatever appetites have become inflamed.

23

One of the seminar subjects Lieutenant John Llewelyn had recently attentively studied was "How to RePrioritize for Personal Achievement." It was aimed at the kind of mid-echelon-level exec who found that much of his/her workday was occupied in the pursuit of goals and agendas imposed by superiors whose priorities were inevitably perceived as of greater importance than theirs. It was a valuable subset within a course aimed at busy department heads of metropolitan cop shops, but for the life of him he could not find an application to the dilemma that faced his metro squad, supposedly an elite unit within a major enforcement agency.

At 1125 Locust, there were many priorities, but for Llewelyn only one, and it had just been impaled by a rocket from high above in the brassy stratosphere. The goal had—until some twenty minutes before—been the apprehension of a serial killer.

Now . . . in reality he wasn't sure what the priorities were. Containment? Hardly—with the news of a mass murderer, also a serial killer in the bargain, on every channel and station and front page. Justice? He would have thought so, but twenty minutes ago, in the Homicide Division terminal on-line to D.C., that one had also run screaming into a brick wall.

He had the squad gathered around him, in their conference room, and he looked at the stack of reports in front of him.

"A dozen grenade kills. Thirteen in the shooting and firebombing. Three crucified, mutilated. Six more grenade kills with the long-range weapon. An attempt. A random kill—it looks like. Then Mr. Embry, in back of the parts department at Bonnarella's. Captain Jones, a twenty-nine-year-old guy just back from duty in Kuwait for crissakes. Rick Moore, a kid on the County Road Crew. Miss O'Connell—student. Mr. Beltronena, a forty-four-year-old pastry chef. The goddamn rifle grenades. Here. All in this area—" He pointed to a map sector with a horizontal line in yellow Hi-Liter reaching from the first to the last of the most recent homicides.

"This big son of a bitch is right under our noses here. This is the second fucking time—he's operating within twenty to thirty blocks of *headquarters*. He's rubbing our noses in it! I think he's trying to make us look like incompetent idiots— this asshole. Why doesn't anybody ever see him? He's big as a goddamn house."

"He gets into his positions at night," Shremp said. "That's the only way he could move around without anybody spotting him."

"So what are we supposed to do?" Hilliard asked. "Put every cop in the city on all-night watch looking for big fat guys with large gun cases?"

"Sure. If we had the manpower, that might be a start," Llewelyn said. "But we don't have the legs. So we'll all work a night tour within forty blocks. Everybody's in the same barrel on this one till he's stopped. We'll divide the city up and watch as much of each section as we can. Looking for big fat guys—or anybody who looks suspicious—and, of course, we can forget the low-lying areas. He needs elevation to use this thing—he can shoot a mile and three quarters and hit you with it, by the way. Let's keep that in mind, too. We all got radios. We'll check in constantly. Sixteen hours out of every twenty-four until we nail him. T.J.— you work something up. Couple hours on, couple off—six on, couple off—that type of staggered schedule. We'll all work a full double shift. Anybody got problems with this?"

"Hell, no," Hilliard said. "We gotta get this bastard."

"What about the bounceback?" Morris asked. He meant on the prints.

"Latent gave us a match-up from The Paseo thing. Shell case—real good partial. Kicked it around through all the usual channels—I get red-flagged." Llewelyn looked down at a piece of printout and licked his lips. Picked it up as if it were on fire and handed it to Morris. "Check that out, Marlin. Ever see that before?"

"Deleted? What the hell does *that* mean?"

"There it is."

"For what?"

"You tell me, ace. First time I ever ran into that one. I called around, screamed and yelled upstairs. They got on the horn for me and nobody knows jack flash, okay? The killer's I.D.—which somebody, the feds or whoever, has on file, was deleted. Ain't that a beaut?"

"I don't get it," Apodaca said.

"That's right," the lieutenant said.

"Has to be a computer error," Hilliard said.

Llewelyn kept silent.

Trask woke up on the outside of a dream envelope, the memory of the mental excursion already fading, something about calling his daughter, and Kit telling him everything he already knew, that he hadn't been worth a damned dime as a dad—things like that. It was the phone.

"Yes?" he said through cotton.

"Vic, I'm very sorry to disturb you but—uh, we've got

a bit of a situation down here at the station. Would you be too ill to come in for a few minutes?" It was Metzger. "We need to talk." This last in Babaloo's sucky voice that he reserved for ultimatums and such. It gave Trask a chill for a second.

"Sure. Absolutely."

"I hate to ask, man. I know you're under the weather. But, you know, if you can . . ."

"Hey, no problem. What's it about, Babaloo? Can you give me a clue?"

"Huh-uh. Probably better talk in person. An hour be enough time? Two hours?"

"I can be there in an hour. Sure. I'll see you."

"Thanks, Vic. I won't keep you long." Yeah, Trask thought. He was sure of that.

He went into the bathroom, relieved himself, tried to clean up a bit, was too shaky to shave, and finally just said fuck it and pulled some clothes on.

The drive to KCM was a nightmare, because he happened to catch a half-hourly newscast. The serial-murder thing had busted wide open without him, and—so it seemed—was not race-related. There'd been a couple more random rifle grenade kills—as the radio story termed them—long-distance homicides in Penn Valley Park.

He started to wonder whether it might be something they were planning to do on the show. But he instantly realized Metzger would have handled that on the telephone and told him to bring his research in with him. They'd never so much as asked about the piles of shows he'd prepared on the theme of violence—the fact that he'd screwed up this one thing had been sufficient to put his ass in the doghouse forever. He sneezed and it felt as if his head might come off. How could everything be so groovy one minute and so grunty the next?

He paid for parking and schlepped to the station. He knew it was bad before he got off the elevator. As the doors opened, he saw Adam David's face. David happened to be looking in his direction and he saw the news director's grimace of anger and distaste as he quickly looked away.

He turned the corner by the music studio and felt the oppressive vibes hit him like a wall of bad news. The first person he saw was Jerri, typing something at her desk.

"Morning," he said, entering. She jumped as if she'd been shot.

"Oh! You scared me."

"Sorry. I have that effect sometimes," he said, while she smiled with that look one reserves for relatives of the departed. "The man in?" He leaned his head a fraction of an inch toward Sean's office.

"Hm-um. He's over at Five. They're taping something—a panel or some show—I dunno."

"That's okay. You wouldn't have an aspirin or something, would you?" She didn't but made a big production out of finding him some and bringing them to him. He thanked her and took them without looking, not caring if they were cyanide or what. She'd even brought him a little cup of water.

"Thanks," he said. Trying to recall the name of the Dylan tune about the Mystery Tramp.

"Sure!" she said, overly solicitous. He knew he'd been fuckin' cut off at the knees right then and there. Flynn gone—as he always was when there was a dirty job to be done—Babaloo's forte.

He gritted his teeth and headed around the bend. His office door was closed, as was Barb Rose's. Nobody home. Metzger looked up with a small, tainted smile, which was even gloomier than his usual expression of dour cynicism.

"Oy vey! What a thing to do to a guy when he's got the flu—" Metzger began, with a cloying civility that made Trask want to become ill on the desk.

"No big deal. What's cookin'?"

"I'm sorry, Vic. We gotta let you go." He shook his head several times as if this were the worst news he'd had to convey in his entire broadcasting and journalistic career. "It's out of my hands completely."

"You mean because I fucked up on one goddamn story?"

"Hear me, now. You could be in a great deal of trouble if it wasn't for the fact that you had some people here who were fond of you. I know you have had some problems on the job. But—wow! Two problems with the police in a matter of days—we have no choice. You know some little dweeb of a board man over at the Z—Doug Reid?"

"Yeah." Trask felt needles stick him in the kidneys. "Buzz Reid?"

"Vice-squad guy was by pure luck tight with Chase or you might be sitting in jail right now trying to line up a bail bondsman." Chase? Trask's mind wasn't working. He tried to swallow. His throat was raw. Metzger watched him try to breathe. "This cop calls Kincaid and says, 'Hey, I came on a conversation with one of the KCM employees talking to this little pimp I'm busting about a plot to burgle the radio station.'"

"Aw, bullshit, man—it wasn't like that at all. I just—"

"He apparently overheard somebody who works at the station, thinks his office and phone are bugged, asking all this crap about how to break into Security?" He said it incredulously. "How to do illegal wiretaps? I mean, Chase said he couldn't believe it when he listened to the tape. You—"

"But I was right, wasn't I? You guys were taping me?" He was in a fog. His mind had become Gouda cheese. He couldn't even mix a metaphor.

"You're still missing the point. We weren't taping you— some vice-squad guy was taping the other guy. He was pimping his wife out of their home or whatever. You just got nailed on it. The point being—have you any idea what would have happened if the vice dude had gone to Higgins with this? You'd be locked up now, Vic. You're one lucky guy."

"Okay," he said in a quiet voice. "I just wanted to know—"

"Don't even bother, man. It doesn't matter that you weren't really going to try any of this stuff. Or even if you were just doing a piece of research, which, by the way, is what Chase told his buddy. You were just researching 'Intrusions of Privacy'—so stick to that. Anyway, the point being—you've lost your judgment and your professionalism. We just can't have it.

"Kincaid had to tell New York about the two incidents and they said you're gone. That's it." Metzger got an envelope out of his desk and handed it over. Trask felt ill, sloppy, blank, and embarrassed, all at once—if that were possible. There was some panic as he peered inside and saw an absence of many numerals.

"What's this?" Trask snarled ungratefully.

"That's your severance pay and I had to argue with them downstairs to get you that," Metzger explained. Trask just nodded. "I need your keys. I'm to tell you that you're *persona non grata* at KCM. If you show up after this—and you're to take your stuff, which we have all in one box in your office—you'll be reported to the police immediately. I'm sorry, man, but they are *not amused*. I'm sure you'll be pissed off, but all I can say is—count your blessings. As bad as this ending is, considering your lack of judgment, it could have been much worse."

"Okay." They stood up and Babaloo offered his hand. Trask shook it and walked out. Took his key off his ring and came back and put it on the desk and left again. Went in his office. Got the box. Walked down the long chilly corridor to the elevator, not seeing anybody.

The last face he saw was the gorgeous puss of Monica Heartbreak, just as the doors slid closed.

Metzger was right, he supposed. It could have been worse. They'd never learned that he'd bugged the office of a Homicide guy. Wouldn't that be fun—say the lieutenant would find a hidden microphone among the volumes in his bookcase. Trask could imagine him talking about it to other detectives, and the vice guy adds two and two. It could keep on snowballing. Maybe the cops would decide he was the mass murderer. What a fucking *nightmare!*

Yet, as Metzger had said, it could have been worse. Think of the bright side: they'd never learned about that time he'd parked in VIP Sales Parking. Also . . . he was still clean on the Lindbergh kidnapping case.

24

The hillside shooter, driving a rental, is loaded for bear. Polar. A nice fat polar. That fucking uncouth, stinking slob of a heavyweight, heart-gobbling, carnivorous, ursine motherfucker who was contaminating Price's ice—he had something for that big boy. A big, grave-digging antivehicle dumdum with Gangbang's name on it. After all, they were tank killers, right? And Bigfoot—shit, if he wasn't about as big as a tank. Gonna blow his fat mountain of blubbery lard to the sky.

A young girl walked by and Shooter opened his car door, winking at her. He carried his impotence around like a challenge, now, flashing it in the direction of every attractive woman he saw, metaphorically opening his trench coat and showing them his big gun.

She was right behind him. Screwed together and locked tight as young snatch. *"To eliminate parallax . . . loosen her forward end . . . insert . . . into female aperture L5 . . . move the head in slight increments . . ."* She waited in the back seat, waited for him to take her from beneath the covers.

"Hi."

"Howyadoon." A college-age boy. Shooter glanced around. He liked this hillside.

"SAVANT accessories include case cover, ammunition case, shooting gloves, entrenching and hide-excavation tools. Hole-digger, awl, spade, posthole tool, shovel, axe, pick, hatchet, lopper, saw, hammer, nails, wire pliers/grips, lumber, metal supports, sandbag, net, tarp with grommets, canvas sheet, paint, brushes, ladder, drainage tubing, auger, detection monitor, synced auto-pager, radio transceiver, auto-destruct . . ."

He was crazy as a fucking loon and he'd switched himself to auto-destruct.

"Hi," he said, friendly as hell. More passing trim.

"Hi." She smiled, and her pretty mouth made a phony curve. He would wipe that shit right off her face, he decided. Teach you to smile at me. This lady is a jealous bitch, he whispered to no one, reaching under the canvas cover for the weapon.

The second he touched her, that was all it took. He was instantly hot.

The smiling phony's back might as well have had a bull's-eye painted on it.

The master's touch. He glances around carefully—not that he really cares who sees him—out of long professional habit. He is alone with his lady and a primary target. He wonders if he should see if he could just graze the skull with that antivehicle round in his lady. Mercy!

Touch her. Feel her skin. Slick and hard. Smooth and where one's hand curves she curves, a tough familiar coolness that will grow warm with the pressure of flesh.

Rest the cheek just so. There is no doubt of her sexuality when one's face is pressed so close. She reeks of animal lust and controlled power. The cheek and jaw mold to her, and there is the pleasurable familiarity present with any pair of old lovers. Everything fits perfectly and feels so right to the touch.

She is without morals. She makes no judgments. Renders

no decisions. Casts no jaundiced eye. She takes all comers without preconception, partiality, bigotry, bias, or subjective discrimination. She is, after all, the ultimate kind of whore. What she gives she offers to all equally. Her dark hole is always open.

Yet, conversely, the bitch is capable of the harshest, most deleterious, incapacitating, and destructive urges. She will lash out with incredible hostility, striking with nothing less than the most extreme prejudice.

He huddles close, warming her. Touching her in the most intimate ways.

Her unblinking gaze is stern and sharp. He sees as she sees, and her vision—as with everything else about her—is perfect. Nothing escapes her sight.

There is a special place underneath her where she begs to be touched. He cups her smoothness, the fingers resting near the spot that sets her loose. He does not trifle with her as she brooks no capriciousness or teasing. If his desires are genuine, however, she will know, and sensing his sincerity all it will take is a gentle, even pressure.

Without preamble she will explode at the touch, and she gets off with a bang. There is no feeling of raw power quite like it: the rush one feels as a mighty shudder blasts through her long, sleek body. The master's pleasing caress sets the beautiful bitch loose once again.

In the rearview mirror of the Buick, Daniel Edward Flowers Bunkowski sees the bleached hair of a former identity almost gone. He is on a sidestreet now, and turns down an unpaved access road beneath a hill. Just the sort of place that Shooter would enjoy killing from.

He slows. A movement or a sense of something makes him turn and he sees nothing, but the moment of intuitive feeling does not go ignored. He stops. Kills the engine. Freezes like stone; patient.

He began at the easternmost edge of the concentric circles of shooting sites, working his way to the west, basically, from Lee's Summit, various historic homes, centers, parks, landmarks, north to Sugar Creek, south to the freeway, angling back parallel to the Big Blue feature, and back south to the Sports Complex, circling the stadiums but never getting the vibes, heading west now on sidestreets abutting the Interstate, moving past Wabash . . . Euclid . . . Tracy . . . near the heart of the punk's comfort zone. At the corner of his vision, he'd seen something, felt a hidden presence, and it had drawn him to this unpaved road.

Finally a quail jumps, flying across the road in front of the Buick, but Chaingang's paranoia is not totally appeased. The flapping of wings and subsequent lack of vibes only infuriates him. After a long delay, he starts the engine again and slowly drives off.

Reaching the Big Blue wet feature, he parks. Gets out. A large "salami" wrapped in butcher paper is cradled in his arms. He sees a desolate river rat shack and is drawn to it. There is no sign of any presence but the heart-eater waits patiently, listening with his mind, and a watcher could not possibly hope to understand why he wastes time on a lonely unpaved access road, or near a rotting shack at the edge of the river.

He buys unleaded for the gas-guzzler. As he pays, the back of a dollar bill nudges him with its pyramid graphic art. "Eye in the sky." A taunting thing he pushes back for now.

Chaingang knows many things, Dr. Norman: ontology, cosmology, epistemology, *trigger*nometry. He carries his killer salami back to the car and a quarter ton of monster lurches down on the springs; he grinds it to life and eases back out in the world of monkeys.

Passes low lifes. Urban rot. Doorway winos twitching in the throes of the jittery jim-jams from Sterno and muscatel and subripples of wet Missouri skid-row dreams. Pig eyes watch as a black whore moves her arm in play despair and a clinky jingle of *bijoux* can be heard from the trinkets she wears. Two hours before sunset and the Kansas City sky is like looking at sunlight through the bottom of a lithophane beer mug. He smells faraway rain.

The huge beast keeps driving the quadrants. Waiting for

his unique sensory banks to hum, excited by the proprioceptive stimuli that make him sui generis. Moves back along the blue—drawn to it himself, truth be known. It is here he would set up if their roles had been reversed. Here is where he would feel most comfortable performing those SAUCOG-otomies with surgical precision.

Bunkowski's bibliomania has taught him many things, Dr. Norman—and as his weird mind scans for traces of a dangerous presence, he sees that a more appropriate analogy for the overcast sky would be Meissen bisque porcelain. That in turns makes him think of Elaine Roach and he visualizes her identifying him to a chief postal inspector, but intenerates his reaction to this treachery. He cannot help but think of the poor lady fondly. Certainly, she is as out of place on the planet of the monkey men as is he. He should have removed her from mortal coil. He sees himself leaving a trace at Mr. Hy's in Crown Plaza, recalls a moment when he burnt in an image, how that description will lead to a Mr. Cunningham who advertised for help at the Hyatt Regency, and, of course, to Tommy Norville of the Norville Galleries on East Minnesota Avenue.

With a start, he jerks his mind to matters at hand. An old woman, staring at him boldly from a street corner, looks—just for a half second—like *Mrs. Garbella*. Daniel is quite disappointed. He will find her in due time and extract an appropriate measure of her life force.

Back on another access road. Another knoll overlooking miles of monkey targets. Macroscopic floating vegetation weaves slimy green pleustonic mats across the surface of the water. A happy little goldfinch flutters across the road. Anything that is alive, he will sense it.

He looks up and sees, on a utility pole, a huge nest—probably built by sparrows but as big as two squirrel's nests placed end to end. Nearby a cluster of white gourds, bleached by the sun, hang from a pole. The holes are hotel rooms into which mocking birds, indigos, and others he cannot identify check in and out. He sees sign—animal and human sign—even from the moving car. The vibes are still.

If you see him perhaps you will have sensed him before—if only momentarily. When he lumbers into view, if he is on shank's mare, you will recoil as you're caught in a stinking downdraft of raw body odors and unspeakable vileness. If he is in a vehicle and catches your eye, look away. The heart-eater hungers for a kill.

In the front seat of the stolen car is a map decorated in circles. But Chaingang heeds neither azimuth nor monitor. He has slipped beyond graded rings or grids of probability. He is somewhere east of Oceanus Aethiopicus, south of Septentrio, north of Lis Incognita, on a heading west, his back and shoulder to the Mar del Norte.

Distance is no longer measured in miles but by bathymetry. He is a shark swimming in lazy dangerous circles, drawn by the smell of blood in the water as he goes down deeper into the land of the lost.

25

Trask supposed that it was pointless to continue working on the notes about American violence, considering that he had no outlet for the research. But at this juncture it was as much momentum as anything that had kept him working on the story—if indeed it was a story. He was too logy to begin looking for another job yet, and he couldn't sit around watching television, so immersing himself in the homicides was a harmless obsession, he felt. He was razoring clippings and assembling his voluminous notes chronologically when a knock surprised him.

"Hey," he said through the opening in the door, astonished to see the attractive face of Barb Rose, of all people.

"Hi. Any chance I could talk to you for a second?"

"Yeah. Come on in." Why the hell not? He opened the door wide and ushered her in.

"Thanks. Feeling about the same?"

"Pretty much. I'm a little better. I don't get many colds or flu bugs but when I do . . . they take forever to shake. Have a seat." He pointed to the only available place besides his own chair where he was working, and was suddenly conscious of all the clippings and work-ups adorning his apartment walls. No reason to hide them now, he supposed.

"I'm not going to stay, hon. I just—" She held out a small bag. "Brought you something for your cold. Go ahead and have some while it's still warm."

"Thanks." He almost said—jokingly—what is it, a cup of hemlock? But he sat it on the little bar between the kitchen and living area and took the lid off the container. "Ahh! Smells good." Yellow thick broth of some kind.

"Chicken soup," she said, with a smile. "Fix you right up. I thought you might need some." She was rather self-conscious all of a sudden, and moved toward the door. "I'm going, Vic. I just wanted to tell you I heard about you leaving and stuff and wanted to say goodbye."

"Come on. Stay for a little while. Sit. If you don't mind the mess—and aren't afraid I'll give you whatever I've got. I'd appreciate the company." He meant it, surprising himself as he said it. Every time he was able to think clearly, he could see more and more what a total horse's ass he'd been. He thought he'd been particularly shitty about Barb.

"Okay. But just for a minute." She sat on the edge of the sofa. "I'll stay to make sure you eat that." She laughed warmly.

"Right." He got a spoon and tried some. "Umm. That's very good."

"We Jews are great believers in the healing properties of some good hot *chick*'n soup!" She gave the word a comedic emphasis. Trask took a few more spoonfuls. Tried not to slurp, but it was difficult.

"This stuff is delicious." The more soup he ate the better Barb Rose looked to him. "I gotta say something to you before you leave. And not just because you brought me *chick*'n soup. I've been a real asshole. Toward you."

"You're right. What can I say?" She had a beautiful smile.

"Don't cover up your feelings like that, Barb. You gotta learn to say what you really think." They both laughed. "But I know I have. I can't explain it. I . . ."

"That's the past. Forget it. I wasn't always such an easy person to work with. We're a lot alike. Very competitive."

"Yeah. That's for sure. I haven't been thinking clearly . . .

about a lot of things, of which—of whom—you were one. Anyway—hope you'll accept my apology."

"Not necessary. I thought you got a real bum deal at the station, by the way. Not that my opinion is worth anything. I suppose you know I'm leaving?"

"No. Leaving KCM?"

"Yep. Gave my notice a few days ago."

"I hadn't heard. May I ask where you're going?"

"New York."

"New York?"

"CNBC."

"All *right!* Congratulations. That's great."

"I'm pretty excited."

"You should be." He was happy for her. "That's wonderful, Barb. I'm jealous. How the hell did you get that—not that you're not good at what you do—but wow! New York!"

"It was weird. A guy we worked with in Memphis went out to the Coast. His specialty is business and entertainment news. And CNBC just hired him to create a new department and he called me."

"That's terrific. I'll bet Babaloo is grief-stricken!"

"Babaloo is Babaloo. He had the gig filled by the time I was out of his office. Ditto with yours. He knows a million young writers and broadcasters just crying to crack a market like Kansas City, so it's pretty easy. Even with the crappy money KCM pays." She gestured around the apartment. "I like your wallpaper. Who's your decorator—the *Kansas City Star?*"

"Yeah." He laughed. "I'm still wound up on this story and I can't stop. I don't have anywhere to go with it but—what the hell. Gives me something to do besides worry about what to put on my résumés."

She nodded. Got up from the sofa and eyed her watch. "Gotta run, kid. Let me know when you land somewhere. Okay?"

"Sure. I don't—I haven't even begun to think about a gig. But I can always get a thing reading news at a little station somewhere. You know—just to put beans on the table. I may not be in too big a hurry to relocate. I've been wanting to write for a long time—and I might try that while I've got the free time."

"Let's keep in touch," she said.

"I'd like that. Really." He moved around the counter and reached out to give her a friendly pat. She leaned in to the side of his cheek, making him wish that he'd shaved.

"I won't give you a real kiss because I don't want the flu," she said, smacking air. "But—bye, hon. Take care and get well."

"Don't be surprised if you get a phone call from me one day. Okay?"

"Okay," she said. He opened the door for her and she went out. "Have fun," she added, in the old-time radio lingo for goodbye.

"Likewise." He'd never really let himself think about how well-built this woman was. Barbra Rozitsky was a looker. He felt better than he'd felt in a week. *"Kill* 'em in the Big Apple," he said to her departing back, and she smiled and waved.

He closed the door and finished his soup. Then he looked up a telephone number in the Rolodex on his desk, and pressed the buttons on his phone. After a few moments, a man's voice said hello.

"Hello. May I speak to Kit please?"

"May I tell her who's calling?"

"Her father," he said.

26

Death is alone. An impossible monster. A hybrid killer with a core as inhuman and beastly as can be conceived. Like an inexplicable strain of pathogenic bacteria, the core continues to evolve almost independent of the host being.

Death's thoughts are of food—burritos at the moment. But on other levels, its dark, poisonous, ectogenous malignancy continues to feed on information and remembered pain and pleasure, changing, growing, spreading within the vast host body. As it feeds and evolves it strengthens.

Death feels the changes and vibrates with the power. Hums with the virulent malignity that makes it stronger, more noxious and fatally toxic, more impervious to antidote.

Beneath the part that hungers for beef and cheese burritos by the bagful, visceromotor-nerve response quickens, sensations heighten, systems accelerate as they electrify and zap the phrenic controls.

Beneath the surface of the beast, there are the tiny paroxysms of microelemental transmutation that Dr. Norman would have given his eyeteeth to understand. With each quivering electrocharge there occurs down inside the core another subtle transformation.

Beneath the skin of the monstrous anomaly that the doctor persists in calling a physical precognate, the godless and godforsaken macrogrossness mutates. Modifies. Powertrips. Nurtures.

The mutating giant was born for the stalk. Its repulsive goals are abhorrently simple: vengeance and annihilation.

On its back, inert, it thinks of burritos, and of death-dealing. Its pleasant daydreams are of those upon whom he'll feed. The other food—that is a mundane biological need that intrudes on his deeper motives.

A massive mound of man sprawled on a filthy camouflage tarp, he turns the pages of *Utility Escapes,* seeing the name of the cruel stable owner, the daughter of a man who performs certain lab experiments, the father of the boys who killed the animals in the petting zoo, the man who joked of bleeding hearts, the buyer, the clown who keeps creatures in his trailer, the freaks he will ultimately find and dissect.

Look inside the wrinkled obscenity that is his mind: you will see a landscape so alien that it will shock you. What do you recall from the age of seven? Think back. Memories of Daddy? Begrimed in oily dirt, toiling in the garage, as you watch from the safe haven of Mommy's lap? Remember your sixth year? Watching Aunt and beloved Granny planting hollyhocks, Grandmother amid the larkspur? Can you conjure up a vague remembrance of age five? Perhaps you were alone in your crib and you made a noise with your mouth. Mommy and Daddy rush in to confront the early whistler. "It's baby!" Mother says. "He whistled!"

Look inside at the beast's first memory: darkness. Warm, soft, liquid darkness. Heat. Critical mass. Pain. An explosive force. Jarring shock. Sudden light. Dazzling, shattering, soul-rending brightness.

What can you ever hope to understand about such a being? From his first memory there is only pain.

He recalls the roar of madness and noise, the inundation of horror, the whiplash of overpowering reality, and he remembers being torn, thrust from his mother into the blazing world, ripped from a dark and warm womb of a screaming woman.

He remembers soaring aloft in the inescapable clutches of a powerful giant who holds him like a dragon, in long slimy claws, soaring into the blinding sky in a sudden nightmare of birthing cataclysm. Pictures the red deluge. The violent, concussive beginning in bright light as he was wrenched from the hot current of his mother's blood.

He can go back to the beginning but he chooses not to do so. *Superior Court of Kansas . . . in the matter of setting aside the adoption of Daniel . . .* vague fuzz of details blur. Mommy—dead at birth? An adoption that fails to take. A foster mother who says the baby must be *disciplined.* The word inches across his mindscreen as he gazes, unseeing, at the pages of his Bible.

Around the word *disciplined* the edges are seared, blackened, where the child was subjected to the intense heat of a stove burner, cigarettes, matches, lighters, soldering iron— oh, the list is long and memorable.

And those are his good memories. He has had enough of this. He has mutated to the power edge. Chaingang is up and moving to the Buick, which he has come to rather appreciate, now that he's made his peace with the seat controls. It is close enough to the hotsheets to make him continually wary, but when he first went back and moved his Olds from the parking lot of the mall, he affixed homemade plates to the Buick, which effectively protect it from the casual "wants and warrants" DMV check, or from the zealous officer or trooper who matches it to a recent sheet.

The assembly of a fake tag is remarkably simple—child's play, in fact, so long as you have the regional prefix key codes, which are changed each license-renewal period. Once the codes are known, fabrication of a plate is a few minutes handiwork. The easiest way to buy a couple of days' time with a spurious tag is to find a matching model in the area in which you wish to operate, fake their tag, and replace their plates with the fakes, putting theirs on your vehicle. And

Chaingang knew a hundred more sophisticated variations on that theme.

But for all of that, he was sure that within twenty-four hours he'd be in another ride. The thing that watched over him kept him, in most instances, from taking imprudent chances.

The Buick cruises on a jagged northeast course, the Missouri River to the north, the Kansas City Stockyards a distant stench to the northwest.

Madison.
Belleview. H 11.
Tarkio. H 12.
Holly
Mersington. H 13.
Overpass.
Viaduct.

Hard eyes scan the rooftop vantage points. He sees a complex of industrial buildings that tug at him. At such times he is wide open to the inner clockwork that ticks within the nervous system, and he stops the car. Pulls his poundage from behind the wheel with a grunt of effort and scans.

The rooftops would be ideal for a sniper. A weapon with an effective range of two miles could smash down monkey men from Kansas to Missouri in an arc of gunfire. His face beams at the pleasant contemplation of an unimpeded, wide swath of death cutting down the monkeys.

He sees a beauty parlor—talk about bizarre misnomers, a dog kennel from the sound of the barking, an arts 'n' crafts store which appears to be closed. No sense of danger, but he is tugged forward and goes with it, moving closer.

There must be fifty or sixty dogs barking. Yet he sees no kennel signs.

Chaingang walks around the building. Sees what appears to be a private residential entrance to the building. It is a small, stale-smelling entranceway. There are wooden stairs. The loud barking of dogs is coming from behind the door to the right. He knocks—the gentle tap of a sledgehammer-size fist—more out of curiosity and irritation than anything else.

"Whatever it is we don't wa—" The man, more effeminate than Tommy Norville could have ever hoped to be, yet oddly macho in his demeanor, was taken aback. He looked up at Bunkowski's size and regained his composure instantly. "What is it?" he snapped.

"I was looking for a place to board my little pup. Is this a private kennel?"

"It most certainly is not."

"Oh, I'm sorry. I heard the barking and thought—" The man was starting to push the chipped wooden door closed and Chaingang slapped the door with the flat of his hand. It ricocheted off the man's chest, knocking him backward into the room.

"You *bastard!*" the man shrieked, charging at his huge adversary.

"Stop," Bunkowski commanded, giving him a firm backfist in the face, but pulling it so as not to hurt him badly. Had Chaingang known what he was about to find, he would have broken his spine in half instead of trying to be easy on the fellow. But at the moment he had gained entry, he was still thinking the occupant might be an individual who cared for animals. This was sufficient cause to spare a monkey's life, in Chaingang's twisted world.

The hard fist only made the man mad, and he came at him again, scratching, kicking, a whirlwind of hands clawing and striking out, cursing the intruder: "Fat fucking shit ass bitch pig fucking cocksucker—" Chaingang simply pinioned him in a pair of arms that were meant to do only one thing: crush.

He held the man immobile, one hand over his mouth and nose until it would kill him to continue to do so. He dropped the man, who weighed perhaps 225 pounds, in a limp pile, and as he fought to stay conscious, Chaingang bound his wrists with a cord from his pocket, did the ankles with a nearby extension cord, and—as soon as the fellow had stopped blowing like a whale—gagged him with a shirt found on a nearby chair.

He was immediately aware of the stench, which had been overpowering the moment he burst in, but which was now so stingingly potent as to put him on guard as he moved toward the barking.

There is no smell quite so overpowering as that of sewage, and on more than one occasion he had opted to live down below the streets in various sewers and catch basins. Second only to the raw poisonous odor of concentrated sewage, the stench in the next room was the worst in his experience, as was what he faced.

It was true that perhaps sixty dogs were barking. But there were well over a hundred in the pen. The sight hammered his heart as badly as anything in his adult memory—even worse than the children he'd come upon in Hong Kong that time, or the animals the clown kept in the trailer. This was instantly worse and closed off a part of his mind.

THEY
WERE
IN
A
BABY'S
PLAY
PEN.
OVER
100
STARVING
OR
DEAD
AND
OR
ABUSED
ANIMALS

SQUEEZED
TOGETHER
IN
THEIR
OWN FILTH.

He did not know what to do could not think had never had such an experience was not prepared could not force his mind back into operation did not know what he was seeing did not understand could not would not did not should not.

Before he could think he was back in kicking the bound faggot like a big football, 15EEEEE kicks low on the legs so as not to kill him, oofing noises escaping the gag, forcing himself to move back, rip the sides open, forcing his mind to deal with it. They were packed in slimy shit. Dead ones. Live ones. Collected from the streets, he supposed. Should he feed and water them first? He walked around through the barking puppies and dead bodies and newspaper—**the fucking shit slime monkey dick-sucking faggot had fed them strips of newspaper.**

Newspaper.

He realized he was spinning in circles. Mad as he'd ever known himself to be. He'd kill any human he saw this second—**anyone.** Went in and pulled the wrists and ankles into a severe hogtie, yanked the gag, pinching the throat in case he screamed.

"Where's the dog food in this hovel, you piece of scum shitass queer aw fuck—" He got a handful of shit and newspaper scrap and shoved it into the bound man's mouth.

"Newspaper! You son of a bitch, I want your skin, your slimy hide up on these fucking walls." He had to force it down and concentrate now. Fifty-seven alive. Opening food. Not enough food. Water in dishes, trays, cups, anything that would hold liquid. Clusters of small wiggling things all over the floor, underfoot. Barking—some of them still afraid or too hurt or ill to eat. Some not able to drink water. All of the animals still alive were badly dehydrated.

He began looking for containers. More food that small

puppies would find edible. He found a dead mother dog and starved litter. Wanted to go back and hurt the man but couldn't yet. Was afraid to. Not yet. He had to fight to remember to breathe. Chaingang Bunkowski—in over forty years—had never been so totally confused.

He could speak, function, deal with it. He went out to the Buick and got his duffel and returned. Sorting for things he could use. Fifty-seven alive. Nine near death. Syringe. Lethal injections—as humane as any way to put them to sleep, he hoped. Forty-six dogs? Forty-eight? He'd lost count. He let them try to eat and drink as best they could, did a bit of sorting, put a few of the weaker ones in the bathroom where the others wouldn't bother them. Walked around trying to decide what to do next. Ended up figuring out how he would handle the killing of the man. Decided to learn why he'd done this. Tried to find some clue to motivation before he interrogated him.

He put together a picture of a man named John Esteban. Bisexual. Had an odd assortment of muscle mags and porn. Body-builder crap. Kid vid. Freak stuff with animals. There were homemade videos, too, but he could not bring himself to view them.

The beast returned to the bound-and-gagged man and pulled him upright, carried him into the bedroom.

Went back and gathered boxes of dogs up and sorted them according to category—apparently able to recover, in urgent need of a vet, and seemingly frisky. The Buick stunk like an exploded outhouse when he'd finished packing them into the car.

"I'll just be a minute or two. We'll attend to you. Be good boys and girls," he told them in a cracked voice, all the doors of the car wide open. He was oblivious to passersby. In fact, at that second he gave a shit for little or nothing. Mercifully, he saw no one in the street. He walked back inside.

He put the man on his stomach, tethered to the four corners of the bed with cords. Pulled the gag away for a moment with a hand which looked like a large human hand but which had the power of pliers or vise grips. Out of sight was a coiled length of wire and another object.

"Hello," he said softly in his rumbling basso. "I fed your dogs. I gave them some stuff out of the fridge. I couldn't find any scraps of newspaper to feed them."

"You listen to me, you—"

"Oh, my. Oh, my, Mr. Esteban. I don't suggest you speak again unless I ask you to do so," Chaingang said in the quietest voice with which he was capable of speaking.

"Gravida—that's what I'm going to call you. Our pet name." He cooed. "Gravida, be a good girl and tell Daniel why you put all those dogs in the pen and gave them only pieces of paper to eat. Do that for me, Gravida. Why? Try to make me understand."

"Fuck you, cocksu—"

"I see. All right, Gravida. Perhaps you're not in the mood for an intimate conversation at this time. You might prefer sex. Eh? Is that it? Would you like some physical intimacy?" He did something and the gag was reaffixed.

"I wish you'd speak with me first. I know you must have some reason for starving all those helpless little puppies but, frankly, I'm not feeling too well myself. I just want you to know, before we have a little sex together, how much I hate you. If I had more time—if I didn't have other pieces of monkey shit to deal with—I'd take you out and peel you, kill you inch by inch, keep you alive for days, but . . ."

Chaingang could hardly breathe. He had to get out of there. This was a luxury he could not afford.

"I see from your pictures and things you're into *buttfucking,* eh? So that's the way we'll go, Miss Gravida." The man felt something large and hard inserted in his rectum. "My goodness, we're large back there. You're a real donut, aren't you? Do you know what's inside you now?" The man on the bed squirmed and moaned.

"Obviously, you're really into it. Ready for your last

orgasm? Good. I think you'll find this a genuinely moving experience."

He forced another deep breath. Uncoiled the end of the wire out the door, pulled the thing as hard as he could and flattened against the outside wall as the concussive blast from the last grenade—the frag up John Esteban's butt—got his ass off for the last time.

27

Trask finally kicked his cold, but his chronic stupidity—that he hadn't kicked. It was crazy, but he was still locked into this story that had cost him his gig at KCM, and that was continuing to threaten him with a jail cell. Once again, he was in his ride, parked near the police headquarters, monitoring that damned hidden mike. He'd told himself the reason was that he was going to get up the nerve to go in and get it—but deep inside he knew there was no way. He wasn't really waiting to see Hilliard, or some other cop he knew by name, leave the building so that he could go up to the metro-squad room and ask if they were in, using that as an excuse to be in the building. He was here because he was drawn by that damned bug—he wanted to know what was going on in a case that had become an obsession.

Crucifixion Killer Strikes Again!

That was the banner headline across the front of a morning tabloid, which he was perusing as he sat monitoring background noise in Llewelyn's office.

Federal agents today joined investigators from the Kansas City Metro Squad, the Homicide Unit of the

Crimes Against Persons Division, the Bureau of Alcohol, Tobacco and Firearms, and the Violent Crimes Task Force, in an investigation into the death of John Esteban . . .

It is believed that an explosive device, such as the military fragmentation grenade which police say caused the explosion of a fleeing motorist's abandoned car . . .

He finally realized he was seeing something that was part of a submerged iceberg. It was pointless to listen for scraps. The cops—assuming they knew anything of substance at all, which he doubted—had no real handle on the apparently senseless and disconnected homicides.

It would be suicide to go up there after the microphone. He'd forget about it. When and if it were discovered, even if they managed to trace it back to Bob's Electronics—his name wasn't on file there, and after a while, it was unlikely his face would be remembered. If he didn't go back to get it, or return to the electronics shop, he could write his indiscretion off as a real bad idea and go on from there.

Trask started the car, pulled out, and drove to the nearest Dumpster, where he ripped out the tape and deposited both it and the earpiece. The radio receiver went into the first creek he crossed.

Lieutenant Llewelyn was far from the cop shop. He and a cluster of coppers and forensics people were at Mount Ely, where Kansas City Homicide detectives had found the place where the sniper blew off the heads of the bikers.

"The killer had to come up here after they were on the crosses," Llewelyn said. "For what purpose—target practice? It makes no sense at all. He'd killed up close—Ms. Hildebrande. If he was the one using the rifle grenades, he'd have taken the head shots down there. Somebody went to a lot of work to get into this position. The doer who did the bikers was under surveillance, it appears to me. We're looking at *two* killers, at least. Maybe more. The grenade guy, the guy with the machine gun and a .22 pistol, he's just part of the picture. The rifle grenades—that's somebody else. And when we match up forensics through the national computer we run into a wall.

"We got reporters now crawling all over the place. They say the mutilation murders—the hearts ripped out—and the size and description of the grenade perpetrator all match the M.O. and appearance of Chaingang Bunkowski, who as we all know is slammed down on death row. We're telling the reporters—yeah, we don't know if it's a copycat killing spree or what. But we got a partial off a shell casing and the national printout came back as 'I.D. deleted.' Ran it by the feds and got zip.

"I'm just guessing—but who do you know ever killed like this but the infamous Mr. Bunkowski? Suppose, just for the sake of being the devil's advocate, he escaped from prison? They decide not to publicize it, for all the obvious reasons. When we inquire to the warden at Marion he says, 'Yeah, Bunkowski's in solitary.' But he's really *here*. Whacking bikers and other citizens. Wouldn't that theory explain why some asshole decides to delete his fingerprint identification? Figure it's for 'national security' or some such bullshit?"

"Yeah," Hilliard said. "That could fly. But who's the *other* asshole?"

Everybody just stood there. Nobody was speaking. They had the expressions of animals at night, when they're caught in the headlights of a fast-moving car.

28

Mr. Conway," the veterinarian explained to the tall, heavy-set man, "we'll certainly do our best. But what do you want us to do if in a reasonable time we can't find good homes for all of the dogs?"

"How much would you want to continue to board them, say, for a year? If you couldn't find homes for them?"

"Just the cost of the dog food, I suppose. We could donate the care and feeding." The vet had been carefully selected by Daniel, who had tried to find someone who genuinely cared about animals. His sense of it was that the puppies would do as well here as anywhere, until homes could be found. This was the second vet who'd taken twenty dogs. He'd told them they'd been rescued from the Rutledge, Missouri, Animal Auction, which was a notorious marketplace frequented by "dog bunchers," who specialized in selling large numbers of animals to medical laboratories.

The care for these forty mutts had severely depleted Chaingang's war treasury, but it was of no consequence. He found money absurdly easy to acquire and of no interest in itself. After paying for a warehouse full of dog food and medicine, and impressing the vets with the fact that he'd eventually be returning for an accounting of the animals' welfare, he proceeded to drive back into Kansas, and found himself once again on the dreaded Bunker of his childhood.

He'd removed forty-nine starving, dehydrated pups from Mr. Esteban's home. Three hadn't survived. Forty were in good hands. But he hadn't found other vets he trusted sufficiently to use—and his bullshit detector was second to none. Six dogs cavorted in the back seat of the Buick. He parked, opened the windows so that there'd be ample air for the puppies, and reached back into the furry tangle of wiggly bodies, selecting one, tucking it into his voluminous shirt and starting up the stairs.

Had someone been watching him—this behemoth making his way up the rickety stairs of the crumbling tenement —they'd have seen him apparently talking to himself. He was reassuring the little dog.

He knocked and heard an old woman's frightened voice. "Who is it?"

"It's me. The man who gave you money—remember?" he asked, rather unnecessarily. After a few moments, he heard her unchain the pathetic thing that held the door.

"Un?" She was less than overjoyed to see this nightmare, money notwithstanding.

"I wanted to stop and see how you were doing. Did those boys bother you any more?"

"No." She thought for a moment. "They never came back."

"I don't think they'll bother you again. I brought you a present. To replace your cat." He reached inside his shirt and got out something brown and wiggly, which he handed to her. The old woman took it like it was a lit firecracker, but smiled when she saw what it was.

"Oh! A little dog."

"You like dogs?"

"Uh-huh." It apparently liked her as it was giving her kisses on her wrinkled, veiny hands. "But I can't afford to buy dog food."

266

"That's all right." He pulled two cans from his voluminous pockets, and then handed her some money. "This will
buy lots of food for you and your new pet. Don't forget to
give him water and plenty of affection." Doctor Bunkowski
found a dirty dish and put water in it, and spread a
newspaper down. The old woman was petting the dog,
somewhat dutifully, but he was certain they'd become fast
friends.

"Thank you," she said, as he turned to leave. "Um. Wait."
He turned back to her. "You asked about that lady who lived
here. I asked my friend about her. She said she knows where
she lives now."

"Mrs. Garbella?" he asked.

"I wrote it down somewhere." She went over to an old
table and sorted through things for what seemed like an
eternity. "Here it is." She held a scrap of paper out to him in
her frail hand. The dog had found an old shoe and was
busily chewing it to shreds.

He couldn't read her scrawl and made her decipher it for
him. He mentally noted it and told her he appreciated it.

"Thanks for getting that for me." It was by far the longest,
most uncharacteristic, and seemingly normal sequences of
conversations—with the vets and this old hag—that he'd
had in years. It made him think of the time they'd drugged
him and freed him from prison, and he'd gone around
acting like a monkey. It pissed him off totally.

He stomped out of the building ready to kick someone's
ass to the fucking max.

The dogs were going nuts by the time he got the car
started again. This was all he needed—he was busy trying to
kill a professional assassin and he had *five fucking dogs* on
his hands! Completely intolerable.

He forced everything out of his mind for the moment,
concentrating on finding Mrs. Garbella. Within ten minutes
he'd found the address the old woman had obtained for
him—it was an empty lot full of rubble. It looked like a
place where a building had burned to the ground in recent

years. It was precisely what he'd expected—nothing. He shrugged and headed for his hideaway. He had to get rid of these dogs. Tighten up. Regroup. Get his shit together.

That night he fed and watered the dogs and gathered them around him in the small stone enclosure, telling them all the bad things were over. He told them about the bad man, and how he was gone now, and how some of their brothers and sisters—the ones he'd tried to feed with an eyedropper—had gone to sleep. Huge hands that had killed many hundreds of times cuddled and stroked the five little dogs.

He shared his body heat with them under the massive tarp, willing himself not to roll over on them by accident while he slept.

He dreamed of the crucifixion and his mindscreen conjured up images of recent cross killings in the Persian Gulf, Mexico, Central and South America; most of them were torture killings with political overtones. He dreamed of Dr. Norman.

"I know many things, Dr. Norman. Chemistry, math, the general sciences. I know of the medical conclusions reached by your colleagues in the Reich Phylogeny College during World War Two: that the cause of death from a crucifixion is suffocation, since one cannot exhale sufficiently when the arms are held up for long periods, and the facility of expelling carbon dioxide from the lungs becomes impaired.

"I know that to crucify properly one should employ expedients such as driving a wooden peg into the upright, so that some of the body weight is taken between the legs. Nailing the feet to the upright also supports the body and prolongs the suffering. Would you like to learn more about this subject, Dr. Norman?"

The enormous figure under the tarp, five tiny dogs packed in around him, smiles in his sleep. He begins snoring like a couple of chainsaws, which momentarily frightens the pups, but they settle back in around his falling and rising mound of belly.

He dreams of eradication, escape, and survival. In a vision black as the darkest midnight, he pictures a white, virgin piece of paper—blemishless white, smoother than the surface of a lake of milk.

Inside the whiteness, it is hot. Burning white fire. An incandescence of white hot vengeance scorches the raw borders of the dream.

Heat envelops him in a sphere of perfect, infinite white fire. The beast punctures it with the sharp edge of his imagination, and the white, milky balloon bursts, as he allows the blackness of his dark thoughts to fill the sphere, cooling it with its inky liquidity.

A stream of black fills the round whiteness of the mental image as the ebb of black water would rise in a tub of perfect white, rising as it cools upon touch, and the curve of the black is an essence that stills his beating heart and slows each loud, deep, ragged breath from his mighty lungs.

The snores abate. A subtle change in his rhythms begins. There is an imperceptible and inexplicable slowing of his lifeforce. Slower, the measured *thu-bump, thu-bump* of his heart beats slower, as he wills, slows, wills the strong pulse down to a crawl.

Willing his heartbeat and respiratory system to slow, becoming a silent, still, invulnerable mass. Efficient. Ruthless. Precise. The breathing so slow and measured.

He waits now for the red mist to come, and dreams of the taste of another fresh human heart.

Shooter Price could make out a large yellow van. A pack of people walking together. A blue over white Mustang. A maroon T-Bird on which he could read the vanity plates. *"The removable accessory vault, which is located in the butt of the stock, forward of the shoulder recoil pad, contains spare brush and bore cleaning rod, lubricant, patches, lens tissues, spare eyepiece shield, Allen wrench, spanner—"* An autographed picture of Annie fuckin' Oakley. He saw a girl in red shoes. Her bright red high heels were like splashes of fresh blood against the dull gray background of pavement. He squeezed one off for the corps. *Ouch!* Girl fall down go boom.

He could make out a sign for the Happy Time Day Care Center. A billboard. The Laco brought an orange-and-white warning sign up close:

"Dumping oil or waste in parking lot violates state and federal laws. Offenders will be prosecuted. Fines can be up to ten thousand dollars. Please help us STOP POLLUTION." He loaded another APEX(X) in and did his part.

He swings over the parking lot of the truck stop. A figure on a nearby slope catches his eye from the middle of a half-acre garden plot. Flapping arms, large brimmed hat, his crosshairs touch the image of a garden scarecrow and he squeezes.

Moves, scans. *"Under emergency conditions clean water can be substituted for bore cleaning fluid . . ."* He's back in the sniper hide on Hospital Hill Park. It is a bad mistake. Chaingang is there, too, and this time when he squeezes, he is observed.

Price sees another college girl. SAVANT kisses the curve of breast, gentle swell of tummy, and he imagines a pouting bulge of unshaved cat under that pair of blue jeans and he squeezes one off for the commandant. *Yeah!*

Chaingang feels the danger claw at him but he cannot see any evidence of Shooter. The first thing he sees is a flight of sparrows who jump when the sign far below them explodes. He hears the noise of impact. Sees the sign—or rather sees where the sign was. Target practice. Shooter is up on the hill somewhere, the little fuck. He stares with full bore concentration, double-barreled vision trying to spot the sniper.

The hide is well done—he'll give him that. Had Shooter not popped the cap on another round he probably would not have found him. But he saw something. A puff of smoke or a branch disintegrating as another high explosive round blew through the shrubbery. He could see the gun pit. He was moving fast, those big hard tree-trunk legs churning, moving him faster than anyone alive had seen him move.

Unfortunately, Shooter saw him as well. Caught the

elephantine killer lumbering up the hill at him and yelled with delight as he slid the empty brass out, inserted a round, and firmly snicked the bolt closed. Eye to the Laco. Crosshairs on the humongous target, which was too fat to even zigzag, like shooting ducks on a pond—an easy squeeze and his worries were over. The big weapon gave him a satisfactory thump as it tooked Chaingang Bunkowski off the count. All Shooter could see on the grass was fresh blood!

Daniel had been shot several times, including a couple of up-close-and-way-too-personal incidents. He wasn't a virgin, as these things go. But there had never been any pain like this.

It was chain pain. The sort of pain he had inflicted many a time—where there's nothing for a few moments and then, as the numbness begins to wear off, it's such a screaming terrible hurting that you think you'll pass out from it. Imagine the pain from a hundred chain whippings.

He had to bite down on it or it would kill him. He had been hit by SAVANT, but his warning system had jerked him to the side just in time, and he'd taken a bad shoulder wound, high on the left shoulder just above the Kevlar vest. Three inches to the right and it would have blown his head off. In his mind, he fixed all his powers on that one point of focus, as he worked his way, on his right side, back to the car and his duffel.

The body is divided into four quads, subdivided again. The small section where he'd taken the hit was walled off inside his brain. He had to stop the pain. Isolate it there. He imagined the shoulder floating above him, freezing the rest of his upper torso in ice. Cutting off the flow of blood from the pain, slowing his vital signs as he made it to the Buick.

There was an up side. He was alive. Functioning. He didn't have the dogs with him—they'd been left at his hideout. This mess was going to be over. He would now do away with a long-time enemy. Battle dressing. Fighting to keep his mind chilly. He had to stay calm. There was a lot of blood but he liked blood. No problem. Bandaged himself and then wrapped some duct tape over the dressing—he was going to be doing some heavy work, he felt sure.

Got the line tracker out of the duffel. The photo interrupter eye had been tampered with. The robot was now a slightly modified toy. It no longer resembled what the store had sold. It was now rather deadly. He got out his coil. Det cord. Clacker. Three-in-one.

Keys. No problem with the right side of his body at all. Experimented with the left as he started the car. Not bad. He could stand it.

He bit down on the pain as if it were a big, mean steak sandwich. Chewed up the hurt and swallowed it. Drove away from the scene of this accident, around the hill that led to the street above the gun pit.

Parked. Got out. Shooter was still scanning the brush below with the weapon. Biding his time on lock and load. Patient and ready.

Chaingang got out and put the line tracker in place. Doused the can of oil on the wheels and bearings. Put it in place and started off to get an angle on the hide which was less than a hundred feet away. If Shooter had seen him crawl to the car he would feel another shot hit him soon. But he made it to the nearby trees and nothing struck him down.

He was close now. He gritted his ugly shark's teeth and switched on the remote control. The line tracker started forward, and momentum carried it straight ahead, tracking no line at all but moving silently on the oiled wheels, rolling in the direction of the gun hide, a Claymore mine wired to the base of the tracker. As the killer robot neared the gun hide, Chaingang triggered the clacker, and the command-detonator fired out nearly seven hundred steel balls in a sixty-degree forward arc. Shooter was down in the hide when it went off, and the projectiles missed him, but his reflexes were lightning fast and he whirled and squeezed one off in the direction of the blast.

That was what Chaingang wanted—that one moment when Shooter Price was caught with an empty weapon. Chaingang came charging and puffing and screaming like a rhino of death, and Shooter was scared shitless, trying to eject the shell and jam that next round in the mouth of his bitch before the fucking son of a bitch could reach him, click—the bolt back, the expended brass flying into the dirt, fumbling for a round, the rhino almost on him. Got it! Big cartridge in the chamber, snick! The bolt closed. Just in time to take the shot and cancel this fucking target out, but his hands were stinging and the rifle was fifteen feet away—*ooh, man*, that chain was big . . . and hard.

It only took an instant for Chaingang to throw a yard of tractor-strength chain at his target. But an instant can be quite long. This particular one was of sufficient duration for Robert Tinnon Price to register the reality of the chain that was probably going to end his life.

The image snaked into his field of recognition with blinding speed, so as the moment of shattering impact occurred he had time to realize what had come whirling out at him. He did not have time to reflect on it as it smashed into his weapon.

And then there was the big boy himself doing something he would not have thought possible—dropping down beside him and picking up the weapon, not the chain, and roaring like a crazed animal and *bending* the super-tough tungsten carbide barrel with his bare hands, blood seeping through the wound near his shoulder, putting an *L* in his lady's throat.

"I'm glad I didn't kill you," Price said to his old comrade of sorts. No longer afraid. "I admire you very much, you know?"

Chaingang, bloodlust coursing through him, only wanted one thing then, and words had no meaning.

"I've always liked your work." Price turned his back, not to run, but to present his neck to be snapped. Inside, there was no fear, only respect and—what surprised Shooter the most—genuine affection. "I'm ready, Daniel," he said, as Chaingang moved forward to rip the sniper limb from limb.

That evening Chaingang woke up, the wound bleeding, something hot and wet in his face.

"Stop that. Stop that, you naughty little boy. What a *naughty* little boy you are!" He was talking to the pup that was standing on his face. One of its four paws had slipped into his open mouth while he snored. "Those little feet don't taste good. Those paws stink! Those little paws stink!" he said, kissing the dog.

No one who knew the beast would believe that he might be capable of the tenderness he shows these puppies who cavort around his huge form.

The wound looks all right, and he has seen many such wounds. The battle dressing is difficult to change as the duct tape has melted in the heat and movement, but he manages, and throws the bloody bandages away where the puppies can't get at them.

With a grunt he falls back on his sleeping bag, and the five little dogs wiggle against him.

"Don't you worry. You're safe now," the huge beast tells them. And they give him kisses in gratitude, but he yawns and moves suddenly and five puppies scamper for safety. "You're all right," he assures them. The friendliest one returns and tries to paw his mouth open.

"Stop that!" he says, making a noise like the cough of an engine being started. His version of a giggle. "You little devil."

The monstrosity opens his mind, fully relaxed, as he plays with the pups, letting the ideas flow past his mindscreen. How will he call the good doctor out from his fortress? All the usual con games are of no use—the sissy is smart and extremely wary. A woman? He doubts if Dr. Norman even likes women. There must be a way to draw him outside. . . .

On another level, he must find some homes for these little mutts, somewhere they'll be loved, where a child will learn to give each dog gentle, loving care, and as he thinks of the children he is presented with his answer. He knows how he will take Norman down. The barking cough that explodes from him has no relation to the sound of a human laugh, and, wisely, the five little dogs once again run for cover.

29

Trask finished reading the news account that blamed the spate of Kansas City homicides on a pair of killers, a man described as a renegade sniper, an "ex-mercenary" named Robert Price, and the legendary mass murderer and serial killer, Chaingang Bunkowski, who authorities claimed had escaped from federal prison. It was quite a scandal, and Trask wished he could have been part of the team that finally broke it in the press. He read about the terrible long-range weapon called SHERFSAVANT, and the cache of unique ammunition that had been found. It was some ending to the violence piece, if he'd only had a show to produce it for.

He turned the radio on and heard his ex-boss ask a guest, "Why is there so much violence in America today? And what can we do about it?"

"I'll tell you one thing—we better get serious about putting the crooks and rapists and killers in prisons that can hold them. We coddle them too much. If somebody rapes a child, for instance, they oughtta be castrated, or if it's a woman—you know—something else like that."

"Go back to an eye for an eye?"

"Well—"

"There's no proof that deters crime."

"Lock 'em up then for life and make sure they can't break out. Make the prisons better."

"Who's gonna pay for all these better, bigger prisons? You and I? The taxpayer? You really want to pay for some more prisons?"

"I'll pay for my share if they take away the damn TVs and the privileges. Make prison tough again. And stop worrying about overcrowded prisons. Stack 'em in there like cord wood. Why worry about being so humane to animals who rape and molest and murder? Worry about the victims for a change . . ." Trask turned the radio off.

All heat and no light.

The room was still papered in notes. He looked at the chronological summary of the violence material. It was as thick as a book. He pictured Sean Flynn at the mike. Listening to himself inside the old pair of Stanton Dynaphase Forty cans he always wore on the air, big vinyl, chrome, and blue steel headphones, plugged into the air monitor. A researcher—probably some kid fresh from Tennessee—and Babaloo would be in there making notes to slip to him. The idea of going back to radio was a repugnant one. He'd had his share of radio.

Trask picked up the story about the sniper weapon and the serial homicides and thought out loud: "I wonder if I could get a book out of this?"

It wouldn't cost anything to try. God knows he had the research already done. Not to mention the dubious distinction of his nightmarish experience as an eyewitness to a kill.

He took some paper and put it in his machine and typed *"THE SHOOTER"* by Victor Trask. Changed his mind. Pulled it out and inserted a new sheet of paper, typing a fresh title page:

SAVANT